GIRL IN THE WALLS

GIRL
IN THE
WALLS

A Novel

A. J. GNUSE

ecco
An Imprint of HarperCollins *Publishers*

GIRL IN THE WALLS. Copyright © 2021 by A. J. Gnuse. All rights reserved. Printed in the United States of America. No part of this book may be used or reproduced in any manner whatsoever without written permission except in the case of brief quotations embodied in critical articles and reviews. For information, address HarperCollins Publishers, 195 Broadway, New York, NY 10007.

HarperCollins books may be purchased for educational, business, or sales promotional use. For information, please email the Special Markets Department at SPsales@harpercollins.com.

Ecco® and HarperCollins® are trademarks of HarperCollins Publishers.

Originally published in Great Britain in 2021 by 4th Estate, an imprint of HarperCollins Publishers.

FIRST U.S. EDITION

Designed by Michelle Crowe
Tree illustrations by Elizabeth Yaffe

Library of Congress Cataloging-in-Publication Data

Names: Gnuse, A. J., 1990- author.
Title: Girl in the walls : a novel / A. J. Gnuse.
Description: First U.S. edition. | New York, NY : Ecco, [2021] | Originally
  published in Great Britain in 2021 by 4th Estate, an imprint of
  HarperCollins Publishers.
Identifiers: LCCN 2021002237 (print) | LCCN 2021002238 (ebook) | ISBN
  9780063031807 (hardcover) | ISBN 9780063031821 (ebook)
Subjects: LCSH: Orphans—Fiction. | GSAFD: Suspense fiction. |
  Bildungsromans.
Classification: LCC PS3607.N87 G57 2021 (print) | LCC PS3607.N87 (ebook)
  | DDC 813/.6—dc23
LC record available at https://lccn.loc.gov/2021002237
LC ebook record available at https://lccn.loc.gov/2021002238

21 22 23 24 25 LSC 10 9 8 7 6 5 4 3 2 1

For my family

PART 1

SUBJECT: YOU ARE NOT ALONE

Listen. We know there are people who hide in our homes.

They crawl into attic spaces. Tuck themselves behind yard equipment in garages. Flit between the rooms of the house just outside the reach of sight.

Some of us have found nests tucked in the backs of bedroom closets behind the hanging clothes. Or in the void space beneath the stairs. In that sliver between a living room sofa and the wall.

We have found half-empty water bottles and candy wrappers and the remains of leftover food cooked the day before. I found my own wrinkled clothes pressed flat to the floor and stinking like somebody else's sweat.

Look in the places behind furniture. The spaces beneath beds. Every deep crevice of a house. No guarantee that once one place has been checked someone will not sneak right back into it.

You can stay home all day and still not find them. They are clever and patient and they know the insides of your home better than you ever will. But you have to find them.

You have to root them out.

J.T.

A NEST BENEATH A HOUSE

THE CAT, BLINKING IN THE AFTERNOON LIGHT, PADDED AWAY DOWN the long length of the gravel driveway. Her paws found the small, flat spaces between the rocks, and the girl, from her vantage point at the guest room window, could hear nothing—it was like a silent film she was lucky enough to look out the window to catch. But she thought about how, even if she were out there, lying on her back on the lawn with her eyes closed, beside the lilies the boys' mother, Mrs. Laura, had planted along the edge of the driveway, she still wouldn't hear any sound that would cue her that the cat was passing just an arm's reach away. She loved that.

The calico had appeared in her view as it trod free from the azalea bushes along the side of the house. The girl knew enough about the house—not only the rooms but the insides of the floors and walls between them—to know a small hole in the house's foundation that could allow enough space for an animal to crawl in.

Had she already seen the cat's nest? There'd been a flattened gray mound of half-decayed insulation she'd noticed a few days back beneath the floorboards. The girl would need to keep an eye out for the animal so she could learn its routines and schedule. She didn't want to encroach by journeying down below when it was napping, when it was clearly trying to be alone. But the cat was across the road, trotting up the steep side of the levee and disappearing over its lip into the batture. Now, since it was gone, the girl wanted to see where it had been.

Tuesday afternoon, the day the youngest of the Masons, Eddie, took piano lessons. She'd go down anyway, even though she heard them there, Eddie and the piano teacher, sitting at the piano in the dining room. They'd both be facing that wall, the one in which she would descend. Tuesday afternoons used to be a safe time to take the trip, as Mr. Nick was at his afterschool meetings, Mrs. Laura outside in the garden, Marshall at the car wash, and Eddie, typically, tucked away in his bedroom, reading. The piano lessons, an early birthday present, had changed that routine.

But the girl was stubborn. She left the guest room and entered the hallway, the balls of her bare feet treading silently against the floorboards. She opened the door to the attic and climbed the stairs. Pulled free the plywood floorboard and revealed the entrance down into her walls. She'd time her descent along with the piano teacher's melodies, and with Eddie's attempts to mimic them. This was her house. She'd done things much harder than this.

Inside the walls, the piano's keys sounded as though they were underwater. In the dark, she pressed her feet against the wall studs and traced her fingers along the wooden laths to find the miniature grips she'd scraped weeks before. She lowered herself, an inch at a time, patient. More than once, the teacher's melody cut out while the girl's toes were still reaching for the nearest grip, and she held herself still, awkwardly, until the muscles in her forearms and fingers burned. More than once, her elbows and knees grazed the laths a little too firmly, causing some part of her to wonder whether Eddie's mistakes—the faltering, hesitant strokes—were from having heard her, and pretending to have not.

"Come on, little guy," the piano teacher said, his voice rising into a higher pitch than necessary for a boy who was nearly thirteen, almost two years older than the girl. "Just play the notes," he said. "Come on. Watch my fingers! Just do what they do."

The girl rolled her eyes. As if the trick to playing well was knowing you were supposed to use your fingers.

The teacher went through the melody again, and she touched

her toes down on a floorboard. With relief, she eased the rest of her weight down. Slowly, careful not to bump against the wood on either side of her, she shimmied through with her leg out before her, leading her like a divining rod through the dark.

Two. Three. Four. She counted her steps, brushing the dusty floor with her heel, until she found it. The loose board.

The girl paused. She waited until both Eddie and the instructor began playing their melody at the same time, their rhythm slightly off, Eddie's stumbling fingers filling the silent rests between. While they played, she pushed down on one end of the thick floorboard, causing the other side to bow up. The board was nearly as tall as she was. She lifted it, gently. Then she slipped down beneath it into the hole, her legs pushing through itchy, rotted insulation until she felt cool dirt under her feet.

Simple. Hardly anything to it.

UNDER THE FLOOR

THE CAT'S NEST WAS TUCKED AWAY IN A CORNER OF THE CRAWL space beneath the house, just beyond the reach of the thin beam of light that bled from the hole in the house's foundation. The nest was hard to find, hard to know what it was even if someone were looking right at it. The cat had left few signs behind. The shed fur upon the flattened insulation. The faintest imprint of its paw in the dirt. The light warmth beneath her palm. Anyone else would have missed it. Since the girl had moved back into her home, into the walls, she liked to think she saw the world differently.

She lay on her back and stretched out her arms and legs, imagining herself a sea creature undulating out over the dark ocean floor. It smelled like earth down here. Wet, rich earth. She relished the scent. It wasn't easy for her to get.

Down here, the piano's keys were muted, but she could still hear the thumping of the instructor's heel banging the rhythm for Eddie. He banged and banged as though the kid were an idiot. She took a deep breath of the musty air, feeling it cling to her tongue, and let out a tired sigh.

She knew it was none of her business, but it still frustrated her when people talked to Eddie that way. It was how the mailman talked when he handed over the mail, or their neighbor Ms. Wanda the few times she came over when he was out walking in the yard. Even Marshall would talk to him that way. That was the most ridiculous of all because, in the girl's opinion, it was Marshall, the long-armed ape, who was the most deserving of being talked down to. But Eddie was smart. She knew this because she read his books—the best ones in the house—about ancient histories or (her favorite) mythological stories about mysterious, magic worlds. She appreciated someone with a good imagination. Even if he was strange.

While the rest of his family ate their meals together at the kitchen table, he ate his alone in the dining room. And there were other things: how sensitive he was, how quiet, how much time he spent playing board games against himself—even the most boring ones, like Monopoly and chess.

But then, what if she were to map out all the strange and annoying things she knew other people did when they thought they were alone? Mr. Nick, with his lingering stares into empty rooms. Mrs. Laura's mumbling. Or Marshall, cursing at himself in the guest room mirror, rubbing the short bristles of his hair between both hands. Even before she'd moved into the walls, the girl would watch her classmates at school during quizzes, when their sense of the world around them shrank and their minds pulled in upon themselves. She'd seen boys' hands creep up through the bottoms of their shorts. She'd seen girls bite the tips of their fingernails until they bled.

She shrugged. When it came to being strange, Eddie likely fit right in.

The girl rolled over onto her stomach and arched her back. She allowed herself a small grunt, and enjoyed the pull on the tight, wiry muscles. All things considered, as the girl crawled on her hands and knees under the floorboards, blinking in the near dark, smelling the sweet, musky scent of the house's underside, her hands and knees kicking up faint, floating particles of dust . . .

Well? She figured she wasn't necessarily in a place to judge.

THE LATE AFTERNOON

OUTSIDE, THE LOUISIANA SPRING HEAT HAD COME IN SWIFT. THE buzz of cicadas filled the humid air, their calls pulsing loud as a siren. But to the girl, it was monotonous and steady, predictable enough to be soothing.

Along the edge of the tall grass that surrounded the backyard, a muscled, black snake could be seen, even from the house's third-story attic window, inching its way toward the patchy grass beneath the broad shade of the live oak trees. Mrs. Laura stood over rows of moist earth in the vegetable garden with her hands on her hips and mud on her knees. And around the corner of the attached garage, just visible over the lip of weathered roofing, Eddie. His piano lesson over, his tousled black hair bobbing as he paced back and forth.

From somewhere, a barred owl let out a garbled call.

It was quiet inside the house. The sun, resting orange above the levee on the other side of the road, cut in across the front yard through the upstairs windows, leaving the speckled outlines of cypress trees on the hallway floors. The clock in the foyer tolled a single, deep note, signaling a quarter of an hour until six. Back from work, Mr. Nick lay downstairs on the library sofa, napping, and Marshall, let go early from the car wash, had sealed himself in his bedroom, silent except for the occasional flutter of his fingers across the computer keyboard.

As the heat of the afternoon slowly faded, the old house exhaled. Warm air respired from the pores in roofing shingles and white strips of siding, and rose invisible into the pink sky. The wood in the floors and walls cooled, making occasional, gentle popping noises. Downstairs, the dryer rumbled to a sudden halt.

Softly, so easy to ignore unless someone was still and listening for it, the attic door hinges chirped as they opened and shut again. The sounds of bare feet followed, quiet as an insect, treading in intricate steps across the patterns of light on the floor.

She had decisions to make for the evening. Whether it was to be a night for reading, or for something else. Her current book was a collection of Norse myths, a thick and battered paperback that she had tucked in the nook of her arm as she listened at the top of the curving staircase. Months ago, from a conversation Mrs. Laura had on the phone, the girl had learned that this book was meant to be a Christmas present to Eddie from a great aunt in Indiana. But it had only arrived earlier this week, after having been lost all this time in the mail.

The girl had been the only one home to receive the yellow package when it finally arrived on the front porch. The doorbell rang, and there it was. Its wrapping torn along the seam, the silver lettering of the book's spine peeking through.

That day, she had squinted out toward the levee and road to make sure no one was passing by. Then she reached her pale fingers into the warmth of the sunlight cast upon the welcome mat, and she snatched it inside. She studied the book, saw that it had gotten wet at one point (from a snowstorm, she guessed—some mail truck barreling through an Indiana blizzard and slumping into a ditch after catching black ice), but even though the corners of the book were warped, and ink bled blue on certain pages, the stories were readable.

Eddie wasn't waiting for the book, wouldn't notice it was missing, unlike any of the other books on myths and fantasy on his bookshelf, since everyone in the family had thought the present had been lost before it came. Sometimes she reread a chapter two or three times before moving on. No need to hurry through this one.

The staircase steps creaked as she descended them. Bothersome. She could hoist as much of her weight as she could onto the wooden banister that bordered the curving stairs, but the steps would still find some way to complain. Some sounds in the house were unavoidable.

Downstairs in the foyer, the front yard loomed, framed through the windows like an old landscape painting. The acre of green lawn and flowers, and a road with the steep green levee beyond. Up there, on the dirt path along the top of the levee, a boy in overalls floated into the frame of the window, and in a few moments, drifted effortlessly out again. Beside the girl, the antique clock ticked, and from the next room over, the library, she heard Mr. Nick shift his weight on the old sofa. He let out a single snore.

She might listen to television tonight, if she wanted—the void space beneath the foyer stairs was close enough to hear most of the words if Mr. Nick had the volume high. Or, she could draw in her notebook in the enclosed back porch, sprawled behind the wicker love seat on her stomach with her pencil and paper. There, once it grew dark and became hard to see, Mrs. Laura would come in from the laundry room and flip on the porch's overhead bulb, as if for the girl, and leave it on until Mr. Nick did his rounds of the rooms before bed.

Those were some options. In the meantime, she was thirsty.

She went through the living room, with its plush sofa and armchair and its quiet, carpeted floor. Into the kitchen, where the refrigerator opened with a small suction sound. A tink of the drinking glasses touching as one was removed from the cupboard, followed by the soft thump of the fridge closing again.

The windows of the kitchen looked blindly out at the trees that grew up along that side of the house. The neighborhood was mostly undeveloped, in a parish just south of New Orleans, and the only neighbor's house that was visible from any of the windows was Ms. Wanda's single-bedroom home, which rested far back across a field, beside the woods' tree line. Still, the girl ducked her head, careful, and squinted through those windows to see the afternoon sky, as much as she could manage. There were only a few thin, pink clouds trailing. Looked like it promised to be a clear evening. In that case, she'd have to come back at some point tonight, after the Masons had gone to bed. She'd lie on the kitchen countertops. From here, shielded by the bulk of the house from the white glare of the roadside streetlights, she would see stars. Above the mass of oak and hackberry branches, there'd be Orion, the Big Dipper, others. Constellations the girl's mom had taught her, when they'd stood outside in that same yard. The girl tucked in a warm arm, tracking her mom's finger as it traced the dim pinpricks of light.

But for now, there was nothing but the gentle whine of the dishwasher opening, a glass with a film of orange juice pulp appearing beside the Mason family's dirty dishes, and a padding of feet on the tiles, leaving the room.

The antique clock in the foyer struck six, and its mechanics let out the loud cries of a nest of baby finches. Mr. Nick at once sat up and placed his feet on the library floor, stretched, and walked through the foyer and living room. He entered the kitchen and rummaged through the cabinets for pots and pans as he began to prepare dinner for his family. A few minutes later, Eddie's and Mrs. Laura's voices could be heard just outside the back porch as they wiped their shoes clean on the mat. Upstairs, Marshall's stereo, without warning, soared to life with heavy-metal electric guitars and double-bass pedals.

In the laundry room, between the thick silver tubes behind the machines, the girl opened her book to the earmarked page. In that chapter, Odin, the oldest of the gods, journeyed beneath the roots of a great tree to a witch and paid her one of his eyes in order to gain wisdom.

"There are many ways to see," Odin said, as a pair of ravens rooted up from under the ground between his feet. The birds shook their dirty wings, wrapped them around the god's legs, and pulled themselves to his shoulders. "An eye on its own," Odin said, "can give you only so much, and now I have so much more."

THE LAST DECEMBER

IN THAT COLD, STRANGE TIME BETWEEN CHRISTMAS AND NEW Year's, when even the adults didn't seem certain what it was exactly they should be doing with the different parts of their days, and the house showed their disarray. Strips of torn wrapping paper peeked out from beneath a sofa and coffee table. Decorations half-taken down, stockings emptied of their contents and carelessly folded on the seats of chairs or the mantelpiece. The Christmas tree beginning to dry, as her father forgot to water it, its needles slowly flaking free to fall and brown on the floor.

They went to City Park to see, one last time before the end of the season, the lights that decorated the botanical gardens. She had gone with her parents twice already that month, but before they had always arrived after dark. Now, she wanted to see what *Celebration in the Oaks* looked like in the afternoon, when the sun still illuminated each of the bulbs and cords that weaved between the hedges and formed the outlines of reindeer and snowflakes. She wanted to see the skeletons of the lights. They walked along narrow, manicured paths, bundled in coats. She trailed a few yards behind her mom and dad, sipping from a Styrofoam cup of hot chocolate, the warmth rising against her face. Hardly anyone else was there.

At the live oak in the center of the park, a huge octopus of a tree, and her parents knew already: the hot chocolate relegated to her mom's hands, her dad waiting by the base of the trunk. He hoisted the girl up by the armpits, lifting her high enough to find a grip into the oak's fork. For the moment he held her: his tangy-sharp cologne, the scent of fresh paint lingering beneath. Followed, as always, by his complaint that they'd both grown too old for this kind of labor.

"A hundred years old with a broken back—I'll probably still be lugging you around."

And up in the tree, she shrugged. Wind blew and the leaves flapped around her. She pulled herself higher into the bobbing branches— "Careful up there!"—her cold palms squeezing the chunky bark. With the sky having grown darker and the shadows lengthened beneath the branches, the light of the blue and yellow bulbs below and around her strengthened. She watched the shapes they formed grow flesh and life.

Later, on the drive back, she'd fallen mostly asleep, only lightly aware of the familiar bumps of De Gaulle Drive under the car, and of her mom's voice in the front passenger seat, murmuring about New Year's plans.

"I think the Wilsons' party will be going on through midnight, if you wanted to stay."

The seat belt pressed against her neck as the car slowed for a stoplight. The cloth of the seat had grown warm beneath her.

"Or maybe we could go back early. It might be nice to celebrate at home. Like we did last year, at the old house? I think we still have that jar for bottle rockets."

The whir of the engine as the car accelerated again and the beat of the tires on the road. Her dad's and mom's voices taking turns. She slipped in and out of consciousness, as if she were moving back and forth between her bedroom and the hall.

ODIN, THE ALL-KNOWING

MONTHS AFTER, HIDDEN IN THE OLD HOME WITH THE MASON FAMILY scattered around her, the girl read in her book of Norse myths that Odin—now Odin the One-Eyed—had become the wisest of all the gods, able to know what was going on in any place in the world. In the story she read, Odin sent out his ravens, who soared up high to spy on the events of the world while hidden in the clouds. When they returned, they tucked into his beard to warm themselves from the icy temperatures of the high altitudes. Once they caught their breath, they whispered in his ear what they had seen.

In this way, Odin saw the whole world through what they told him—storms raging in the mountains, giants stirring beneath the earth, animals rustling in the underbrush of the swamp—all in the near-darkness of his throne room.

When the girl finished the story, she closed one eye and scratched the back of her neck. A good story, but then again, as she sat and let its images drift through her mind, the feeling welled in her that something seemed off. Fishy. If she were in Odin's place, when he first made the agreement with the witch beneath the great tree's roots, would she have taken the same deal? Traded an eye for that?

The girl leaned her head against the laundry room wall, rubbed her eyebrows with her thumb and forefinger, puckered her cheeks, and made soft popping noises with her mouth.

It's not that she didn't believe the magic, or think it was worth the cost. For limitless knowledge and wisdom? She'd give an eye for that. Heck yeah—and she felt pretty attached to her eyes, too: light green with brown specks. But the girl also had two of them. And once, her dad had given her a book about Ann Bonny, the lady pirate. On the cover, she was illustrated steering her ship through the blue Caribbean Sea with a wild, free grin and a big, black eyepatch.

The girl wouldn't mind that look. She'd trade an eye for magic birds.

Well, maybe not for ravens. She figured those were loud and squawking birds. She hadn't yet had the chance to read it, but she had heard about that old Edgar Poe "Nevermore!" story.

Something quieter. Smaller, too. Like a wren. She liked their puffed-out chests. It was like a pillow they could rest their faces on, one they carried with them and could use wherever they chose to sleep at night. And their size meant they could fit anywhere, go wherever they liked.

But still. The birds weren't what was wrong with the story. There was something else. What was it?

The whole exchange with Odin and the witch. It didn't make sense.

The witch. What was she doing down there, beneath the roots of a tree? Why did she give the man this power to see the whole world over—seemed like a pretty big deal—and only get an eye in return? What does anyone do with an eye anyway?

And even then, did Odin actually become that all-knowing, after all? The girl had read a couple of other myths about the Norse gods (Eddie already owned a collection of short stories that had samplings of almost all the good ones: Egyptian, South African, Greek, Native American, Middle Eastern), and she knew that Odin, even with all his knowledge, had no idea what kind of tricks his wicked son was up to, even when they happened in his own home.

Then—the girl held still. Mrs. Laura padded through the library toward her into the laundry room. The dryer in front of the girl reverberated as it opened, and she heard the brush of fabric against the metal well as Mrs. Laura pulled the dried clothes out into a basket.

The door of the dryer clicked shut, and as suddenly as Mrs. Laura entered the room, she left. The woman trailed away, now humming the theme music to *Survivor* and bouncing the laundry basket against her knees.

The girl flipped open her book again. Turned through the pages and squinted at the illustration of the old man and the witch, shadowed by the massive roots of the World Tree. Maybe the lesson to be learned from the story was simply that adults, even the smart ones, were kind of dumb. It was a lesson the girl had learned before. In her experience, adults had often demanded fairly stupid things of her. Adults like her old teachers, who talked to her as if she was an infant. The foster guardian, Ms. Brim—one evening with the woman, yet the girl still remembered her name—who suggested that families and homes are things people can recreate. Even her mom and dad had required pointless chores of her (sweeping the back porch, though it would only get dirty again half a day later; dust-mopping the rooms they hardly used; and, worst of all, their own constant projects on the house—the girl's earliest memory was coloring in a book while lying on a plastic-covered floor). Ridiculous to think of the hours her parents had wasted of hers. But she stopped herself from dwelling too much on the thought. Of course, she'd take their chores and projects as a trade-off. Hundreds more, if she could.

But—the story. So, why didn't the witch just take all wisdom for herself? Down beneath the roots of a tree, she must have wanted it more than anyone. To close her eyes, listen to the whispers of her ravens, to see each facet of the world appear before her like a flickering television screen. Why would anyone give the birds up?

What made her go down beneath the tree, and what was she doing down there? If she made Odin the smartest of all the gods, what else was she capable of? Seemed to the girl like the story had skimped on the most interesting character.

She liked this witch. She felt like she was being winked at from the page. There was more to this woman than she was letting on, and she was keeping it hidden from everyone in the world. Except her.

The girl turned back to the beginning of the story. She rolled her neck, feeling the gentle pops as it loosened. Then she read the story again.

Here, in her home, time moved as she wanted. Here, in the world she found, the one she created—who knew? She might as well stay a little girl forever, as long as no one else ever knew to find her.

BOYS

LONG AFTER ALL THE LIGHTS IN THE HOUSE HAD BEEN PUT OUT that night, the girl watched the stars through the kitchen window. When she was finished, she brushed her teeth in the downstairs bathroom with the toothbrush she kept hidden behind a rack of magazines. Then she pulled herself back into the walls, like pulling a bedsheet over herself before sleep. Inside, she felt the vibrations of the building, a tremor of a pulse beneath her fingertips. She scaled the space between the walls. But as she neared the second story, she stopped.

How could they still be awake? Sounds of their feet creaking on the carpeted floor above her. The older boy kept his voice low, so as not to wake their parents.

"You think I can't hear you moving around in here? The fuck were you even doing?"

Eddie's returning voice was soft, frail. She couldn't make out what he said. Before he finished, Marshall cut him off.

"Shut up."

She pictured Marshall standing over Eddie, his pointed knuckles whitening as he gripped the doorframe. Narrow face turned gray by the dark of the bathroom that connected their rooms. She imagined him leaning in close as he spoke.

"You weird, idiot, little kid," he said. "For the love of fucking God, why can't you just be a normal brother? Wake me up again, and I'll beat the shit out of you."

THE HOUSE

THE OLD HOUSE HAD BEEN CALLED A PROJECT BY EACH OF THE half-dozen families who had lived there through the decades. Over time, each had left their mark when renovating their home, in shaping and reshaping the floorplan. They added cabinets, constructed a back porch, and, later, closed that porch in to become an interior back patio. Utility closets had been converted into pantries, a playroom transformed into a lounge then into an office, and the kitchen at some point doubled in size and expanded into the garage.

Inconsistencies abounded; the house was like some hybrid, ridiculous creature from an ancient myth. The white Ionic columns in the foyer were followed by the living room's 1970s cream drop-ceilings and fluorescent lights. The exposed hardwood floors of the upstairs hallway changed into the thick brown carpet of the separate bedrooms. In the library, an unusable fireplace without a chimney. In the master bedroom, an ornate wrought iron heating system, without any gas hookups, jutted from the wall. The look of the house resembled its history: of people trying, and failing, decade after decade, to make the house their own.

As long as the girl had known the home, something had always been about to break: a plumbing pipe or a rusted water heater, a ceiling leak or cracked gutter, a garage on the verge of being infested by carpenter bees, or an attic with a pair of nesting squirrels. For her own parents, and the Masons now, she figured this was why so many projects stood half-finished (the broken upstairs-to-downstairs intercom system, the stained-glass kitchen window above the stove that led into the darkness of the wall).

Throughout her childhood, her mom and dad had always complained how, as soon as they began one project, they'd need to stop halfway because, somewhere across the house, another one became more pressing. Too many memories, like the one of her mom: screwdriver between her teeth, rushing down the stairs to the kitchen where dinner boiled over on the stove. Of standing beside her dad as they looked up at the pantry ceiling, where once again it had darkened from moisture. "Is the leak coming from your bathroom? Ours? Or somewhere else?" The house's insides unfurling above them, a cave system through walls. "Let's think."

So, it'd been a kind of déjà vu, a month ago in early March, when the girl listened to Mrs. Laura coming to terms with the house's stubbornness. The Mason mother had wanted to add an extra door to the office to help bridge the divide between the boys' bedrooms and their own. A single hallway led through the upstairs, curling like a horseshoe, separating the rooms, making them feel like they belonged to different homes. (A problem the girl knew well: when Marshall's room had been her own, she'd felt stashed away, and would strain to hear the murmur of her parents' voices in their bedroom before sleep.) That day in March, Mrs. Laura brought in a contractor, and his saw shrieked through the bones of the house, revving and spitting for most of the morning. After lunch, Mr. Nick lost his temper with the noise and took the boys to a matinee. Mrs. Laura stayed and sat out in the Adirondack chair by her vegetable garden. The girl could only cup her hands over her ears and wait.

Around two in the afternoon, with a withered sigh of its motor, the saw eventually gave out. The worker stomped over to Eddie's bedroom window and called out for Mrs. Laura to come up.

"I mean, I thought I'd just cut through the studs," he said in an accent thick with the southern parishes. "But, would you believe it? It's like that wood has petrified. Bent the teeth of my saw blade!"

The contractor picked up a hammer and smacked its side against a stud for effect. The noise was as if he'd struck stone. The girl, who had pressed her ear against the side of the office closet when he began to speak, bit her tongue in surprise.

"This house might as well be a mine shaft!" the worker said.

The girl spat into a small basket of Marshall's old video game controllers. Decided she wouldn't mind the loud man himself being thrown into a mine.

"Well, it sounds like you're saying you can't do it." Mrs. Laura's voice was heavy with disappointment. The girl could imagine her already bending over, feeling the texture of the wood, wondering whether her own saw might fare better.

"I'm saying that nobody's cutting through, short of using explosives."

"Let me see."

It was Mrs. Laura's turn to thump the hammer against the wall. This time the girl was prepared.

"Hard as rock," the mother said. "Jesus. We're learning something new about this place every day."

Here, the Masons would temper their expectations as to what could be done with the home. The girl had learned enough herself to know some things wouldn't change. She counted on it. She had felt those walls on their insides, traced her fingers along their grooves and indentations.

The Mason parents could spend their weeknights curled up in bathroom cabinets breathing in paint fumes, or bent over a table saw on the back porch. The boys could be called down, grumbling, on Sunday evenings to help with the latest project, whether it was to re-align the lazy Susan cabinets in the kitchen, rip up cracked tile in the master bedroom and caulk in new, or lay fresh insulation in the attic, or hook up new ceiling fans to the old wiring that veined through the walls, or dig through the back of the deep living room closet to sort through the leavings of families who had lived there years ago.

But none of them would ever know the house like she did.

A CLOCK OF BIRDS

THE ONLY CHANGE THE MASONS MADE THAT THE GIRL IN THE WALLS liked was the clock. Loud enough to be heard throughout the first floor's rooms, so that ears, grown sensitive in the quiet, would hear it in the attached garage when coiled within the foot space of the kayaks, or upstairs, tucked in the plush quilts in the hallway's linen closet, or even higher, in the dark heat of the attic.

The antique clock was so unlike what she had imagined one should be. They were supposed to be dusty things, decrepit and cockeyed, something Ebenezer Scrooge would own. The clock wasn't as huge as one would expect, considering its volume. It stood just above waist-height for a man, or as tall as a short, eleven-year-old girl, and was nearly pyramid-shaped, with a smooth, glossy curve that sloped up the sides to frame the face. Its cedar was bright, almost shiny when the overhead lights were on, and at the clock's bottom, a narrow glass strip revealed the swaying pendulum, painted with the image of a southern short-tailed shrew.

It was a granddaughter clock, or at least that was what she had heard Mrs. Laura call it. The name sounded made up, but the girl liked it. For some reason, it brought to her mind some other young girl—not so different from herself—who, by magic, had metamorphosed into two separate things at once, changed into a mixture, like a mermaid or sphinx. In her mind, the clock perched in the corner was both a child and a smirking old woman.

On its face, instead of numbers, were twelve painted types of birds. A mockingbird, a cardinal, tight clusters of finches and star-lings, a great horned owl, a blue jay, and at the top, a painted bun-ting with colors like stained glass. And other birds, a couple the girl didn't know, hadn't yet found in the hefty *Illustrated Guide to North American Birds* that was kept on one of the bottom shelves in the small library-study. Every hour, by some process of gears and pulleys more than a hundred years old, the clock thunked, then let out whatever bird's call the hour hand faced.

The clock began her morning: the faint sound of a blue jay from downstairs that woke her from sleep. In yellow light from the attic dormer window, she would pull herself out from the nook beneath the floorboards. She'd fold up the layer of quilts and winter coats she used as a mattress and tuck them back into the Masons' storage bins.

Below her, on a weekday like today, her rise was soon followed by the light squeak of Mr. and Mrs. Mason's bedsprings as they sat up to rest their feet on the ground. The girl waited until she heard them, then she stepped carefully along the plywood that formed the attic floor, swinging her arms in windmills to loosen them. She looked out the dormer into the backyard where oak branches bobbed in a breeze. A leaf tumbled between the parked cars beside the attached garage in the driveway. In a few minutes, Marshall's alarm clock began its routine of wailing and stopping, wailing and stopping, as its owner slapped at the snooze button again and again.

Below, the hiss of the boys' shower as Eddie bathed. The AC unit rumbled beside her as it turned on for the morning, and the girl hoisted herself on top and spread herself across to feel the cool metal along her neck, back, and legs. Downstairs, Mrs. Laura had begun cooking breakfast—the girl could smell it, couldn't she?

Biscuits in the oven?

Sometimes, she imagined the scents of an entire meal wafted up through the rafters: the maple syrup on the boys' pancakes, strawberry jam spread over Mr. Nick's toast, the spray of an orange as Mrs. Laura split it into its separate parts. But later, when she went downstairs to the kitchen, she'd be disappointed to find in the dishwasher only the remains of instant oatmeal or cereal and milk.

This was its own cold reminder. Whenever the girl ate breakfast with her parents, her dad always cooked. Hash browns. Plump, crackling sausage. Scrambled eggs with Crystal hot sauce. While they ate, sometimes she'd kick beneath the table, one leg catching the small flags of her dad's cuffs, the other grazing her mom's stockings—the feel of them like firm, soft sand. Her mom's smirk, her cocked eyebrow. "Having fun?"

After the Mason breakfast was finished, shoes stomped up the stairs, rushing to one of the boys' bedrooms. A few moments later, they thumped back through the hall and down again. Marshall or Eddie must have forgotten a textbook, or a calculator.

Through the dormer, she watched Mr. Nick and the boys appear, the father dressed in his white, collared shirt, Marshall in a black T-shirt and jeans fraying at the heels, Eddie still in his middle school uniform—blue polo and khaki shorts. As she watched them leave, she remembered how, when they left together in the morning, they all went to three separate schools, Mr. Nick teaching at a high school far from their district, east of the river. That thought always surprised her in a small way. Easy to think that, when they were away, they were all together—but they hardly ever were.

When Eddie reached the car, he paused to wipe the soles of his shoes along the rubber seal at the bottom of the red Saturn's back door. He seemed to count as he wiped, deliberately and patiently, one sole before the other. She'd seen him do it for a full minute on other days. This morning, Marshall wouldn't wait. He stepped up behind Eddie. And after Mr. Nick got into the front seat and closed his door, he shoved a quick elbow into his younger brother's back.

"Hurry up!" Marshall said, gripping Eddie by the shoulder to usher him in.

The girl threw an uppercut into the air, imagining a well-placed swing into the older brother's teeth. After their car pulled away, Mrs. Laura was soon to follow, flashing into the backyard in a dress and heels, dressed for her real-estate job. As always, when she reached the car door, she paused to bend, place her briefcase between her calves, and comb her fingers through her shoulder-length hair. She found what must have been a speck of dried paint, and she pulled it loose with her thumb and forefinger and flicked it into the lawn. Soon, her blue SUV kicked up dust in the gravel driveway.

The next round of birdcalls rose up from the granddaughter clock below. This was the wren's hour.

Her time.

Throughout each day she'd hear the clock, its singular, weighty tones on the quarter and half hours, and the birdcalls when the minute hand pointed up, toward twelve, and higher as well, up toward the girl's own nest in the attic. She counted time by their calls.

THE BIRDS

WHEN THE WREN CALLED, IT OFTEN MEANT A SLICE OF TOAST AND A hard-boiled egg in the kitchen, and cereal when she wanted to be careful. It also meant going to the bathroom, washing her face in the sink, and wiping down her armpits and the dirty soles of her feet with a moist washcloth. She kept the green cloth in the very back of the cabinet beneath the bathroom sink on the first floor, behind the extra toilet paper and cleaning supplies.

Starlings meant she could be as loud as she wanted. It meant music and exercise. Meant turning on the radio in the living room, and if there was a good song on, it meant dancing, and cartwheeling in the upstairs hallway, lying belly-down on a rug and sliding between rooms as though she were on a sled. New songs could be hit or miss. "Don't Phunk with My Heart" was good enough that she had to stop whatever she was doing to run to the living room and jump on and off the sofa. "Hollaback Girl" might get the radio turned off for the day.

The call of robins meant it was a good time to check out television, since *The Price is Right* was finally over, and sometimes reruns of *Hercules* and *Xena: Warrior Princess* came on. This was usually when the mailman came by, and if there was a package to be delivered, his truck would churn down the house's long driveway, and he'd leave it on the front porch. The girl had to be careful here. She kept the remote in hand while she watched, in case she needed to put the television on mute. Poised to duck down to the floor, out of the view of the windows, on a moment's notice. Once, a month or so past, a mailman had heard the TV inside and had knocked and knocked until she thought he would never leave.

The low, moaning honk of the Canada goose meant microwaving whatever leftovers she could find in the fridge. Sometimes, it meant eating trail mix or an apple, or digging through the back of the freezer to find an old bag of peas or strawberries. It also meant prepping: making peanut butter sandwiches, or popping popcorn on the stove and keeping it in a brown paper bag in her attic space for her dinner.

The solemn hoot of the great horned owl meant it was her time to read. Or, if she didn't feel like reading someone else's stories, it meant she might make her own. The girl went through each of the rooms, imagining other people living around her (sprawled out on the sofa with a crossword puzzle, or singing in the shower, or a couple of older folks chatting to one another—like dolls in a dollhouse). Sometimes, the people she imagined were ones she had known: her mom and dad, of course, and others. Elderly relatives with canes and walkers from the small family reunions she had attended as a little girl, or ones she had only heard of, like the great uncle who had owned the house, way back, who had given it to her parents after he passed. Other times, the people whose stories she invented were ones completely made up. Imaginary families, like ghosts, wearing button-down coats and floor-length dresses, ones she imagined must have lived in the house generations ago. Other times, the people she imagined weren't even human. Centaurs clomping through the foyer. Odin, bending over in the kitchen to open the fridge and pour himself a tall glass of milk. A mermaid in the parents' bathroom, adjusting the temperature of the water in the bathtub. Giant spiders who whispered to one another in the walls.

When the cardinal, the bright red bird, chirped, it was a warning. It meant she should expect the Masons to come home.

And now, their time.

TODAY, DIFFERENT

WHEN THE CARDINAL SANG THIS AFTERNOON, THE GIRL WENT BACK to the dryer, where she had left her book. She hopped on the machine, curling at the waist over the controls at the back, to reach down and snatch the book from its hiding place. But as she lifted the book, its cover caught on the silver exhaust tubing and pulled the tube free from the wall.

The girl hated mistakes, inconsistencies that the Masons would find when they came home. This one, a disconnected dryer tube, was small, considering. She'd broken a plate before, had spilled a glass of water on the couch and had to spend the greater part of an hour kneading the dark spot with beach towels. The dryer tube at least seemed like something that might take a while for a Mason to notice. Maybe. The girl honestly had no idea what the tube was for.

Regardless, she had to fix it. The thought of it there, unhooked, open to the world, was a steady, solemn whisper saying, "Something's changed. Something here has changed this"—and the girl knew she wouldn't be able to think of anything else until night, when she got the chance to fix it, and shut the bleating thing up. She had a few minutes to spare before the Masons drove in. Might as well fix it now.

On top of the dryer, the girl lowered herself, her belly sliding further past the control panel, until the dryer's timer display was digging into her thigh. She felt the tingle of blood rushing to her face. Her fingers fumbled with the tubing, trying to stuff it back over its fitting. But it wouldn't go. Her hair caught in her face. She needed to pinch the metal wire around the tube, but her fingers were too short to get a good grip. Then, at once, the girl's legs slipped free from the dryer and she felt herself drop—sickening lurch—but she caught herself, one hand on the floor. A small wave of nausea passed through her. And then she saw it. In the exhaust hole in the wall, a patch of pink in the dark.

The girl dropped the tubing. With her other hand still propping herself from falling to the floor, she reached into the hole and snatched the pink thing up. A simple, old sock. Dust and curling strands of grayed hair clung to it in clumps. It was exactly what she had hoped for. The girl squeezed it between her fingers, shook the thing off and pressed it to her exposed neck. She knew who it had belonged to. It'd been her mom's.

The Masons would soon be home, but the thought didn't worry her as much as it had moments before. Priorities shifted. Growing dizzy from the blood in her head, the girl twisted the rest of her body down into the crevice behind the dryer and righted herself on the floor. She reached as far as her arm would go into the exhaust hole. Was there anything else? She clawed at the sides, top, and bottom. Sifted through the build-up of dryer lint and dust. Anything else left at all? She reached deeper, as far as her fingers could go, until the tips were rubbed raw. Her wrist and forearm scraped against the metal rim. Sharp pain as the soft skin was cut through. When she heard the gravel churn in the driveway, the girl kept looking. What if there was something she was missing? It wasn't until the keys turned in the front door's knob that she heard her mom's voice.

Elise—hide!

The girl pulled back, as if shocked by electricity.

Her imagination only, but enough. Keys were turning in the front door's lock. She looked around her, heart thumping. She looked to the walls to engulf her.

THE MASONS ENTER
THEIR HOME

THE BOYS DROPPED THEIR BAGS ON THE FOYER'S TILES, BESIDE
the granddaughter clock. Mr. Nick dropped the mail on the small,
oak table. And from the foyer, they separated, splitting in three
directions.

Marshall dragging his feet to the living room—drumming his
large knuckles against the molding. Mr. Nick heading upstairs, each
step measured and slow, hand clapping the banister. And Eddie,
his short strides passing into the library—toward her. He stopped
abruptly to spin the small globe on one of the bookshelves.

From the living room, *Judge Judy* resounded from the television.
Marshall switched the channel. Mr. Nick's weight on the second story
above, going into the office, his desk chair rolling across the floor.
Then Eddie entered the laundry room, where she hid. Eddie passed
the washer and dryer. His shoes squeaking against the tile. He left the
room and stood in the back porch, plucking at loose reeds in the wicker
armchair. Then he opened the door and went outside.

And she was safe. Crouching in the tight, dark space of the laundry chute, she let the clenched muscles in her legs and arms relax. She
shuddered, adrenaline still coursing through her limbs. She'd been
stupid, and she'd almost ruined everything.

It didn't happen often. She shouldn't make mistakes. She was supposed to be an extension of the house itself.

Be better. Only her own voice now. Her own admonition. She
wished she had someone else here to scold her, to put their hand

firmly on her shoulder and shake their head slow. It didn't feel like enough coming from herself.

Be better. She took a breath, deep, slow, quiet. She imagined her body growing dusky, translucent. She liked this place, the hidden chute. One of her secrets; it felt closer to the house than many other places she might hide. Like a heart, or a stomach. She held her mom's sock in her hands. And while the Masons settled into their separate places in the house and yard, she held the sock against her cheek.

Elise held her mom's sock and wept.

WAKING IN SMOKE

LAST DECEMBER, ON THE ROAD HOME FROM CITY PARK, ELISE crawled on her hands and knees over broken glass. The fire behind her roaring so loud she wasn't sure she would ever be able to hear anything else. Her palms burned as she pulled herself on, and the fumes of gasoline were strong enough to choke on. She reached the tall weeds of the neutral ground and she sat there, her hands stinging and the length of her back aching from the heat. The feathered heads of weeds itched her cheeks, and her legs soaked up the hard cold of the ground beneath her. She watched the black smoke from the two vehicles, the truck and her parents' car, pumping in a column high into the sky.

She was a smart girl. She was mature for her age. She knew well enough what she was watching. That her mom and her dad, they were already gone.

When she was found, she was walking on the roadside across the Woodland Bridge, nearly two miles away.

Even then she felt them expanding into the world around her. They were in the roadside weeds brushing against her legs. The dark trees along the sides of the road, those swaying branches like hands, waving. The impact of the barges docking beneath her, far down below the bridge. Their floodlights flitting up into the sky. The clank and thud of the docking chains. In every single thing, they were speaking. But their voices were too soft to understand.

Do you know where she was going? She crossed that whole bridge on her own—that accident was miles away.

Where were you going, little girl? The address we have for you says you live back the other way.

She told me, when she was brought in, that her old house was down there in Plaquemines. It's another family living there now.

Elise, is there someone else we can call? Anyone in town you know, or your parents knew?

She won't say.

Is there a relative you can stay with tonight? Or, maybe for a while, while people sort this out?

Chief, you can keep asking her yourself, but she won't say.

THE CHUTE

THE GIRL ELISE WOULD HAVE TO WAIT THROUGH THE LONG HOURS of the afternoon in the hidden laundry chute until night. They wouldn't find her here—the chute had been blocked off long ago, rendered useless when some previous owner had added a large cabinet to the upstairs master bathroom. It was Elise who'd brought viability to it once again. A couple months back, when the Masons were away, she'd taken a small saw from the garage and cut through the thin wood in the back of the bathroom closet (the cut slanted, uneven, but her dad would still have been proud). Just the stack of old towels and spare toilet paper hid the crevice that she had created, large enough for a young girl to squeeze through on her belly. Once inside, with her feet using the small crossbeams as grips, she could work the wood cutout back into place. Though the scar across the wood would be visible, and the white paint had flaked loose in the corners, someone would have to be specifically looking there in order to discover what hid behind. Inside, the chute was narrow enough that she could pin her back against one side to help her descend or climb the tall chimneystack.

But the bottom of the chute, its entrance, was why, maybe more than all other places between the walls, she loved this space. The entrance was the reason she knew the chute existed. When her parents still owned the house, the bottom had been sealed with a square of plywood so ugly that Elise's dad had used a crowbar to pull it out, which revealed the old, obsolete chute. Elise's mom was at work, and he'd called his daughter downstairs. They investigated the narrow tower with his biggest flashlight.

"So many odd things here," her dad had said. An artist, he brought the board to the attached garage, and he painted it a deep, forest green. When it dried, he took out a delicate brush, and with quick strokes, added a white tree to its middle. A weeping willow in white bloom.

At one point, the board had been beautiful, but being beside the washer's water hookups, the wood had gotten wet, and over the years the painted tree had swelled and begun to crack. Elise knew it likely wouldn't be long before Mr. and Mrs. Mason made it their next project, to touch up the tree, or to paint over it, and in the process they would discover the chute behind it.

Until then—Elise could hide here.

Outside the chute, the dryer's exhaust tube was still unattached. And her book of Norse myths left there, tossed behind the machine when she'd heard the doorknob rattling. That was more concerning. And with the Masons now home, leaving the laundry chute wasn't easy, or quick to do; the plywood board would have to be wedged out, a corner at a time. She'd have to find a way to catch the board before it fell to the floor. The process took time—she could do it, but not during the family's waking hours, risking someone passing through, finding her half-exposed. Elise would have to wait until night to fix the exhaust tube. Her book would also have to lie there, waiting. This was her punishment.

No more mistakes.

A faint impression of light encircled the board with her dad's tree, and what bled through shone on the pale hairs on her forearm. The inside of her arm burned. Small beads of blood had formed along the scratches gouged by the metal-rimmed exhaust hole.

Elise didn't cry from scratches and bruises anymore. The last time she could remember was for a skinned knee, one or two years back, from when she'd fallen from a tree. The flash of memory like a photograph to her: Elise seated on the rim of her parents' tub, crying, watching her own reflection in the mirror. Her mom cleaning and bandaging the cut. Elise's hair, then combed, pulled to one side with a pink clip. Below, her mom's back hunched over her leg.

In the chute, the girl brushed lint from the cuts. She pressed each wet droplet with her thumb to stop their flow. Later this evening, she would scale the long chute up, patient and quiet, to that same bathroom, now Mr. and Mrs. Mason's. While they watched television downstairs, Elise would pop free the false wall at the back of the cabinet, push through the rolls of toilet paper, and crawl into the bathroom, where the rubbing alcohol was kept. She'd ignore the mirror and, with it, her dusted cheeks, the unkempt hair that'd grown too long. She would douse the cuts over the sink and grit her teeth as her stinging arm seared.

These are the consequences of living alone, Elise had come to realize. Of being all alone. You take care of yourself. You learn to take care of yourself.

If Elise ever hurt herself, punctured a palm with a nail, twisted an ankle in a descent, she would still be alone. If she caught a cold, she would recover on her own. She could suppress a sneeze (those loud, bellowing sneezes were for dramatic people, she'd learned, for cartoon characters ridiculously failing to hide), but no hand would ever press against the heat of her forehead. No ice water, cold compresses, or aspirin brought to her bedside. Elise worried most about coughing. About nausea. She worried about what it would mean if she grew too weak to pull herself back out into the light.

Even so, she'd be here. Until?

She would be here.

Elise told herself this for months. Every day, she was resolute, even if it had grown harder to hear.

BEGIN AGAIN

IT WAS LATE BY THE TIME THE POLICEMEN DROPPED ELISE OFF. HER extended family—a grandfather, an aunt she'd never met—lived in states far to the north, in a time zone earlier than her own. They hadn't answered their phones when the policewoman called. So, for tonight, Ms. Brim. The woman met them on her porch in a bathrobe, pulled tight for warmth. Her hand suppressed a yawn. The face of the house behind her was narrow across, like all the others around it. Stubby, and stunted-seeming, to see it from the street, but Elise had seen this kind before, a common house in the city. She knew it was deep inside. Long, like a massive snake; the big door was its mouth pinched shut. Her dad and mom always called them shotgun houses. Elise hadn't ever asked them why.

On the porch, Ms. Brim knelt down on the mat and looked Elise in the eyes. She spoke swiftly, without inflection, the way teachers did at school with instructions for the standardized tests even they didn't want their students to take.

"You'll be with us tonight. Maybe for a few days while they figure out who's getting you. And when. But this is your home, for now. And we can be family. Home's where you're loved, and you'll get that here."

She handed Elise a small, stuffed elephant. Then a toothbrush still in its packaging.

The wind blew—cold outside—but the snake's insides were little better. Cool, dark, the air smelling sharp with the remnants of bleach. Ms. Brim kept the overhead lights off and led Elise through, their footsteps like knuckles knocking beneath the floorboards. No doors between any of the rooms. They passed through a room where she saw impressions of bodies turn in their beds. In the next, one shape sat up and stared. Each room a half-room, a hallway.

"It's late," Ms. Brim whispered near the end of the long house. "Early, actually. Tomorrow, we'll see what'll happen." Ms. Brim reached through a doorway and flipped on a bathroom light. She pointed elsewhere. By the glow: a small mattress, a blanket balled up at its foot. Elise's new bed.

"In the meantime," the woman continued. "Undress. Brush your teeth, and sleep. Try to. You got a whole new start in the morning."

In the other bed across the room, another girl rolled over and covered her head with a pillow. Ms. Brim's hand touched Elise's shoulder. She tensed. When the woman left, Elise went into the bathroom and did as she was told. Brushed her teeth. Laid her toothbrush beside the other four on the counter. Turned out the light and groped her way to bed.

Through the window, the streetlights shimmered orange. As she lay on the stiff sheets, a sudden gurgle from the bathroom—probably water in the pipes—but like nothing she'd ever heard before.

Elise closed her eyes, and she tried to imagine that opening them in the morning meant returning to a corrected world. One that realized what it had done, and taken its choices back. But there would be no sleeping that night.

Eventually, with the night wearing on, seeming never to end, and with the breath of that other girl growing steady in the bed near her, and the wind against the loose windowpanes, and the morning seeming impossible, increasingly like some pockmarked creature, needy and biting, with fingers grown far too long to actually exist—the girl had to catch herself.

Ms. Brim's words in her head: Home is where you're loved.

Elise needed that place.

She needed to go home.

THE MASONS AT WORK

SUNDAY AFTERNOON IN LATE APRIL, AND MR. AND MRS. MASON HAD the boys pull loose the guest room's carpet. It was a wilted brown mess, old and almost sticky, long past its due date.

"How did we put this off for so long?" Mr. Nick said, his voice muffled through one of the white ventilator masks he and his family wore over their mouths. "We've been keeping an *armoire* in here. An antique armoire—nineteenth-century—on carpet?"

Mrs. Laura cut a long segment with a *thwuck*. She beat across the floor on her knees, rolling the old carpet into a bundle, which came detached with a sound like paper being crumpled into a ball. "There's a hundred thousand things in this house that need to get done. There's a lot of ridiculous things happening here," she said. "Hey—Marshall, use something smaller. A flathead screwdriver is more than enough for the corner tacking. You don't need the crowbar."

"The trim's already scratched up," Marshall said.

"Marshall," Mrs. Laura said.

Across the room the crowbar clattered to the floor.

Mr. Nick's voice: "Watch your attitude, kid."

While the family worked, Elise was beside them, reading with a booklight inside the wall. She was close enough to listen in, to hear their conversations, and the strange, comforting sound of carpet being torn from its tacking. It reminded her of the Little Mermaid shoes she owned as a little girl, and the sound their Velcro straps made when separated.

"I don't see why we have to do this," Marshall said.

As Mrs. Laura rolled another stretch of carpet, she answered him. "Because, you dingbat, this carpet is nasty. Not that you understand the word. You can't seem to notice whatever dead thing in your room is making it smell that way."

Mr. Nick laughed. Inside the wall, Elise had to do her best to stifle her own snort.

"What the hell are you smiling for, Eddie?" Marshall said.

"All right, boys," Mrs. Laura said. "We don't have time for it. Actually, yeah. Can we please pick up the pace? I'd like to get this part finished by dark."

Thwuck.

Like with most of their projects, Elise could see that Mrs. Laura seemed to enjoy the work more than the rest of her family combined. Mr. Nick, who was just as likely as her to be found on an early weekday morning on top of a ladder, touching up border trim, had a reasonable approach to housework. Elise, more than once, had peeked around a corner to see him pausing in the middle of a project to look over whatever left he had to do. He'd slump his shoulders and, with a long sigh, let out a hushed, moaning, "Fuck."

That, she understood.

But Mrs. Laura never showed weakness. Over the past few months, Elise had looked down through the attic dormer and seen the Mason mother's hair wild, glowing in the sunlight, while she sledgehammered fence posts in the garden. Had heard her chuckling as she pressure-washed the house's siding. Had smelled the scent of fresh wood stain coming from the attached garage late on a Saturday night. Mrs. Laura reminded Elise of her own parents, in their own projects here, before they gave up on trying to have another child (the pregnancy with Elise had hurt her mom somehow) and decided to move on to a home more in line with their needs. This was all to say Mrs. Laura went about each project with an enthusiasm Elise thought pathological.

But to be honest, she didn't mind Mrs. Laura as much as someone like Marshall, even if the mother seemed to be the driving force for most of the changes (awful changes) to Elise's home. She had grown to realize she enjoyed watching and listening to Mrs. Laura, like Weather Channel footage of a tornado. Enjoyed, as long as Elise wasn't subject to the torrents of wind herself, like when the woman, on a whim, replaced the set of thick curtains with a pair of sheer ones (impossible to hide behind). Or how she would get on her hands and knees to vacuum under tables and behind the sofa. Or, worst of all, how she had taken to probing with a flashlight the oddly sized holes in the backs of closets and the access panel in the pantry ceiling.

"I don't know why we always have to do it ourselves." Marshall grunted as he tugged on a patch of carpet liner that was stuck in a corner. "We could hire someone. Sunday's the only day I don't have to go to work or do homework, and it's kind of bullshit you have me doing this."

"Watch your language," said Mr. Nick, across the room.

"Neither me or Eddie," Marshall said, "want to have anything to do with your stupid projects."

"Eddie's not saying anything," Mr. Nick said. "Do you have a problem helping out with the house, Eddie? No? Marshall, I'm pretty sure the only one complaining is you."

"Stop it," Mrs. Laura said. "Nick, I mean you, too."

In a few minutes, Mrs. Laura had her husband and Marshall lifting each side of the armoire while she pulled free the carpet beneath it. Eddie was somewhere in a corner. He'd hardly spoken the entire afternoon. Nearly silent. So hard to keep track of him sometimes, hard to imagine what it was he was doing. Sometimes it felt like she wasn't the only ghost in this house.

Earlier that day, Mrs. Laura had said this would be a quick project, one they could finish in an afternoon. But, with the day dying, and the wren calling out from downstairs, Elise listened as the family looked over the bare, wooden floor. They paced over it. They stopped in various places to rub at patches with the bottom of their shoe soles.

Elise could tell: something had turned out different than they had planned.

Big surprise.

"Nope," Mrs. Laura said. "Nope. This won't work. We'll need to scrub it down, polish it. We'll need to polyurethane it, too. Nick, add all of it to the list."

The father, quiet for a second. A sigh. "Okay. Consider it added."

"I'm guessing," Marshall said, "this means you'll have us in here again next weekend? So, it'll be every Sunday this month."

Eddie groaned from the corner, the only sound Elise had heard from him in over an hour.

Their father took a harsher tone. "I don't want to hear it. You two should know, we've been more than reasonable. With as much as needs to get done in this house, with as much as we do without you? We need a lot more than an afternoon a week of help, and we're not asking for it."

The boys didn't respond. Something thumped against the wall by Elise, startling her. It must have been Marshall, letting the back of his skull knock against the plaster.

In the moments of quiet that followed, Elise imagined the boys and their parents looking down over the length of the floor they'd uncovered. She pictured it stained, blackened in places from age, or water damage from a summer hurricane. She remembered how it had looked in the kitchen when her own parents had ripped up that mustard yellow linoleum, and how long it had taken for them to turn that wooden floor to the glossy, syrup-colored brown it was today. She remembered lying on it on her belly with her mother when it was finished, rolling Cheerios across the floor.

"Besides," Mr. Nick continued. "If you're going to start a project, you've got to power through. Finish it. Leaving something half-done is worse than not even starting in the first place."

"Really," said Marshall. "If leaving things half-done is so bad, then how come we've lived here for over a year and we still have mice?"

"We don't have mice, Marshall," Mrs. Laura said. "We've talked about this. If we did, the traps we laid would have triggered."

Elise remembered those. Actually one had, in fact, been triggered. On her heel.

"Well, then who's eating all my food?" Marshall said. "I had two Pop-Tarts last week that went missing. Eddie swears it wasn't him."

"Could it be bugs?" Eddie said.

"Yeah," Mr. Nick said. "Have you considered some colossal bugs might have carried your Pop-Tarts away?"

"Nick," Mrs. Laura said.

"Something took them," said Marshall.

"Mice don't run off with entire Pop-Tarts," Mr. Nick said. "You probably ate them yourself."

"Did you eat them, Eddie?" Marshall asked.

"No."

"Did you guys eat them?"

"You really think we ate your Pop-Tarts, Marshall?" Mr. Nick said. "Together, maybe? Sneaking them in the middle of the night?"

"You two act like I'm an idiot, but I'm not," Marshall said. "I'm not dumb. I'm not a child. No, I didn't eat them myself. Something took them."

Elise closed her book. The Pop-Tarts had been a bad idea.

SUNDAY EVENING

EVENTUALLY, INSIDE THE WALLS, ELISE SENSED IT GROWING DARK OUTSIDE.
She could feel it in her own body: a slowness to the muscles, a heaviness, even if she wasn't tired. There were the sounds, too, that cued her in. Faintly, the calls of tree frogs and crickets. That throb of the afternoon cicadas had ended for the day, and now, she thought, they must be tucking themselves in, behind the leaves and under litterfall—wherever it was they went—for the night.

After the Masons' Sunday projects were done, or delayed (more often) and prolonged, each family member went a separate way. Mr. Nick to his upstairs office to grade and Mrs. Laura to the back porch to read, the boys each to their own bedrooms. Marshall's door closed, Eddie's halfway. By night, the home would grow quiet, free from ladders being dragged along upstairs floors, or from the table saw roaring in the garage, or music playing from a paint-speckled radio in the hallway.

Tonight, as evening wore on, the family seemed to grow accustomed to the noises they heard that the house made when everything else was quiet. Sometimes the outside voices of a couple on horseback taking a night ride along the top of the levee sounded loud enough to seem as if they were coming from inside the house, from the depths of some empty room or closet. Other times the floors and ceilings creaked, seemingly of their own accord. Noises heard while dozing off on the living room couch, like footsteps in another room, might simply be something else: branches of a tree tapping against the siding of the house, or the steady beating of one's own heart.

The girl heard them, too. Enough to make her wonder if someone else was here, unaccounted for, slipping through the rooms of the home, like her. Someone here, who'd come to look for her. Someone else, playing a game.

SOMEONE'S ALWAYS MISSING

PEOPLE GO MISSING EVERY DAY. AND WHILE FIRST RESPONDERS, friends, neighbors, and family all search for the missing—walking along roads and the sides of canals; returning to favorite places, the ice rinks, coffee shops, playgrounds, and snowball stands; circling in their cars at night around the edge of parks with their high beams on—there are so many cases where that person hasn't been found.

But people who go missing, they don't always disappear.

Extended family—a grandfather in Minnesota, an aunt in Wisconsin, a second cousin in Illinois—hear that their granddaughter, their niece has been lost. They learn in one call about the accident, both parents dead, and that she's run away from the foster home where she'd spent the night as custody was sought. A bedroom window found open to the cold, and no other sign.

They are shocked, panicked. They are grief-stricken and overwhelmed by worry. What can they do? They drive all the way down to Louisiana; they take flights delayed by winter weather. When they arrive, they talk to police and the foster woman, who is apologetic but useless. They get in their cars and drive back and forth through neighborhoods they don't know. They take roads they imagine her parents drove with her in their car. They go to her home and search it. There, they find lamps left on, still awaiting that family's return. When they're done there, they turn them off and go back outside, into the humid cold, and search ditches and alleyways, following impulse and awful gut feelings. They look at the windows of houses along her street, seeing the gray frames glinting back at them, expecting somehow that her face will appear, grinning at them through the glare.

And, in time, their feet are numb and lifeless beneath them, their thighs and calves ache. They're tired. There's a life for them back home, still going, and she is nowhere to be found. They know the officer in charge of her case, whose number they call for updates. They can continue calling, from home. They tell each other, when they leave, that they haven't stopped looking.

But on the long drive north up I-55 to home, with the interstate stretching out in their rearview, gradually they fix it in their minds, immutable and unforgiving, what they believe to have happened: three lives gone.

Two adults deceased, and a girl missing. Two adults and a girl gone.

An awful thought. That a family—all at once—can be erased. Even though it's wrong.

Two adults gone, and a little girl hidden away.

MAKING IT HOME

NOT THE ONE SHE AND HER PARENTS HAD MOVED INTO MONTHS before, but the old house, the one that had always been her home. The too-big house, with all its rooms, jumbled like a maze on paper. The house that was falling apart. The one with mysteries that had to be solved. The one with memories.

Other houses were brick, and wood, and glass, and tile. This house was more. Each day the house woke her, held her, cradled her. It responded to her, felt each touch of her fingertips, and pressed back against the bare soles of her feet.

That morning in December, she found her way in through the library door with the loose knob that popped when wrenched, and then opened as if it hadn't been locked at all. Inside, winter winds rattled the house's storm windows. The new owners were away for the holidays. She knew it because their lamps were on automatic timers, and the thermostat had been lowered to a chilled sixty-five degrees. Their Christmas tree had all but dried up, its ornaments threatening to fall under its drooping branches. But the girl went to the kitchen, took an old carton of orange juice she found in the recycling bin beside the trash, filled it in the sink, and watered the tree. She lay on her belly as she poured into the tree's base to avoid the prick of the pine needles, the way her father would have.

It was a time of preparation: of returning to the old entrances into the walls, seeing which ones still existed—like the laundry chute her dad had shown her, the crevice in the boards she'd seen when her parents redid the attic floor, or the removable access panel in the pantry installed when the old pipes above wouldn't stop leaking.

She pushed herself, deeper into the spaces between the walls, farther than she ever would have gone before when she had been her most adventurous, when her parents had been distracted across the house, too far away to tell her to stop, come back. She saw how far she could go.

She learned practical things: which door hinges complained, how far the flush of a toilet sounded and how long it took its tank to refill, how to stifle a sneeze into something swallowed and suffocated. She learned about the family by the things they kept in their drawers, the size of their clothes, the types of soaps and shampoos, deodorants and toothpastes they used. With each hour that passed, the house became larger. It stretched out until the rooms were no longer rooms. They were each their own houses. The hallway was a road curling between them. The attic might as well be the sky itself.

Elise wrapped herself in the house as if it were a winter coat. One she didn't plan to take off.

EDDIE'S ROOM

IN THE EVENING HOURS, AFTER HIS FAMILY HAD CONCLUDED THEIR day's work on the guest room floor, Eddie built a castle in his room without any help from the instructions. He squatted barefoot on the carpet, still wearing the fraying jean shorts he'd put on for the work that day, muttering to himself so quietly that anyone near might hear only the light smack of his parting lips. He separated his Legos into different bins around him, all laboriously organized by color and size. Then he laid the castle's foundation.

A couple weeks back, Eddie had come home from school and Elise had seen him through the dormer, alone and sobbing in the backyard, cradling his face in his hands. She'd been thinking of it since: how strange, seeing a boy cry alone. She never had a brother. Sure, Elise had seen little boys cry on playgrounds and in grocery stores. And the one night she spent at the foster home, she had thought she heard an older boy snuffling in another room. But to watch Eddie then had been odd, kind of fascinating, like seeing a dog eat its dinner with a fork and knife. It had felt nice to see someone else break down.

Elise shifted her weight. She squinted through the hanging shirts in Eddie's closet at the crack of light between the door and its jamb.

That voice of hers: *You shouldn't be this close.*

Elise would never have guessed Eddie was older than her if she didn't already know. The boy's limbs were so frail they could belong to a bird. So quiet and, when he spoke, it sounded funny, like he was trying to make fun of the way someone else spoke, except he wasn't. One night, inside the intake vent by Mr. and Mrs. Mason's bedroom, she'd heard his parents talk about whether he would be better suited to a different school, an expensive one that started an hour later, with special activities that lasted into the evening. The conversation hadn't surprised Elise. If Eddie had friends now, he wasn't leaving on weekends to hang out with them. Though, to be fair, Elise had been the same way, when she still had a choice about that kind of thing.

Before, when Elise went to school, she knew of strange boys like him. So often they sat in the back corner of class, ignored, until those times during presentations when they were required to stand before the chalkboard and show, fully, how different they really were. Those boys had never bothered Elise. Like anyone else, she rarely gave them the chance. Classmates, in her experience, were a waste of time. Elise had preferred family.

Her favorite classmate had been a big, sleepy-eyed boy who sat beside her and had kept his mouth shut the times he'd seen her slip out the back door before class, during the commotion of students entering and dropping their heavy book bags to the floor. The boy had been awkward, like Eddie, had once even peed himself in homeroom as the teacher ignored his quivering, raised hand. Elise had never talked to the boy, that she could recall. But she liked him. Once, when she tucked herself in the supply cabinet, he'd pivoted in his desk, rotated completely the other way. When Ms. Robicheaux asked him whether he knew if she had gone home sick that day, he had muttered, stumbling over the words, that he didn't know.

Eddie wasn't so different. Weird, to most anyone. But, here in his room, she could tell this was where he was at his best. Alone. Away from school, and from his brother, and his parents. Elise understood that. Eddie wasn't weird, quiet, or sensitive here. Here, he was good at building.

When Mrs. Laura's voice called up from downstairs to tell Eddie it was time to get ready for bed, he stood with his hands on his hips and looked down on the work he had done. He nodded and went into the bathroom to brush his teeth.

Eddie closed the bathroom door behind him, even if it didn't make much sense, since his own bedroom door was shut and no one would see in. Peculiar, but a trait Elise appreciated. It allowed her the chance to creak open the closet door, to step out. For a couple minutes, she moved through the room as freely as if it were hers, and looked over his bookshelf, through the window, and at the beginnings of the castle. She could do this during the day when no one else was home, but there was a feeling to a room that someone had just left that was different, a little more alive. The carpet was still warm from where he had sat. She dropped to her haunches to study what he had built of his castle: the impressions of walls and antechambers, columns without walls between them, what she imagined would grow to be a ballroom, a throne room.

Over the next few days, the towers would grow tall, and the characters—knights in armor, blond princes, and bandits lurking in the recesses—would populate each of the separate rooms of the castle. She'd watch it grow.

THINGS KEPT

IN HER NOOK BENEATH THE ATTIC'S FLOOR WAS WHERE SHE KEPT them. Under the loose board of plywood, there was a space just large enough for a small girl to lie on her back between the rafters and extend her legs. Looking down, it might seem tight as a coffin. At night as she slept, they surrounded her on all sides.

There were practical items kept here. Several half-filled water bottles that had been pulled from the recycling bin. Uneaten Nature Valley snack bars stacked in the shape of a small pyramid. A gallon-sized Ziploc bag of popcorn. Wrinkled, rolled-up boys' T-shirts. A girl's, with a unicorn graphic and the text, "I Believe in Humans." A tube of men's deodorant. An old, empty emergency car toilet. A pile of folded, unused tissues and balled-up ones beside them.

There were pencils, a pencil sharpener, and a loose-leaf paper with drawn pictures of finches, wrens, and cardinals. A small flashlight and spare batteries. Peppermints.

Also, other, stranger items—incongruous ones—that together resembled a seabird's nest of collected colorful things found out in the ocean.

An old Jazzercise VHS tape. A man's black bow tie.

A stuffed elephant. A woman's earring. A single, pink sock.

Books, fantasy and mythological ones, taken from a downstairs bedroom, their pages dog-eared, hard creases in the paper that remain no matter how hard someone were to rub them smooth. A sun-bleached photograph: two parents and their child.

GAME

ONE WEEKEND AFTERNOON, WHEN NO ONE WAS UPSTAIRS, ELISE slipped down from the attic and saw both of the boys' bedroom doors open. It startled her to find Marshall's door ajar with its overhead lights on, the room as garish as a gaping, open eye. The older brother always kept it closed, even when he wasn't home. Seeing, from the hallway, the sixteen-year-old's clothes scattered across the floor, his bedsheet and comforter balled at the bottom of his bed, like the dried and wilted leaves of some flower, it felt like catching him coming out of the shower, even if she knew the room as well as any other. Already knew its secrets: the magazines stacked beneath the nightstand with long, skinny women in underwear; the pair of switchblade knives kept in a red pencil bag in the back of his computer desk's drawer.

She crept down the stairs, and she heard the boys in the dining room, speaking to one another in voices hard to make out. Plastic pattered across the dining room table—the contents of a checkers box dumped out. Their chairs squeaked against the wood floor as the boys scooted them closer and leaned their chests against the table's edge.

"All right," Marshall said. "Like I said, I'll play one game. Make it count."

Elise stepped into the living room. She heard the boys around the corner, in the dining room. Elise crouched behind the back of the sofa, then crawled, shimmying up the narrow length between the sofa and the wall.

Too risky. That voice, exasperated, in her head.

At the sofa's far end, Elise peered around the corner, between the thick legs of the end table, through the dining room's doorway.

You're making a mistake. Another one.

But Elise had always liked checkers. She couldn't play it on her own.

Eddie sat barefoot and cross-legged in his chair. Marshall slouched with his chin on his fist, his posture a curving question mark. With the board set up and ready, the younger brother contemplated his first move.

"Go ahead," Marshall said.

Eddie stared at the board. He got up on his knees and curled over, looked down on it, his bangs dangling loose from his forehead. He raised his slender arm, elbow high in the air, and pushed a piece forward with his pointer finger. In response, Marshall picked up his and dropped it to its new square. The piece rattled to a stop.

Eddie took his time for the next move. While he thought, he scratched at what must be a mosquito bump on his thigh. His attention was on the game, but he scratched carefully, circling the bite, never letting his fingernail cross the puckered skin. Marshall raised an eyebrow at his younger brother, and investigated his own fingernails. Chewed on the thumbnail.

"It's checkers, not rocket science," Marshall said.

Eddie made his move. Then Marshall, his. As the game progressed, it was too difficult to see what was happening on the board. Expressions needed to be read, posture analyzed. How many jumps were they making? How far did their arms extend when they reached to move their pieces? Elise followed their game this way. Marshall reached behind his neck and felt the short bristles of hair of his newest buzz cut. Eddie's brow furrowed. He leaned on his elbows.

The deeper into the game they played, the longer Eddie considered his moves. Elise imagined his thoughts sliding across his forehead like a child's rotating lamp.

Should the king on the back row hold its position or advance? How much was a piece that hasn't moved worth? Should I fight to keep the pieces I haven't moved yet?

And he was taking too long to move. Marshall picked up the checkers he'd already captured, rubbed them between his thumb and forefinger, stacked them on top of each other, picked them up again. He jutted his lower jaw like a bull, then slumped to lay his head on one hand, toying at his pieces with the other.

It became hard to tell who was winning at this point. She was fairly certain Eddie was, but she didn't think anyone else would think so, with how seriously the younger brother seemed to take the board, how troubled he seemed, and how bored the older brother now acted.

The game ended during one of Eddie's longest moves. Marshall picked up the box top of the game, placed it beside the table and, with one fluid motion, swept all of the pieces from the board. Eddie, startled, yelped like a dog as the world on the board evaporated before him. Marshall sat unfazed. He folded the board up and tucked it into its box.

Marshall stood, ready to take the checkers box back to the rest of the board games in the library. But he paused at the table, and said, "I really can't play games with you. Goddamn, you know I wish I could. But you make it so hard."

He took a few steps more then paused in the doorway to the living room. With the box tucked under one arm, he gestured with his open palms. "Fuck, Eddie. You're thirteen next week. A teenager! You'll be in high school, with me—and you know, it's hard enough as is without having you there to take care of, too." Marshall took the checkers box in both hands, brought it to his face, and shook it so all the pieces rattled inside. "So, fuck, man! Why can't you be a normal fucking brother?"

Eddie stared down at the table, as if the board had never been pulled away at all. He didn't have much of an expression. He put his hands in his lap. Breathed through his mouth.

"I swear you make me weirder, just living with you. I wish you'd grow out of it. I wish you'd grow up. Just be normal? I wish you fuck-ing could."

Marshall returned the board to the library, then went up to his bedroom.

IN THE EVENING

EDDIE BUILT A CHECKERS BOARD ON HIS BEDROOM FLOOR OUT OF black and white Lego pieces. Knights aligned on one side and bandits on the other. He played against himself, jumping the characters over one another. He squinted between moves, as if trying to forget the other player's strategy he'd been using only a moment ago.

At one point, as he stood up to use the bathroom, he paused, standing in the middle of his room in a way that suggested something seemed strange to him. His gaze slid over the dresser, the overstuffed armchair, the closet in his room. He bent over a bit to see beneath his bed. From the look of him, it seemed a feeling had welled up in him, unsettling, some tingle along the back of his neck and shoulders, inspired perhaps by pretending for the past hour to be two separate people.

Eddie opened the door to the boys' shared bathroom and shut it gingerly behind him. He wasn't in there long. The flush of the toilet meant there would be twelve to fifteen seconds of Eddie sudsing his hands with the lemon-scented hand soap, rinsing them in the sink. The rumble of the towel rack meant the bathroom door would soon be opening.

Everything would look the same to him, at first. His bedsheets still made with the top folded back, the way his mother liked. The books on his bookshelf stacked horizontally and vertically the way he preferred. The pieces on his Lego checkerboard still in the same position: the bandits about to promote two kings, their waiting crowns and horses prepared beside the board.

Eddie would play his game for a little while longer before he would notice. The biggest change was a small one, made to the castle he had finished the day before, to its single tower that extended up from the heart. "The Observatory" he had called it to the empty room, when finally it had been completed. Knights and wizards peered out through the various portcullises and windows, but the top of the tower, behind the long telescope with a pearled jewel lens, had been left empty.

Eddie's mouth tightened. In the empty space at the top of the tower, there now stood a single character, whose arm extended to brush the telescope's side. Her torso bent back at the waist as if she were either belly-laughing or looking up to study the sky. Eddie hadn't placed her there. She'd been left in the box. A little witch.

It's hard to tell exactly what someone is thinking when you can only look at him in the briefest, safe glimpses. When you could only catch some of the small movements he made. How can one tell if he is deciding whether to look at the room around him, empty as it should be, and ask, "Hello?"

OUTSIDE IS REACHING

SOME OF THESE DAYS, WHEN ELISE THOUGHT OF THE OUTSIDE AND when she remembered her parents, thinking of one felt like thinking of the other. The sun through the dormer window warming her face and neck and shoulders was the heat of her mom's arms. The breeze that came at night through that same window, cracked open at the bottom, which blew across the floorboards and dried her sticky, hot skin—that was her dad. Like the way he used to check on her at night when she lay in bed in her room, her overhead light still on and her bedsheets kicked down around her feet. She'd sense him there in the doorway. He'd leave, and then she'd hear the click and rumble of the air-conditioning coming to life. When he came back, the sheet was pulled over her, and the light turned out.

Sometimes, the house itself could seem like a ghost. The squeal of the screen door coming open—she'd heard it a thousand times—but each time, for a moment, it was her mom, that time her arms were full with a bag of boiled crawfish, and she held the door open for Elise with a hip.

And when the doorbell rang, the chime was the same. Elise could tell herself every day how things were different, but that wouldn't stop the expectation that her parents' voices would soon follow, greeting whoever had come.

Footsteps above. Voices, out in the yard. At times, they could be anyone.

This massive, cumbersome house. The Masons might try to cut holes in it, or they might rip up carpets, or fill it with their furniture and cover the walls with their own photos, but when Elise hid behind a column in the foyer, or crouched in a closet in one of the rooms upstairs, or bent low to peer down the length of the stairs? It might still be them she was hiding from, in a game. Soon, she'd hear their voices calling for her again, from some room far from hers, when finally they'd given up seeking.

"Okay, where are you?" her mom had once called to her. "Elise, are you even in here anymore?"

Months ago, when she had first moved back into the old house, Elise had figured calendars meant nothing more to her. The shadows would drift across the floor, and weeks would pass, like planets swooping, invisible, across the daylit sky. After all, the Girl in the Walls no longer had a birthday. She no longer would need to count the days until school ended. Holidays meant nothing to her. But here she was, tracking the days on the kitchen wall calendar, increments of life, by what the Masons marked: the weekend, the household projects, Eddie's upcoming birthday, the beginning of the boys' summer vacation, the start of summer school and hurricane season. She adjusted her routines around them. She looked for opportunities to listen. This week, she'd spent her mornings—her time—waiting, looking over the wrapped birthday gifts that had appeared this week in the nook of the library's fireplace. She studied Eddie's castle, waiting to see when he'd remove the witch she'd placed in the tower. Elise kept returning, wanting to see if he'd done anything with it. It looked like he hadn't touched the castle since.

She didn't know what to think about any of it.

She was living in a holding pattern. Her life was a film put on pause while the rest of the world churned relentlessly on. As if she were a ghost.

You're not a ghost, though. That voice in her head. A warning. *You know that, right?*

She knew.

You have to be more careful.

BIRTHDAY PARTY

SATURDAY, THE MASONS CELEBRATED EDDIE'S BIRTHDAY. MRS. Laura cooked pancakes and eggs for the family, but Eddie still ate his meal alone in the dining room as he always did. No friends invited over and, by the sound of it, there wouldn't be any plans for later in the afternoon, besides a trip to Zack's Frozen Yogurt after lunch. A low-key birthday, but it seemed to be how he wanted it.

Elise could understand that. Her last two birthdays, for ages ten and eleven, she had celebrated with her parents alone. Besides presents and a cookie cake, she only requested a drive through Uptown. With the windows rolled down, she wanted to see all the old, colorful homes draped in their Halloween decorations. But even so, Elise had been hoping for a party a little more sizable for Eddie. Or, at least, something more interesting for her.

While Eddie opened his presents (careful, slow, unfolding the seams of the wrapping paper instead of tearing), Elise hid in the living-room coat closet. In that deep, narrow space, Mr. Nick had stored, for most of the week, a large computer desk. He had fit the desk in it longwise, so the square foot-space had parted the hanging jackets and raincoats, which swaddled it on either side. A perfect spot for Elise to curl up, her feet propped against the desk's drawers like an infant in her mother's womb. As Eddie opened his gifts, Elise listened in and played a guessing game of what he opened.

"Oh," he said, after the plop of a cardboard box's lid being removed. "Thanks."

Something useful, but unexciting. Clothes? Pants. Underwear. Probably a pair of underwear.

"Try it on! See if it fits!" Mrs. Laura said.

Not underwear.

Eddie tried on the shirt and modeled it for his mother, standing in the middle of the room, until Marshall cried out that she was embarrassing him. Eddie was quicker about opening the next gift. It must have been one of the smaller ones she'd seen; perhaps the book-shaped one. Elise was interested in this.

"Nice," Eddie said. "A book."

Elise pumped a fist. Yes!

"Oh, it's a chess book!"

Rats.

Why not something more fun? Even a book on history—like African or Native American. Those would have been fun to flip through. But at least it was better than the next one he opened: a pack of spray deodorant. "Essential for any teenage boy," Mrs. Laura said, practically as an apology.

Marshall's gift was last. Elise had seen it, laid beside the fireplace in the living room: a large ball of blue tissue paper Scotch-taped together. The wrapping job was so poor that even without a tag the gift-giver had been obvious.

"No need to say who this one's from," Mrs. Laura said, walking across the room. She must have been holding the present carefully in both hands so that the wrapping didn't prematurely slough off. Eddie had it opened almost instantly.

"A backpack," Eddie said. "Thanks, Marshall. Now, I've got two."

"Now, you've got one," Marshall said. "You can throw away that little kid purple-stripe one you've been using. It's too small anyway."

For a moment, the family was quiet and the only noises were from the large nylon balloon, caught by a draft, scraping against the ceiling, and from the tissue paper as Eddie tried to wrangle it into a ball.

"I like that backpack," Eddie said.

"Yeah," Mr. Nick added. "It isn't that bad yet, is it? We only bought that for you a couple years ago."

"Maybe it's not bad for a child, Dad," Marshall said. "A little kid. Maybe I'm the only one who realizes he's not one anymore."

"Marshall," Mrs. Laura said, in a placating tone. "It's a great gift. It's a great thought. I'm sure your brother appreciates it."

"He can speak for himself, you know," Marshall said. "Eddie—I mean, he's thirteen now. You don't always have to coddle him like a baby."

"That's enough, Marshall," Mr. Nick said. "Quit it."

"Whatever."

Marshall couldn't seem to remember it was Eddie's birthday. Take a hint, Elise thought, and shut up. If that's what being a teenager was, she might just have to forget her own age, so when she became one herself, she wouldn't know to change.

"In fact," Mr. Nick said, "we're well aware that the youngest Mason here is now officially a teenager. And, accordingly, we decided to go a little big for the milestone. So, we got you one more birthday gift."

"Really?" Eddie said.

Good. Each of the presents he had opened so far had been a disappointment: outside of the book, they were all practical gifts, clothes and things for school. Something fun. A book. Or Legos—something new to build—maybe a pirate ship.

"Where is it?"

"It's right there in the closet," Mrs. Laura said. "Go open it. Check it out."

Elise's eyes went wide.

When she had entered the closet hours earlier that morning, she hadn't seen any present for Eddie. No wrapping paper or bows. Nothing that even resembled a gift. There were only the cardboard boxes in the far back, old picture frames, a storage container of light bulbs and extension cords, and that desk that was being kept there.

The desk.

Oh no.

Eddie's footsteps padded to the door. She heard its hinges creaking open.

"A desk?" he said.

"Like your brother's," Mrs. Laura said.

They wouldn't see her. The desk's drawers blocked her from view. There was a narrow space to either side, but one of the Masons would have to squeeze through and bend over to see her.

"I'll pull it out," Mr. Nick said, coming closer.

Elise felt the vibration along the length of her back as his hands gripped the desk's corners. He pulled, jerking with enough force to free the desk from the friction of the carpet it rested on. The wood thumped hard against her back, and she held in a yell.

Mr. Nick tugged at the desk again, and this time Elise dug her feet into the carpet and braced herself. The desk moved an inch. Half an inch.

"We thought," Mrs. Laura said to Eddie, "now that you're going into high school, you'd appreciate a bigger working desk. Nick, be careful not to tear the carpet with that thing."

"It's stuck on something," he said. He pulled again, and it thumped audibly against the spokes of Elise's spine. She gripped as much of the carpet as she could with her hands. Her back throbbed. He tugged on one corner, then the other. Elise pulled back, equally on each side. Her fingers burned as she felt threads of the carpet in her grip tear loose from the floor.

"Do you like it?" Mrs. Mason said.

"I, uh," Eddie said. He made a noise in his throat.

"Marshall," Mr. Nick said, "get back in there and help me pull this thing out."

Elise heard Marshall sit up in the recliner across the room. The chair squeaked as the footrest returned to its base. He dragged his feet across the carpet toward her.

"Well, do you like it?" Mrs. Laura said.

They would see her, the whole family, when Mr. Nick and Marshall picked the desk up and carried it out into the living room. There was nowhere for her to go. No escape in the back of the closet. Mr. Nick and Eddie blocked the only exit. Only the desk covered her. Nowhere else to hide. They were standing right above her—they all were.

"I don't want it now," Eddie said.

"What?" said Mrs. Laura.

Elise could almost hear his mother and father turn to look at him.

"I don't really want it now," Eddie said. "Later. I want it later. I want it out later."

"Why?" Mr. Nick said. Elise felt his hands grip the corners of the desk again, ready to pull once more. Marshall was in the doorframe now. He tapped on the desktop with a fingernail. Elise gripped the carpet with her fingers and toes tight. She'd been holding her breath, and her lungs were beginning to burn.

"I don't want it now!"

There was a moment of quiet. Right now, Elise wouldn't know how to breathe without gasping for air.

Mrs. Laura spoke. "Hon, it's okay. It's Eddie's birthday. We can take it out later if that's what he wants."

Mr. Nick took a step back from the closet. "I mean, sure," he said. He sounded puzzled. Frustrated but trying to hide it. "I guess we'll give it to him later."

Marshall wasn't subdued. "We can pull the thing out now. Dad, let's just take it up to his room. He can be weird on his own time."

"Marshall, stop." The father's voice was resolute. The hinges squealed, and the closet door shut with a click. Their footsteps moved across the room.

Dark again. The muscles of her back quivered. It would be some time before Elise let loose her grip on the carpet.

WHAT HAD HAPPENED HERE

THE FLOOR HAD FALLEN OUT, LIKE A JAW UNHINGING, TRAIN SQUEAL-ing to a sudden halt. The Masons all above her, and the whole world pivoting to see. She felt it throughout her entire body. Picked up by a gust of wind and thrown.

She'd been careful.

You hadn't.

No way she could have known they would come looking in the closet.

No reason you should have been so close.

SPYING

AT EDDIE'S REQUEST, THE MASONS ATE PIZZA AND CAKE ON PAPER plates on the back lawn by the garden. The boy stood and paced while he ate, away from the others, a patch of dark, curly hair passing through the frames of windows in the sun-stained yard. When they'd finished, the Masons came back inside and took the desk from the closet. Bringing it up to Eddie's bedroom was no easy task, with Mr. Nick and Marshall and Eddie all grunting and stumbling as they maneuvered the desk up the stairs. Sounded like three people were too many—that the extra body only complicated the process of moving the heavy oak desk around the curving staircase. But Mr. Nick, in what must be some attempt at a finale for Eddie's birthday celebration, insisted they all do it together.

"You're a man now, Eddie," he had said. "Help us out with this guy. You can tell us where you want it."

Once upstairs, there were the moans of furniture dragged and rearranged throughout his room. Another set of lumbering footsteps climbing the attic stairs. When the Masons finished, they each returned to their routines. The attached garage soon shrieked with Mr. Nick's table saw. Mrs. Laura watered plants in her garden. Marshall watched television until he'd be taken by one of his parents to his afternoon shift at the car wash. Eddie, the only one upstairs, was in his room.

The whole length of the horseshoe-shaped hallway was still and quiet: the parents' side, the boys'. Passing clouds made the outer lines of shadows on the floor grow dim, and sharp again. Eddie's door was slightly ajar. Inside, a curtain flapped against the molding.

What was he doing?

Through the crack, she saw Eddie's window was open, and he sat in a chair before it, hunched over, his arms and chin resting on the sill. The curtains filled with wind, plumped like the chests of overgrown toy soldiers guarding him on either side. Unmoving. He might have been asleep.

A floorboard popped beneath her feet. Eddie stood up.

Elise froze in place.

But Eddie only went into the bathroom, shutting the door slowly behind him.

Elise looked around her. She took a breath and went into his room.

Eddie's furniture had all been rearranged. The oversized armchair taken out, the squat dresser in its place, bottom drawer open and gaping at her. Everything had been moved. The huge desk stood where the bookshelf had been, the bed had been turned toward the center of the room, away from the wall.

Elise dropped to her elbows and crawled through the dust ruffle to hide beneath his bed. There was no sound of water running yet from the other side of the door. Could Eddie sense her in there? No matter how hard she tried, there was always a little noise. The soft press of a body against the plush carpet makes sound. The fabric of the dust ruffle brushing against her jeans.

After what happened that morning, after she had almost been found, Elise should be hiding in the attic, in the walls. She knew that.

But Elise couldn't wait. Something had expanded inside of her, like a balloon filling with air. She couldn't take it. She needed to hear, to see a sign, though she wasn't sure exactly what it would be.

That voice: *Does he know?*

The sink faucet in the bathroom ran for a few seconds. The towel rack rattled. Eddie opened the door and sat back down in his chair by the window.

Outside, the trees rustled in the breeze. The hiss of Mrs. Laura's hose. Downstairs, Mr. Nick's power saw wailed on and off again.

Through the sliver between the dust ruffle and the carpet, Elise saw his new chess book lying on the floor. Beside it, Eddie's bare heel rose up and down, slow as the second hand of a clock.

The breeze must have felt cool through the window, moving across Eddie's face, through his hair. Voices now outside—amplified but broken by static. The words hard to make out, but coming over the levee from the river. Two tugboat captains talking to one another, piloting their barges along the river's shore.

Eddie had saved her this morning. When Mr. Nick and Marshall were about to wrench her from her hiding place in the desk, he stopped them. The thought wasn't at all comforting for her. But there was a kind of relief, too. Like the breeze.

If Eddie knew, he would keep her secret. He had already shown that this morning. He wasn't afraid of her. What if he had known for a while? Those times he could have turned and looked as she moved behind him, the mistakes he made when he played the piano when she moved through the walls. Was it the plastic witch she had left for him?

A part of Elise wanted to share things with another person again. Things she'd seen: the owl perched on the oak tree outside the hallway window one night, looking inside with its big, yellow eyes. The cat that was hiding beneath the house. Or the secret things about the house itself—the hidden laundry chute, the nook beneath the floorboards in the attic, the spaces between the walls, and its entrances. There was something nice to seeing someone else react a certain way, like to a glimpse of a coyote skulking through the front yard at night—to see that excitement and fear on that person's face, to know what you are feeling is really worth feeling.

But, then again, she shouldn't.

Then again, he still might not know she was here.

What if the reason he had told Mr. Nick and Marshall to leave the desk in the closet was just that, in the moment, he didn't want it? As odd as he was, maybe he thought too many presents at a time was overwhelming. Or maybe he didn't like the desk, wasn't in any rush to look at it, run his hands across its top, feign excitement at opening its drawers? What if his saving her had just been a coincidence?

And even now, he was only sitting there, looking out the window, motionless, oblivious to anything else around him. A shadow passed across the sun, turning the world gray.

Through the open window, Elise heard the back door open, and Marshall speaking to his mother in the yard. Soon, the water cut out, and the car doors opened and shut. The engine started, and she drove him away to work. Downstairs, the saw buzzed intermittently, three or four more times. Then quiet. Mr. Nick had finished that stage of his work.

With each passing minute, the world floated on. Elise closed her eyes, and listened.

HIS VOICE WOKE HER

ELISE WASN'T SURE HOW LONG SHE HAD BEEN ASLEEP. SHE STIRRED, her eyes still closed, as Eddie spoke nearby. She brought her hand to her face and rubbed the bridge of her nose. As the drowsiness bled away, she focused on the conversation, trying to figure who else was in the room.

It was an odd thing, listening to him then, speaking in a voice so much lower and gruffer than she had ever heard from him before. His voice usually so much softer—not high-pitched or girlish, but less forceful and pushy, harder to hear, more yielding, uncertain. Eddie must have been talking to Marshall, because it sounded as though his voice had somehow merged with the older brother's. Like how in an old cartoon she had seen, the hero's love had been possessed by a warlock, and while everything still looked the same about her, the princess had taken on the villain's gruff voice. Elise figured she must not be fully awake yet. Her mind was doing strange things, blending the sounds she heard, still in that blurry-gray gap between sleeping and waking.

Who was he talking to?

Elise tilted her head back as far as she could to look toward the doorframe. The door was still partially cracked open, but no one stood there. She rolled her head over, scuffing the tip of her nose against the bedsprings. The door to the shared bathroom was closed, so it wasn't Marshall come back from work, picking a fight.

Elise scanned as much of the room as she could see, lifting her chin to peer above her crossed legs, and risking the shift in her body to see if there was someone standing on the far side of the new desk. No one.

"I'm too old for something like you," Eddie said, in his grumbling, low voice. "I'm grown up now, and I have to act like it."

Elise saw he was standing, his bare toes pointed toward the bed, a few feet away. She looked at the neatly trimmed nails on his feet. Eddie wasn't moving anywhere. He just stood there. It took her a few moments to realize that if he were speaking to someone sitting on top of the bed, she would have felt that person's weight, sinking down through the bedsprings. But there was nothing above her. There wasn't anyone there. Eddie was speaking to her.

He stepped closer, his heel stomping into the carpet.

"I don't want you near me anymore. I don't want you in here. I don't want you reading my books. I don't want you touching my stuff."

Elise couldn't move. The impulse shot through her to twist and wrench her way out. But the bed was tight above her. She couldn't move.

"I want you to leave me alone," Eddie said. He spoke now as if he were growling. "I want you to get out of here."

Elise inhaled, a small gasp. Too loud. Couldn't help it. The muscles in her face gone taut. Fists clenched at her sides, fingernails digging into her palms. The bed was like a stone on top of her. For a second, Elise saw the muscles in his thin calves strain, and it looked as though he were about to drop to one knee, to lower himself and put his furious face right next to hers. Her eyes watered. She wanted to scream.

But Eddie didn't. He went to the window instead, to that same chair he had been sitting in before. He dropped down hard, so hard she thought the chair legs would snap under him.

Facing the window, he said, "Get out."

She was still.

"Get out."

So she did.

Elise pulled herself free from beneath the bed, and she stood up. Her legs weak beneath her. He didn't move. She stepped backward toward the door, watching him the entire time, ready to break into a run the second he turned back from looking out the window to see her—but he never did. Eddie only looked down at the backyard. She squeezed through the narrow space between the door and the frame, and her spine brushed against the doorknob. The hinges let out a soft moan.

"I can't believe in you," he said. "You don't exist."

She watched as Eddie, his back still turned, lifted his hands to his ears and covered them.

She turned down the hallway, her pulse thumping loud as heavy footsteps in her ears.

Elise kept going. Every doorway gaping. She looked back over her shoulder down the hallway's length. Her calves tense beneath her, ready to sprint.

But he wasn't following her.

Elise turned the corner. Lost, for a moment. Not sure where to go.

The attic door creaked open, but no one heard. The stairs leading up were dark. With the overhead bulb left off, there was no seeing where they began and ended.

She didn't exist.

Elise brought the door closed behind her.

She couldn't.

SHE LEFT A TRAIL

SHE WAITED IN THE ATTIC UNTIL SHE HEARD THE SQUEAK OF THE pipes below—Eddie in the bathroom, brushing his teeth. She went into his bedroom once more, her heart beating in her throat, and she stole each of the books off his shelf she had loved.

The Myths of Ancient Greece, Hans Christian Andersen: The Little Mermaid and Other Fairy Tales, a three-book anthology from *The Chronicles of Narnia,* and others, as many as she could fit into the small purple book bag she had brought with her when she had first returned to the home. She left, and waited until later, when the family was asleep. Then she went downstairs into the library and opened the side door into the night.

Not the best plan, but if Eddie were to tell anyone else about her, he would have to tell them that she was now gone.

The next morning, before their alarm clocks rang, Mr. Nick thundered into the boys' bedrooms, shouting loud enough for the whole house to hear, wanting to know who had last used that door. Who had left it open? Mosquitoes inside—there was a goddamn toad on the coffee table! Anyone could have come along the levee, down into the yard, and strolled right into their house. Right inside! Growing up meant growing responsibility, and responsibility meant closing the damn doors behind you.

Elise heard the fear in the father's voice. For him, it had to have been one of his boys who had done it. The idea of someone else opening the door and moving around their house in the dark—Mr. Nick insisted it must have been someone from the inside, who made a mistake.

"If I used it," Marshall said, "I think I would have remembered to close it."

Eddie, though, was quiet.

"What were you even using that door for?" Mr. Nick said to him.

Elise listened with her ear tight against the attic floor. She could picture him there, still lying in bed, trying to think.

Eddie took his father's anger in silence. Like any other Sunday, they readied themselves for church. Eddie, in the yard, brushing his shoes off with the back of his hand before climbing into the back seat and closing the door. Whatever Eddie thought she was, he hadn't bothered to explain her to the others. Maybe he thought she was not something he could explain.

Was it enough? Would he still listen for her?

Would he hear her?

And with that thought, Elise realized what she had been doing. Some part inside her—slowly growing—had wanted to be heard.

Now that she knew, Elise would muffle it.

MAKE YOURSELF LESS

GIRLS EAT THREE TIMES A DAY. ELISE DIDN'T NEED THAT. SHE COULD do two: a breakfast when everyone had left for school and work, and a dinner in the attic, something cold that wouldn't smell or go bad during the day, like dry cereal or baked beans in a Ziploc bag. Lunch was too close to the time she might expect someone home. She readjusted the meaning of the bird clock calls, her afternoon limit for being outside the walls sliding back from cardinal to great horned owl, its solemn hoot in the early afternoon now ominous, threatening.

Girls move through a home; they take up space. They move on whims, compelled by light, by the gathering of voices down the hall. She didn't need to move as much as she had before. Trips outside the walls through the rooms, when others were still home, were extravagant and unnecessary. She had been giving in before. She'd been surrendering to things that only little girls feel. Elise wasn't one anymore.

The Masons moved through the house below her. And while they did, she would lie on her back each day, all day. The smallest movements, that's all she needed.

Hardly alive. Not alive. Hardly breathing.

PART 2

SOUNDING BOARD

Once, when I was coming home from work, pulling into the
driveway, I'm certain I saw the upstairs lights flick off. My
husband swears I'm imagining things. I had to stop mentioning
it to him. I'm not sure what to do. I'd tell a shrink, but I don't
need a diagnosis. I'm not looking for Proloxin.

*Sometimes I'm hearing my heating ducts tapping above
me. But it's more than just metal warming or whatever
I've heard it's supposed to be. The ducts are too small for
anything like this but the sound is like someone crawling on
all fours up there. I can sit and read a book but each fiber
of my body's pulsing like someone's watching me through
the cracks in the vent.*

Each day and night is hard and I've done
everything I can. It's like I'm drowning.
How does anyone do this on their own?

Will someone else come here and look?

ive been hearing that sound too. are any of your things
missing? like food from your pantry? fridge?

*Been trying lately to switch them out in my head. Imagine
whoever's hiding here as having the face
of a person I remember. Somebody I've lost.
Not always very easy but I think it helps.*

SUBJECT: I HEAR THEM TOO

I know how hard it is to find someone else who believes.

Not easy to expose yourself as afraid. And seem like a child. Scared of the little bumps in the night.

You have to be careful about who you tell. People will write you off. Say it is your paranoia. Your anxiety.

Just make-believe.

Can you believe that? As if it were just our imaginations. Gone berserk!

But no matter what they say we still will see signs of them. We hear them bumping and stepping all around us. First thing before the sun is fully up. Through the dead afternoon. All night.

You know I see signs of them even in other homes. I pass down the road and notice a light on late in a downstairs room. Or a television glowing when the driveway is empty. Or else hard to say why but so clear they are there. Sometimes I have to pull up on the curb. Cut the engine and watch. Do they see me through the window blinds? Does no one else really have any idea?

And then sometimes I get out of my truck. I circle around as much of the house as I can. Look into each of the windows. Study all the narrow slices that show.

Eventually it will happen. A closet door will unlatch and glide a little open. A head of hair will show around the edge. They will step out into the room and arch their back. Stretch their skinny arms and legs.

Look.

When finally you find them you got to drag them out. Man or woman or child by their ankles or their hair.

Pin them beneath you and feel their skin beneath your hands. Feel the relief to have them there.

One day when I hold them I will look into their eyes. Hold so they cannot turn away. They will understand I have known the whole time. They have hardly been hiding at all.

I want you to know I am out here.

Let me know when you find them. I want to help. I need to see them too.

J.T.

TERMITE SEASON

IT BEGAN MOTHER'S DAY'S NIGHT, NOT LONG AFTER THE MASONS had returned home from dinner downtown. The gravel churned in the driveway, and weather stripping shushed across the foyer's tiles. The Masons weaved through the rooms of the house—bees through honeycomb. The lights, flipped on, bled out through the windows onto a lawn where insects teemed and blades of grass cast their own slender, black shadows.

Eddie's father poured a pair of glasses of wine in the kitchen. His mother curled up in front of the television to watch a recording of *The West Wing* they had missed that week while they finished the guest room's floor. Marshall was upstairs, and already the ceiling pounded beneath him. A set of clapping pushups likely, the way the ceiling in the dining room shook in rhythm—Marshall would be on the floor of his bedroom, forcing himself up just enough to slap his hands together.

Thump.

The veins of his long forearms would be bulging. The window open for the breeze.

Thump.

Or was it jumping jacks?

Eddie, at his place at the table, squinted into the overhead light of the small, quivering chandelier. He could hear the chandelier: the squeak of the chain as Marshall exercised, each of its bulbs emitting the softest hum, like the buzz of a wasp trapped between windowpanes. He could hear it—or at least he imagined so—above the sounds his teeth and tongue made chewing through mouthfuls of lukewarm jambalaya. In the next room, a commercial played, and his father pressed the fast-forward button on the remote. Eddie hadn't paid attention to the show, but he could always tell when the commercials came on—their volume just a little louder, even if he couldn't understand what was said. Sometimes when watching television himself, he preferred to lie down on the sofa and tuck his head beneath a pillow when the commercials came. Their colors always too bright, too sudden and loud, as if someone had kicked in the front door to shout at him. He ate the rice from the black Styrofoam box the waiter had packed, and cupped a palm over an ear.

There were no windows in the dining room. It was part of the reason he enjoyed it. He'd eaten each of his meals there alone since they had moved in. He needed space from his family when they ate—their chewing, smacking that awful wet sound. Eddie saw the teeth in his mind, saliva stretching in thin strands between the mouth's roof and the brown, soft mass of food on the tongue. The miniature hairs of a chin, rising and falling. At Brennan's this evening, his parents didn't need to ask him—they knew the routine: three meals for here, one to-go, to be eaten later at home. While his family ate, he tucked his head between his arms on the table.

The dining room always gave him distance. The evening buzz of cicadas was subdued here more than anywhere else, and rain, when it came, was softened to a whisper. The room even looked gentle, with the light green paint and an ivy-patterned wallpaper border that ran around the base of the ceiling. The piano's wood glistened as if oiled, and the large oak china cabinet with a glass front revealed clean, white plates with gray birds around their rims. The room had been his favorite in the new house, maybe even more than his own.

But since the week of his birthday, Eddie had become aware of something new about the dining room. It was positioned in the middle of the house, surrounded on all sides by more rooms, more house.

Maybe once that had seemed comforting as a warm, weighted blanket on his chest. Now? Suffocating.

While Eddie ate the meal, listening as he always did, unable to ignore the sound of one of the dying, half-deflated balloons, blown by the living room's fan blades and dragging along the wall; unable to stop listening to the rooms around him as if any moment someone unrecognized might appear in the doorway—hearing so many things in the heart of the house. Yet, he couldn't hear them, the insects. That night, with as many as there were, taking flight from between the blades of grass in the lawn, and floating up, drawn by honey-colored light—it was odd to Eddie, later, that he hadn't heard them at all. Later, in bed, he had to remind himself that the sounds he remembered were ones he had imagined: the fluttering of two thousand small, golden wings against the windowpane.

"Termites!" Eddie's mom called out from the living room.

"Oh, no," his father said, followed by the smack of a palm against the leather armchair. "Shit! Yeah, they're in here, all right."

His mom cried, "Boys, cut the lights!"

A stumbling over furniture, and the doorway to the living room went dark. Eddie's father appeared in the frame, pushing his glasses up the bridge of his nose. Without apology, he reached over and flipped the switch to the dining room, sending Eddie and the remainder of his meal into darkness.

"Marshall, cut the lights up there!"

The television in the living room gave a dim blue glow, and when Eddie leaned over in his chair, he saw the shapes of his parents passing one another as they moved to separate rooms. The sound of his father thumping up the staircase.

Eddie blinked. He nudged his chair back from the table and felt his way into the living room, a hand placed on the corner of the piano, then the doorframe. One of his parents, before they left the room, had pressed stop on the remote to the VCR. Eddie watched a small insect crawl across the television screen. They were drawn even to the blue light. Eddie's face was close enough to the set to feel static on his cheeks. Two other bugs appeared on the glass.

His father and brother shouted upstairs, arguing about a window.

"Seriously? How couldn't you notice? It's wide open! They're flooding in!"

Marshall's window. While Eddie's brother worked out, he would have had it open for the cross breeze, with his bedroom light left on. This wasn't the first time his family had dealt with the swarming termites, but it was the first time in this house. Before, in the old home on the Northshore, Eddie had once left his own window cracked, and woke at night to the tickle and itch of a half-dozen of them on his arms and legs. He figured they'd been drawn to the heat of his body. Fortunately, tonight Eddie's own light had been off in his room. Unless it had been turned on. Not by Marshall, but another way, when the family had been away from home.

But had his light been on when he walked from the car across the driveway? Eddie shook his head and pushed the thought from his mind. He rearranged the pillows on the sofa and took a seat. His light had been off. That was all there was to it.

His room was safe from the insects, and upstairs, his father wouldn't be mad at him. Recently, after the side door in the library had been left open overnight, his father had canceled Eddie's piano lessons, saying Eddie could request them again when he showed more maturity. Of course, Eddie wouldn't ask for them back—he never had enjoyed them. He'd only put up with them for his parents. They'd seemed pleased by the hobby. Maybe his father knew that he didn't care for them, and had used the open door as an excuse to end them. Eddie wasn't sure. It was hard to know. It was hard sometimes to understand why anyone did things.

His mom entered as a dark shape into the living room. She reached around him as he sat on the sofa to close the curtains, the fabric of her shirt brushing against his hair. He watched as the outline of her head turned into profile, looking down among the furniture for the remote. She found it on the old ottoman and turned the television off. The high-pitched whir of the machine—too high for the others to notice, even when the television was on mute—went silent. Eddie closed his eyes. Opened them. For a little while, he couldn't tell the difference. His mom left the room and he waited for his eyes to adjust.

A house is porous, he decided. Surprisingly so. Cracks beneath ill-cut doors and along the bottoms of the old storm windows, and holes in the foundation. Rainwater dripping through the ceiling, or bugs skittering across the linoleum: there's not much separating inside from the outside. Eddie lay down on his back on the sofa and squinted until he could make out the turning fan blades above him. His parents still thumped through the house, catching any lights still on. The clock in the foyer chimed for the quarter-hour.

A wall doesn't create two separate places, it's just a thing in the middle of the same place. How many bugs were in the house already? There'd been a spider in the ceiling corner of his bathroom above the tub for months—it had to have been living off something. Maybe those somethings were simply good enough at hiding that no one knew.

What else is in the house?

He didn't want to think those words.

Who was it that had been here?

Don't bother. It's over, and gone. Half-made by imagination, or more, or all—done and gone away.

"I don't even think about it," he said aloud to the empty room.

NIGHTWALK

LATER THAT NIGHT, AFTER THE SWARM ENDED, EDDIE FELT THE ITCH of filament legs on his body. But when he turned on the lamp, nothing crawled over his skin. The door to the bathroom was shut, and a towel stuffed along the bottom crack still blocked any of the termites that had entered through Marshall's window from entering his own room. Eddie climbed out of bed and stepped in the hallway. It was all in his head. Like his mom told him: when a nightmare scares, a walk shakes the fear away.

In the hallway, Eddie rested his forearms and chin on the thick frame of the storm window. He inhaled, and dust tickled his nose. Outside, the moon was big and bright, like a bulb of a flashlight between the trees. The moon never really had looked like a face to him. There were holes for eyes, but where was the mouth? The whole thing seemed covered in eyes.

"Who is that?" his brother hissed through the guest room's doorway. "Is that you, Eddie?"

"It's me."

Eddie heard the bedsheets shift. He looked through the doorway and saw in the gloom his brother sit up and rub his face.

"What did I tell you about walking around at night? The fuck are you doing out there?"

"I was . . ." He didn't want to admit the nightmare. Marshall would laugh. Eddie said, "Just looking."

"What? What's that mean—looking?" Marshall said. He shook his head. "Actually, I don't care. Quit skulking and go to bed."

"Okay," Eddie said.

"I'm serious, you scare me like that again, I'll gut-punch you."

"Okay."

Marshall pulled the comforter over his head, and Eddie went back to his room and closed the bedroom door. Inside, he stood and listened. He wouldn't be able to sleep until he looked. Eddie went into his routine, the one he had begun the evening of his birthday, when he packed up his Legos into plastic bins and stored them in the attic. When he counted the books on his shelves, so he could ensure they were all still there.

Eddie dropped to one knee to look beneath the bed. Peered behind the overstuffed armchair. Pushed the hanging clothes in the closet to either side.

Nothing. So, Eddie crawled into bed and turned off his lamp.

SOME TROUBLES OF THE GIRL
WHO DOESN'T EXIST

ELISE SAT AT THE KITCHEN TABLE EATING A BOWL OF RAISIN BRAN. The Masons were out of milk, so she ate the cereal dry, picking raisins out first with her fingers and placing them on a napkin beside her bowl. What remained was the brown flakes, dry, on their own. A terrible breakfast.

One of the Masons, earlier that morning, had spilled orange juice on the table, and the small puddle sat beside her cloth place mat, yellow and sad, soaking slowly into the table's wood grain. By afternoon, the liquid would likely turn the wood beneath it a brownish-gray—unfixable probably—puckered into small moisture scars.

Not Elise's problem.

She might once have been bothered to slide her napkin four inches over, to clean the spill for the family. Solve a mess before it became one, without them ever knowing. Keep Mrs. Laura's wrath from whatever dumb boy couldn't notice the spill he'd caused. Now, she couldn't be bothered. Girls who don't exist can't clean up the mess of people who do.

WHY ELISE WAS BOTHERED, IN NO PARTICULAR ORDER

1. A MISERABLE NIGHT'S SLEEP.

Last night, with the termites swarming, Elise spent the final hours of her evening in the pitch-black of the attic, afraid even her small booklight might attract the bugs. She sat in the dark, hours before the cries of the starlings downstairs, when she normally called it a night. Eventually, when she could no longer take the boredom, and the waiting, and the unsettling thought that insects were somehow gathering in a dark cloud above her head, she flipped on the booklight to investigate. They weren't billowing above her—thank god—but she did find nearly a dozen crawling on the floor below the attic dormer. Their clear, papery wings already shed along the windowsill, their pupilless, red eyes like little drops of blood under her light. Elise couldn't decide what was worse: letting them live to skitter through the attic all night, squirming over her, or to smoosh them, and get bug guts on the soles of her feet. Ultimately, she hedged her bets and did a little of both, which had given her the worst of both worlds.

2. BREAKFAST FOOD.

She wasn't going to let this go. Breakfast is—should be—the single greatest meal. Fried eggs, pancakes drowned in syrup, buttery biscuits, hot grits, grape jelly on toast, bacon with the edges burned the way her dad used to cook it. No child should ever be subjected to the

Raisin Bran in front of her, particularly a bowl without milk. Elise was tempted to walk right over to Mrs. Laura's tear-off grocery list hanging from the refrigerator and write, below her husband and the boys' request for bananas and spaghetti, a two-line, all-caps demand for "GOOD CEREALS PLEASE." Seriously. They didn't have to be sugary stuff. Just not Raisin Bran.

3. TODAY WAS A WEEKDAY.

This used to be a good thing; it guaranteed morning hours alone to herself in the house. But now the afternoon encroached on her like an ominous weather forecast. It drove her to interrupt her reading or television show in order to lean into the foyer and double-check the time. Had to make sure the goose call she just heard wasn't actually the cardinal gone hideously hoarse. Weekday afternoons had become more restricted. Since the birthday of a certain boy, Elise had to spend them in—

The attic.
The laundry chute.
The walls.

—often wedged up and uncomfortable, as quiet as she could manage. This was safest, the only way she could be sure that Eddie wouldn't realize she actually hadn't gone anywhere. That she had, in fact, stayed exactly where she was, and still heard, from her nook in the attic, the same squeak when he climbed into and out of his bed, the same opening and closing of his clunky dresser drawers; and that, from time to time, she still caught sight of him in that part of the yard where he paced, between the willow and oak, where he thought no one could see him. And now that she considered it, catching sight of him was no good because that meant:

She had been in a place to see him, so—
He had been in a place to see her.

Which meant she was still making mistakes, meant she should tone down, curl up smaller, be even quieter than she had been before. She had to realize no time was safe, or fully hers. Even the nighttime was being taken away, like last night, when she tried to sneak down to the first-floor bathroom to scrub her feet clean of the dead bugs, and she'd been startled by Marshall in the guest room rolling over and squinting out into the dark at her. Elise had flattened against the wall beside the doorframe, her heart so loud she could hear it, and listened as the older boy called out to her:

Eddie? Is that you?
Who is that?
Who's there?

And she stood there for nearly half an hour, squeezed against the wall, until she was sure that Marshall had chalked it up to his imagination and had finally gone back to sleep. Finally.

4. SPRING WAS ENDING, AND EVERYTHING WOULD ONLY GET WORSE.

Eddie and Marshall out of school, at home more—maybe all day. Plus, two days ago, Marshall had come home from the car wash to say he'd quit his job because his manager treated him like a child. Mr. Nick's voice rose up from the guest room, cracking with the disbelief she herself felt. Marshall home all summer, every day? Neither of the boys seemed to have friends they left home to spend much time with. They'd both be here, and Elise would need to limit herself even more, even more. And so, she would have to rearrange her schedule. Adapt, shrink.

Find other times for:

Breakfast.
Bathroom breaks.
Stretching.
Moving.
Breathing.
Basically anything considered life.

5. BUT THAT WASN'T EVEN ALL THAT WAS BOTHERING HER, BECAUSE . . .

Dear lord, dear Odin, dear patron gods of nonexistent girls and all that's hidden and lost and stuffed-up-in-someone-else's-crawl-space-somewhere—a crick throbbed along the length of Elise's neck. A big, fat throbber down into her shoulder. Of course, when one sleeps in the crawl space beneath attic floorboards with a balled-up sweatshirt for a pillow, it's something she would expect. But this morning?

"Necks that don't exist shouldn't hurt," she muttered, giving the offending muscle a harsh, two-knuckle rub. "Get with the program, Buck-o."

LIFE IS BORING

ELISE WASHED HER BOWL IN THE KITCHEN SINK, DRIED IT WITH A hand towel, and placed it back in the cupboard. She took one of Eddie's gummy vitamins from the pantry and chewed it, looking out the window past Mrs. Laura's garden and the backyard trees, across the open field, at Ms. Wanda's blue house that rested, half-surrounded by woods. Elise watched a little boy, tiny with the distance, step out from the underbrush, and cross into the neighbor's yard. He crawled up on the seat of a riding lawn mower parked beside the house and, standing on the seat, pressed his head against the dark window with hands cupped around his face. He pulled the window open and squirmed his way inside, legs flailing in the air as he kicked his way in.

Locked out. Elise sighed and shook her head. She understood that. She felt locked out, even being inside. The boy was some nephew of old Ms. Wanda, probably, visiting for the morning. A second- or third-grader at most.

Elise yawned and arched her back, trying to pull loose the tight muscles. Had she ever been this sore before? Had she always been, since she had come back home? Was this growing up? Growing pains? Elise made a mental note to check the pencil marks in the side of one of the library bookshelves her parents had used to measure her height—measurements she tracked now with something less than pride.

In the fall, if Elise were still going to school, she would be a fifth-grader. Maybe once she would have been excited to reach that age.

Maybe. But now a fifth-grader seemed so old. Gangly, out of place. How could a girl that big move in the small crevices of a house? Where could she fit? How could a girl like that exist anywhere?

She sighed and watched the shadows of clouds pass over Mrs. Laura's garden in the backyard. The ground still moisture-dark from the cantaloupe and watermelon seeds she'd seen planted the evening before. Each of the leaves on the trees wiggling in the breeze, as if they each had their own mind.

Elise pressed her nose against the thick storm window, and— *careful*—bunched her shirt up at the bottom to wipe away the offending smear. Elise missed these things. The outdoors. The simple act of going outside.

But to come back to a home after time gone is to push open the door and find that the shadows have all shifted. To be accosted by the house's smells, whether laundry or candles, food or mildew. To find things moved, mail brought in, someone else's shoes left by the door. To come back, at any point, is to return, in a way, as a stranger. Each minute you're away makes you a little more odd, and the house a little more odd to you.

Elise had been that stranger already—when she'd come home that December to find the Masons' furniture squatting in the places where her parents' things had once been. Pungent, orange-scented air fresheners plugged into the electrical sockets. New scratches on the wooden floor. Hair, shades darker than hers or her parents, collected around the shower drains.

Who would want to be that again?

Elise wouldn't, as long as she stayed, and stayed inside.

She'd last here, for as long as was needed. Like one of her dad's old sayings: *Come hell or high water.* Until the very end.

The sun pulled free from a cloud, turned the outside an electric, vibrant green, the kind that continued when she blinked—a flash of the speckled afterlife of lights—reds and yellows lingering across her eyelids' insides. The colors of the last days of spring shifting in the wind, still there as Elise turned back to see a room that had gone gray around her.

Here, the girl stayed, where all that moved was dust, sinking through the air like a cloud of gray, dead midges, visible only in the illuminated shaft through the window.

SWAMP CREATURES

ON THE OTHER SIDE OF THE LEVEE, RIVER WATER ROSE.

For months, as the snow melted up north, the small runs of water fed into streams, swelling half-iced creeks, sloughing downhill, weaving over rock and sand and padded mud, over the days and weeks down into the Mississippi. With it, the brown river ballooned, as it had every spring, until it pushed up against its border levees, swallowed the thin batture, and submerged the cypress trees to their slender bellies.

When the air cooled in the evening, green river frogs and southern toads, large as a man's fist, emerged from the water's edge and leaped in short bounds up the concrete side of the levee. They crested the levee, plunging into the grass. Then down across the road and into the Masons' yard.

Eddie marched along his trail between the willow and the oak even after the sun set. Twelve and a half steps to the roots of one tree, and twelve and a half back, made twenty-five. There and back four times made a hundred steps. He wore the knee-high rubber boots he had received this past Christmas, the ones he wore every afternoon in the backyard, even though his feet had already grown until his toes pinched, and it had become a chore to pull the boots on and off again. Everything changed in time.

Eddie adjusted his pace in order to step over a toad that had appeared in the mud of his trail. A skink wormed over the bark-stripped root where he had planned to step and pivot. Hard to keep focused on his own mind when the world beneath him teemed and wriggled on its stomach.

"Eddie!" His brother's voice. "If you're still out here, Mom says come inside!"

The back door slammed shut.

It was getting late. Eddie had been out here since he had come home from school, counting his steps and imagining himself as a knight. The back field had become overgrown with yellow thistle, and while he had paced that afternoon, the stalks had been spiked creatures, his enemies, peering at him above the tall grass, plotting as he prepared his castle's defenses. Too old to think like that, he knew. He hadn't even done any of his homework, even though there was less of it now, with the school year nearing its end. Eddie looked over at the house, gone gray in the dusk. His father was a shape passing through the office window. A lamp blinked on. He had to go inside now. Eddie realized he'd been avoiding it.

"Hurry the hell up!" His brother's voice again. "She won't let off me until you get your ass in!"

The grass rustled in the field behind him. Shadows leaping throughout the yard. When Eddie pulled open the screen door, he found a lizard caught in the netting. Its limbs twisted in the screen, and its yellow eyes lolled. Skin dried to a dark brown. He couldn't tell if the animal were dead or looking at him.

JUST BEFORE THE WORLD'S END

ELISE SAT ON THE KITCHEN COUNTER, EATING NEARLY THE LAST OF the Raisin Bran from a bowl. A squirrel in the lawn cleaned its face with its paws. The animal paused as though nervous, sensing something moving nearby.

The cat?

Elise craned her neck to search the azaleas alongside the house, the monkey grass beside the attached garage—but she saw no sign of the calico. She hadn't for weeks. She had even broken the promise she had made to herself weeks ago—to leave the cat alone—and had gone down below the house hoping to find it there. If she had found it, Elise had half-expected to turn the animal furious. Its back arching, swiping at her, growling in a voice not unlike the way Eddie's had been. But, of course, none of that happened—the nest had been empty. The cat had come and was gone.

Elise picked up a raisin between her thumb and forefinger and squeezed. Each day was a monotony of dry corn cereal. Just her. And a squirrel. And bran.

Oh, Odin. It was going to be another long, long day.

Some days she wished she could skip altogether, stay in her nook and doze, half-asleep, as the shadows stretched from right to left across the attic floor, and the heart pine grew warm then cool again against her. But as easy as it would be, and as nice as it seemed, she had come to realize that might be riskier than anything else. Skipping meals and water and bathroom breaks put her in a worse position later on, being in need when the Masons were all at home.

And besides, two nights before, she'd had a dream she was a skeleton beneath the floorboards, motionless, watching as the roof rotted away until there were only stars above her, whirling wildly in the night sky. Freaked her out how much she had enjoyed it.

So, Elise couldn't allow herself to sleep in and to mope, to miss out on meals and chances to refill her water bottle. She couldn't let herself get weak or sick. Had to keep pushing on with life, so she could keep pushing on with life. So she could keep on pushing.

Outside, the squirrel lowered its paws and eyed her sadly.

Elise didn't need sympathy. Especially not from a squirrel.

She hopped off the counter. Dumped the rest of her uneaten bran back into the cereal box. She went to the pantry and, climbing the shelves like a ladder, placed the box back where she'd taken it. Outside, the squirrel shot up to a higher branch, out of view, but she could still hear its nickering. Starlings called out from the granddaughter clock she was behind schedule, had been slow to get up this morning. Elise washed her bowl in the sink.

Another day, another dish. The hiss of the water faucet was like television static. The yellow sponge along the edge of the bowl, plunging into the white curve. She toweled the bowl dry and hummed as she placed it back in the cabinet. Distracted, so she hadn't heard: that rattle of the library doorknob twisting in its loose socket, the movement through the library and foyer, halting footsteps over the living room carpet.

Elise was thinking of birds, of real starlings she'd seen a year or so before. She'd woken in the morning to their noise out in the yard—cacophonous, all chittering and trilling at once, like a warning. Elise had never heard birds so loud. Her mom, passing through the hallway, had stopped when she realized Elise was awake. She had entered the room and opened a curtain.

"Look."

The blue-black birds, hundreds of them, hopping across the yard, rustling in the branches, picking at their folded wings. And even more above the trees. Small clouds of them, flying in their tight, orchestrated circles. A murmuration, her mom had called them. She told Elise that she always wondered how they did it: fly so close without ever bumping into one another.

The memory vanished when Elise realized someone was watching her.

She turned and saw him there.

He stood in the kitchen's doorway. Real. He was looking right at her. He wasn't a Mason. He blocked her way out.

"Oh," the boy said. "Wow."

INTRUDER

OUT OF INSTINCT, ELISE TRIED TO HIDE. HER KNEES WENT LIMP, AND she slumped beneath the kitchen table. But among the chair legs, how ridiculous she was—his feet right there! She jumped up and threw open the silverware drawer and snatched the first weapon she could get her hand on.

Elise turned to the boy to see him move only a few feet away. He fumbled with a small radio on the counter. He was young, younger than she was.

"Hey," he asked, "how do you do this?"

"Stay away," she said, thrusting the butter knife out between them.

"Okay," he said. Then he switched on the radio. He twisted the knob through several stations. Country. Rap. Soft rock. He shut it off.

"Your house is really big," he said, and walked out into the living room.

Elise stood by the counter with the small blade still trembling in her hand. After a few moments, she went over to the doorway, but the boy was already gone. He must have turned the corner into the foyer. Elise darted to the kitchen window to look, as best as she could, at the driveway. But there was no car parked there.

Elise slipped behind the side of the refrigerator and listened, her eyebrows scrunched tight enough to hurt. She placed the blade down on the floor and strained, trying to hear voices, adult voices. Some family friend of the Masons who had stopped by. Some contractor had been scheduled, one who had brought his child to wait while he worked. But she heard no one at all.

Was the boy here alone? What was happening?

And why had he looked familiar?

Elise crept into the living room, leaning her upper body from side to side to see around the angles of the recliner and sofa. She pressed her back against the wall and peered into the dining room. Empty. She moved on and did the same for the foyer. First, around the tall white columns, then ducking low to see up the staircase. Inching forward, now on hands and knees, she looked into the library. He was there.

The boy scratched the back of his neck and studied the old fireplace and shelves. Messy brown hair curled over his forehead. His blue jean overalls looked like hand-me-downs from a much taller person. Beneath their muddied cuffs, his feet were bare.

And oh Lord his feet.

They were caked thick in mud that must have dried against his skin, then cracked, then been remuddied with a wet, fresh second layer. The boy shifted them as he turned to her, leaving a pair of new musty prints on the polished floor beams. "Sneaky," he said. "Didn't know you were there."

Elise yelped. She jumped up and ducked behind the foyer columns. She had to get away from him—needed somewhere to hide. She peered around the edge of the column and saw him there, looking at her.

"Hey."

"Go away!"

Elise fled through the living room into the kitchen. She turned in a half-circle, panicked. The whole room seemed wide open, garishly exposed. She threw herself in the pantry and held the handle tight. Wedged her feet to either side of the doorframe. He would have heard the door shut, so she'd have to hold him out. Soon, a shadow darkened the crack beneath the door.

"Leave me alone!" she shouted.

"What are you doing in there?"

"What do you want from me?"

The door handle tried to turn in her grip. "Why are you in there?"

A sudden flash of contempt broke through her, for a moment overcoming her panic. Why wouldn't she be in here?

The doorknob jiggled in her hand, weakly.

"Who are you?" Elise said. "Who's with you?"

She needed to know if there was someone else, someone bigger—or if it really was just this boy. She had the small access panel above her, which would lead up into the walls. One loud noise, one heavy footstep from the other side of the door, and she'd scramble up the shelves to escape.

"Nobody's with me," the boy said.

"You're alone?"

"No," he said. "Not alone."

Elise's heart lurched.

But the boy followed with, "Because you're here."

What was wrong with him? The idea of opening the door and thrusting the palm of her hand into his chest wasn't unpleasant.

Elise asked, "What are you doing here?"

On the other side of the door, the boy hesitated. She pictured him pawing at the handle, slouching, with his odd, bowl-cut hair. And she realized where she had seen him before. "Wait," Elise said. "A couple days ago. You crawled in Ms. Wanda's window!"

"You saw me?"

"Why are you in my house? Are you trying to steal?"

The boy mumbled something.

"What?"

"No?"

"How did you get in?" Elise demanded.

"The door was unlocked."

"You're lying!"

She had always made sure the doors were locked while the Masons were away. Locked doors proved none of them were still lurking in the yard.

"The side door was open."

The side door? Whoever the kid was, he had gotten in the house the same way she had, months ago. That stupid, broken lock! It was enough to make her wonder how many other people had gotten in through that door over the years.

"Are you coming out or not?" the boy asked.

"No!"

"Well," he said. "Okay."

The shadow pulled back from beneath the crack in the pantry door. Elise held the knob tight and waited. She didn't hear his footsteps, or the front door open and close, but it was hard to hear anything in the pantry. Her ears rang from her shouting in the closed space. Her fingers tingled from gripping the pantry's doorknob so tight. Eventually, when she thought it was safe, Elise stepped out into the kitchen.

KEEP THE GATES CLOSED

IN THE FOYER, THE FRONT DOOR WAS SHUT, AND SO WAS THE SIDE one in the library. Elise looked around for something she could push in front of the library's door as a barricade. Alone now, and she had to make sure it stayed that way. Keep him out. Keep whoever else out who might come in that way. Whatever Elise used to block the door, she would have to remove before the Masons came home, but right now, she needed to have it. Another wall where the hole had been discovered. Block it off.

She grabbed hold of the coffee table and dragged it to the door, careful the wood wouldn't scratch. She looked around her at the stillness of the room and realized she didn't feel alone. The spine of each book of the shelf seemed like its own separate eye. The photographs grinned placidly out.

Then she heard them. Footsteps above her. She wasn't alone—the boy was still in the house.

TACTICS

ELISE RESISTED THE URGE TO STORM UPSTAIRS, TIGHTEN HER small hands into smaller fists, and tell the boy to—Go! He'd looked pudgy around the waist, but he couldn't have been more than her height. Elise had a chance.

No. First, she needed to calm herself. Needed to think. Use her head.

Elise could hide. Tuck herself away in the walls. Dissolve from the world and from whoever the boy was upstairs—no problem. The Masons could take care of him. The Girl in the Walls stays safe because she hides. She doesn't meddle in problems she can avoid.

But what was he doing up there? Touching things? Moving them? The thought occurred to her: what if the kid made a mess, then decided to leave before the Masons came back? If Elise let him do whatever he wanted to the house, Eddie might see it, and think it had been her—not good. Might be enough that he would tell the others. She couldn't let that happen. That stupid kid upstairs! She'd have to clean up whatever mess the boy made before they got home.

But then Elise remembered: the footprints. Those filthy feet! She'd have to track them all down and figure out every last place the boy had stepped. Everything he touched, as well. His hands were probably filthy, too.

Above her, something fell and rolled along the floor.

Maybe she might not be cleaning up after all. So, then, what? Hope the Masons would find him here? They'd come home, see him, chase him, catch him—and then Eddie would know the intruder wasn't her. It might work. Maybe Eddie would think it had been him all along; on his birthday, Eddie hadn't looked at her in his bedroom, didn't know whether she was a boy or girl. So, this was a plan, but— Elise checked the clock in the foyer—no, they wouldn't be home for hours! And Elise couldn't exactly call the police to catch him before-hand.

Hello, sir, I'd like to report a trespasser.

Of course, young lady, may I ask who's placing the call?

Oh, just . . . another trespasser.

Well, then, could she stop him from leaving? Wrestle him down? Trap him, or drag him into a closet? How does one realistically drag another person, anyway? By the shirt collar? By the hair? Maybe if she tied him up with the bungee cords from the garage?

Elise knew that none of this would work. Even if the boy left, and by some gift of fate, everything appeared as it should be when the Masons returned home, the biggest problem would still remain.

He knew she was here.

CONFRONTING

FOR A TIME, ELISE THOUGHT HE MIGHT BE HIDING. HER HOUSE WAS large, rambling; it could swallow even a stranger. She stepped slow through the upstairs hallway, arms pinched against her sides, not sure what to do with her hands. The AC system rumbled to life, and the cold air from the ceiling vent brushed across her hair. The parents' bedroom was empty. So were the guest room and office.

She passed the attic door, leaving that space alone for now. The attic's old staircase was unvarnished, and dead bugs collected along the sides of the steps. The light wasn't until you were already up there. The boy shouldn't have gone up alone so quickly. Growing up here, it had taken Elise years to build up the courage. She turned the corner of the hallway, past the linen closet, and went down to the boys' bedrooms. She opened Eddie's door.

With all its furniture moved, the room felt like it belonged in someone else's home. It even smelled different, pungent with the odor of spray deodorant he'd gotten for his birthday. Even from the doorway, she could see it was empty. The dust ruffle had been folded up and tucked under the mattress, exposing the bed's underneath. The closet door left open, with the hanging clothes parted down the middle. The laundry hamper had its lid removed and was angled against the closet's doorframe, showing that only pajamas pooled at its bottom.

Elise passed through and opened the door to the bathroom. Nothing behind the shower curtain. Empty. She went into Marshall's room, and the smell of sweat filled her nostrils. She checked the crevice behind his door. For whatever reason, the fear had formed in her that she'd find not the boy but the older brother hiding there, waiting to snatch her by the shoulders. She felt the house was yawning wide around her. Deepening beneath her feet, hearing her as she moved. She searched the rest of Marshall's room, but it turned up empty as well.

Elise retraced her steps, wondering if maybe he'd made it into her walls, and now tracked her, step for step, through the narrow dark. But on the second look through the rooms, she found him in the corner of the office. She'd completely missed him earlier. He stood with his back to her, holding one of Mr. Nick's computer CDs to the window, catching its iridescent bottom in the light. Sweat darkened the armpits of the boy's shirt, and when he turned, it was beaded also along his prominent upper lip.

With him in front of her, standing there, looking at her, Elise again had to fight the urge to turn and run.

"No," Elise said. Her tongue now felt thick and dry in her mouth. The thought occurred to her: How long had it been since she'd spoken to anyone? "Where do you live?" she asked. "Where are you coming from?"

"Delacroix Street," he said. "The little brown house with the rescue dogs in the pen? It's just past that field and through the woods." He pointed in the direction of the levee, then thought about it, and pointed toward the backyard. "You know, I like your house. I think anybody could get lost in here."

He squinted at the CD, watching the colors slide across the plastic. Crescents of dirt beneath his fingernails. He waved the disk in her face to show her what he was looking at. He'd left oily fingerprints on its bottom.

"I'm Brody," he said.

And with the boy looking at her, and the oddness of that feeling again—being seen—the girl forgot, for a moment, what else she had planned to say.

"So," he said. "Which one of these is your room?"

HAUNTED HOUSE

A HOUSE IS LIKE A TREE, AND ITS ROOMS ARE BRANCHES. EACH movement along them causes the smallest tremors across the length of its bark. In the Masons' house, no one was supposed to be home, but it was as if a hummingbird flitted between the rooms: a door opening and shutting again, a patter of feet along the hall and stairs, a television switched on, a set of children's voices quarreling.

A girl telling a boy, "No."

She said to him, "Leave."

Downstairs, Elise shouldered the screen door open and pushed a hand into the boy's soft chest, ushering him down the back steps.

"You don't talk about me to anyone."

"Okay," Brody said. "But then I get to come back tomorrow."

Elise latched the screen door shut.

The Girl in the Walls needs her secrecy. The Girl in the Walls stays alone.

"Never come back," she knew she must say, and then the boy might listen. Say it cold, with the voice of a ghost. Say it with the certainty of someone who is already dead. Declare it as much to the world outside as to him, and he'd leave.

Stay away from me. You're dangerous.

But instead, Elise's shoulders sank, her back bent. She leaned against the screen door like a cat, bone-tired, buckling in the cold.

"Earlier," Elise said. "Early, but not too early. Tomorrow, ten in the morning for you. Meet me here, at the back. And no one can see you come."

She shut the door and twisted the dead bolt.

When he was gone, Elise stood there in the porch. What exactly had she just done?

The house now seemed so open around her. As if the roof had been torn off, and something dark and large circled above. She went upstairs and crawled into her walls. She took her book and squeezed it tight against her chest.

"What have I done?" she asked. She took a deep breath, shuddering. The empty dark around her. Her eyes shut. With no one in the world to talk to, she told Odin what had happened.

And, from the darkness, the wise god said, "Well, that's a mess."

She'd made a mistake. Another mistake.

But even he had made mistakes before—right?

"Many," the old god's voice echoed, sad, through the empty space between the walls. "I still often do."

But as one sovereign to another, he wished her the best of luck.

Elise stayed there in her walls for a while. She collected herself. Then she pulled herself out.

Had to.

Elise went to the utility closet and snatched a broom. The boy had left gray footprints all over the floors.

"Right," Odin said. "Good luck with those, too."

MORE WORK

"BUT THE GARAGE IS FINE THE WAY IT IS!" MARSHALL SAID. "WE don't even use it anyway."

"That's the problem," his father said.

When Eddie's family moved into the new home, the small garage was already half-filled with lumber and cardboard that had been left by the family before them. Since the Masons were moving into a house much larger than the one they had before on the Northshore, Eddie remembered the words his parents had repeated to one another when they were packing up the U-Hauls and looking over the collection of the boys' outgrown, childhood clothes and toys, a push lawn mower in need of repair, enormous kayaks the family hadn't used in years.

"There's so much space in the new house," they'd said. "We'll sort it all out there."

The house had engulfed their objects easily enough. But the result was chaotic spaces in the attic, and especially in the garage, where white and black garbage bags of clothes and old sports equipment were stacked on top of necessary things, extension cords and tools and cleaning supplies. Bikes with rusted chains were wedged behind their father's workbench, cardboard boxes filled with assorted things already forgotten and lost and being replaced. Marshall's parents had tasked him with cleaning it out.

"I'll be spending my entire summer vacation working on y'all's projects, won't I?" Marshall asked, dropping his book bag in the foyer when they arrived home from school.

His father sorted through the mail. "Maybe you should have thought of that before you quit your job."

That evening, Eddie sat on the library sofa with a book, all the while hearing, several rooms over, Marshall dragging boxes, cursing, and kicking at them. Upstairs, his father worked in his office while his mom dust-mopped the wood floors—Eddie smelled the lemon-scented Endust even down here. A horsefly, likely snuck in through the open garage doors, spiraled above him and hummed relentlessly.

Eddie tried to slap the bug with the back of his book every time it passed through the light of the floor lamp, but as soon as he sat up, the bug slipped out of view. Its buzz distracted him from a book that was hard enough to pay attention to—a dry, historical one from his grandmother about the Spanish-American War, written for adults, that he'd put off reading for months. The easiest solution was to go upstairs, put up with the smell of Endust in the hallway, and read in his bedroom. But since his birthday, he hadn't enjoyed being in his room.

Across the house, Marshall wasn't becoming any more productive. He'd been working for over an hour, but before that had spent as long as he could in his room, delaying the work. He hadn't begun until their father had hammered on the door, demanding he get off his ass and get at it. And even since then, Marshall had come in several times through the kitchen door, calling up to ask whether a cracked Frisbee, a box of packing peanuts, or a bin of soiled cloths should be kept. He lingered inside each time, flipped on the television for a few minutes. He grumbled that if his parents had hired someone to do the work in the guest room, he wouldn't have to do this on his own. He came in the library to tell Eddie it was ridiculous his younger brother didn't have to work on the garage as well.

"It's not like you've got a job, either."

Around dinnertime, Marshall again shot halfway up the stairs, to call up to his parents. "So, what are we eating tonight?"

"Something in the pantry for you and your brother," their mom shouted down. "There might be some leftovers from the restaurant still in the fridge."

"From Brennan's? There's nothing left. You know it."

"Marshall, watch yourself," she said. "I've spent the whole evening cleaning up dirt you boys have tracked in all over the house. Go find something, okay?"

Marshall descended the stairs. He crossed into the library where his loose black jeans and small belt buckle stood at the edge of Eddie's peripherals as he read. Marshall grabbed each side of the book and closed it shut.

"Dinnertime," he said.

SMALL SIGNS

EDDIE SAT AT THE KITCHEN TABLE AND WATCHED HIS BROTHER scour the pantry. Marshall lifted a bag of black-eyed peas, read the back, and dropped it on the shelf. He did the same with a can of corn, and again with one of green beans. The tin of the cans smacked against the wood. Eddie winced each time.

"There's nothing here," Marshall said. "No dinner food."

"I'm not really hungry," Eddie said. Part of the reason was that Marshall had left the garage door open, and the sawdust and mildew smells had begun turning his stomach. The other part was that, if he could choose, he'd rather not eat than be around Marshall.

"Yeah, dipshit," Marshall said. "Me eating and you not will go over real well for me with the parents. Don't be dumb. But, seriously, what are we actually supposed to eat? Cereal? Even these boxes are mostly empty." Marshall stepped out of the pantry and shook the Raisin Bran. "I didn't realize any of us ate this crap."

Eddie's gaze lay on the stained-glass window above the stovetop vent, the one that led nowhere but into the dark of the wall space.

"Do you even eat this junk?"

"No."

"Really?" Marshall opened the box of Raisin Bran and peered inside, shook it. He closed the lid and tossed the box to the top shelf where it toppled to its side. Marshall considered Eddie, his lips pursed.

"Why are you looking at me?" Eddie asked.

Marshall had grown into a way of examining Eddie sometimes, as if seeing him like he were some other boy, not a brother. Like

Marshall was puzzling out what to do with him. The look made Eddie feel like a stranger. He could be sitting next to Marshall on the couch for an hour and a half, watching television, and if he turned to see that expression, he knew he might end up with one of their mother's throw pillows shoved into his face.

Marshall stood up straight. He went to the fridge and opened it, tilted the crown of his head back and looked inside through the bottom of his eyes.

"Hm." He closed the fridge. "Well, someone did." Marshall moved around the kitchen counter, still watching Eddie.

Eddie felt relieved when his brother turned and left the room. But after his brother's dragging feet faded, climbing again up the stairs, the emptiness of the kitchen swelled around him. Eddie was alone on the first floor. The stained-glass window that led into the wall caught the light from the overhead lamp, so its painted fleur-de-lis illuminated as though a candle shone from the other side. The porcelain rooster teapot on the top of the glassware cabinet made bug-eyed, wild eye contact with him.

Now even the teapot was getting to him. Eddie rubbed the bones below his eyes, then his temples. Nothing in the house was listening. It was his imagination. Why couldn't he shake that feeling?

Eddie stood and closed the garage door. He went to the threshold of the kitchen and living room, then passed on to the foot of the stairs. His brother was arguing with their parents. Eddie leaned against the antique clock, hearing its steady ticking, and watched the pendulum swing. The horsefly hummed in another room.

Above, his mom's voice: "I'll get to the grocery store soon, Marshall!"

"Mom, I'm not saying that—"

"Then I'm not following," she said. "Hey, please. You're standing right in the pile I swept up."

"Okay, whatever. Well, I'm trying to say—"

"Marshall!"

Eddie imagined his father opening the office door, still hunched in his rolling chair, leaning out into the hall. "Does it look like we want to hear, one more time, about your goddamn Pop-Tarts?"

"Dad, I'm not talking about—"

"Marshall," his father said. "For the love of God, can you just stop? This isn't *Tom and Jerry*. Maybe can you just give the stupid childishness a break. Just tonight, since we're busy, maybe can you think and act like a normal kid?"

Eddie's mom said something too soft to hear, probably to their father, telling him to tone his temper down. But when Marshall spoke, Eddie heard him well enough. "Dad, you can screw yourself."

Marshall rumbled down the stairs. Their father calling after him. Marshall paused at the base of the stairs, breathing heavy through his nose, his face raging bright red, his lower lip puckered and pouting. Eddie sidestepped him, crossing to the other side of the clock, allowing him a berth to pass.

Marshall watched him. His voice hushed when he spoke. "You're in this house. You're here. And I'm the one Dad's calling a child? Calling weird?" He looked up at the ceiling, clenching his fists.

"You know what?" Marshall said. "I don't need this. Fuck this place. Fuck this family."

BRODY

THIS WAS THEIR AGREEMENT: BRODY COULD COME BACK, TODAY, AS
long as he didn't tell a single soul they'd met. Elise hadn't told him
more than that. When he had asked her which room was her bedroom, she had said she preferred sleeping on the couch. Fortunately,
for a boy like Brody, that seemed to be enough.

At the back door that morning, Brody showed up thirty minutes
early, knocking on the window, and leaving smudges on the glass.
Elise pointed at an imaginary wristwatch on her arm, grabbed two
clumps of her hair, and mimed ripping them out. She opened the
door, but held the screen shut and pointed down at his feet, which
were still bare and caked in mud.

"If this is going to happen," she said, "that isn't."

Elise wiped clean the window and sent him back twice to the hose
alongside the house to spray his feet, the second time demanding the
"jet" setting (worry stiffened his face) until finally they were clean,
the heels and tops and soles, his skin blotchy pink from the harsh
stream. She tossed him a towel and, while he dried off, she had him
answer questions, ones she had prepared the long evening before.

"Who did you talk to last night? Did you tell anyone about me?
Who knows where you were yesterday, where you are now?"

"No?"

"No to what?"

"All? I didn't tell anybody. Auntie's at work, so I came over."

"Why aren't you at school?"

"Homeschool. Auntie doesn't believe in Halloween. She took me

out of school last year after we did jack-o'-lantern cupcakes and decorated the calendar board with bats. You going to let me in?"

"You didn't tell anyone about me?"

"Nope."

"Are you a spy?"

"Yes."

She considered. That was probably the safest response. "You can
come in."

Once he was inside, Elise realized what little control she really
had over the boy. It was like steering a wild goat with nothing but
her open palms. Brody wandered the rooms, opened cabinets and
drawers, chewed ice from the freezer, insisted on seeing how fast the
overheard fans would go. He turned on the television, raised the volume, and darted away to another room, still listening to the shows.
She could make suggestions, put her foot down when he wanted to
go too far (like sliding down the banisters, pretending the floor was
lava), but she felt, more than anything, like a babysitter scrambling
after a toddler.

Elise couldn't keep him out of the bedrooms. He lunged atop the
parents' bed and rolled across the sheets. Marshall's death metal post-
ers fascinated him. "Wicked!" Eddie's room startled him. "Everything's opened up!" Even with Elise snatching at the back of his shirt
collar, he sprang between the boys' rooms, tripping over dirty laundry on the floor. "Does he have video games on here?" he said, running his fingers along Marshall's computer keyboard.

Brody touched everything.

This would be it. No way she could clean this up. He'd gone into
every room—moved so many things. How could she move it all
back? She could hardly catch all of his footprints last time.

"My cousin has Duck Hunters and Alien Invaders. I played last
time I went over—he lives in Chalmette, across the river by the big
oil refineries. How do we turn the computer on to see what he's got?"

"We don't."

Elise was firm here. No way she'd allow him that incomprehensible machine, with its strange chimes and rings. She figured whatever Brody planned to do to it would need fixing, and she'd be stuck having no idea how. She thought of Marshall, the sharp points of his shoulder blades sticking out the back of his shirt like sprouting wings of a dragon. His oversized knuckles. Too easy to imagine him coming home, finding something wrong with it and, in anger, punching a hole in her wall.

"You have to go now," Elise said.

"But you said I could stay until the owl hooted from the clock downstairs."

"You're leaving now."

"I can leave whenever I want."

"No, you can't. Get out."

Something wild and immovable in her eyes. She knew it from the way Brody looked at her. He turned around in the room, resigned to his fate. He hung his head while she led him out.

LIFE, AND WHAT'S MISSING

BUT THE NEXT DAY, ELISE SAW HIM THROUGH THE GUEST ROOM window, walking along the levee, the tuft of his odd bowl-cut bobbing in the glare. He carried a bag of Doritos and the board game Life under his arm.

She opened the window and called out to him, "Hey! Hey! Get in here!"

After he'd circled around back and, once again, had finished washing his feet with the hose outside, he grimaced with his chin tucked tight to his neck, still pouting from the day before. "You never told me your name."

Her mouth full of his Doritos, Elise told him, "It's none of your business."

The less he knew, the better. That voice in her head, nagging at her, was right about that much, even if Elise ignored its howling protestations about allowing him in now. Yesterday's long afternoon, listening to the Masons' routines beneath her, waiting until they finally went to bed, the whole while knowing that tomorrow would be the same dead quiet of the house, then the same afternoon routines, that most days would be exactly the same, hour by hour, week by week— she'd been worn down.

Elise had Brody pour the contents of Life out on the dining room table. And when he did, she discovered most of the pieces were missing, including every last bill of the bright-colored game money. And even if they had them all, playing through middle age was impossible, as the cardboard had been left long in the sun, and much of the text had bleached to illegibility. Elise squinted at Brody, expecting some justification, but the boy only shrugged as if surprised as she was.

"Do you want to investigate your house?" he asked.

"I thought you wanted to play a board game."

"You've got a really good house."

"I already know what it looks like."

"Okay, well, I'm going to investigate."

"No way," she said. "You're going to move things, and switch things, and turn things on. You made a mess yesterday, you know that? Everywhere. You weren't even here that long. Took me forever to get it right."

Brody groaned. "Why are you always fixing things? You're always moving it all back and cleaning right away. Do your parents say you have to?"

Elise wasn't sure how to respond.

"Even my uncle isn't that bad about cleaning." Brody craned his neck to study the chandelier above them and twisted in his chair to look over the antique china cabinet. "Are you homeschooled, too?"

"No," she said. "Well, yes. Sort of. I just don't go anymore."

"What about your brothers?" Brody asked.

"They're not my brothers." She shouldn't have said it. But the thought of lying then seemed exhausting, like its own kind of sneaking around.

"Oh," Brody said. He looked around at the picture frames hung on the walls. "I wondered about that. You're creepy looking. Your hair's all flat and dirty. Looks like you crawled out of the ground. Was wondering how you got allowed to be that way."

Elise patted lightly at her hair. She didn't think it was that bad.

"Are you being punished? Is that why you're always here alone?"

"No," Elise said. For whatever reason, the question stung. "No. I'm here because I want to be here. Nobody tells me what to do. Nobody else knows."

What was she doing?

"Really?" Brody said. His eyes grew. He leaned over in his chair. "Do you sneak into houses, too?"

"What?" she said. "No." She squinted at him. "Is that what you're doing all day?"

"Have you snuck in any other houses around here? Do you live in another home, when you aren't here?" He turned his head to the side. "Which one?"

"No. This is my home," she said. "This is where I live. So, wait, how many houses are you sneaking into?"

Brody didn't answer. He stared at her, mouth agape, eyebrows raised in childish fascination.

That part of her pleaded, *No, don't take this from yourself*—but Elise ignored it, giving in to the rush, the vibrating warmth, of having eyes on her, wide with excitement. Someone wanting to know more, caring to know, about her. Hidden for months—months—when part of the feeling of being alive is seeing someone see you, react to you.

"How about I show you?"

REVEALING A HOME

ELISE BROUGHT HIM TO THE ATTIC, TO HER NOOK BENEATH THE PLY-wood floor, and the scattering of items laid in the place between the crossbeams where she slept. She watched his face, to see how he responded.

"No way!" Brody shouted. "No way you sleep here. This is where you live? Does anybody else know?" Then later, after he stepped in, incredulous, bending and sorting through the space: "This is your stuff? This is junk!"

"It's not junk."

He picked up a roll of toilet paper she planned to use as tissues. He dropped it and picked up a Ziploc bag of crumbs. "It's junk!"

Brody's opinion changed, though, when she showed him the crevice, the narrow mouth that led into the dark between the walls of the house. The cool air from below lapped at their faces, and the boy had to stand two steps away, his curiosity in battle with self-preservation as he leaned apprehensively over.

"It's so close to where you sleep," he said. "You don't worry about falling in?"

"Watch this."

Elise got down to her knees and lowered herself into the dark mouth, her feet led by experience to fit into crevices in the wall that the boy could only imagine. Her limbs worked, and she sank from sight. She sensed a shadow swelling over her face as she pulled away from the attic's overhead bulb, growing until Brody's own face was something pale as a moon, grimacing high above her. Brody shrank in size, until finally, she made a turn, and he disappeared.

"You okay?" he called down to her. His voice bounced through the house's ribs, sounding blunted. "Can you hear me?"

Around her, quiet. A warm water pipe in her grip, and the whisper of the air through the AC vent not far away. She felt her heartbeat in her wrists.

That voice of hers, pleading: *What have you done? Giving everything away. Your home. Your mom and dad's home. For a stranger. Ruining it—why?*

The more she told the boy, the harder for her to keep what she held tight to. The more she gave away, the less safe the Girl in the Walls became, the less secure. She became less. With Brody here, her impulse to hide and duck away had never left her. Every time he turned a corner to another room, the temptation to pull back. At any time, she could have tucked herself away and left him there, to grope through the large house, calling for her. All she had to do was leave him, abandon him there with the large, dim, empty house around him. To him, it would be as if he had been talking to a ghost.

She was deep inside the walls now. She could still forget him. Close her eyes and, next morning, the world might reset. But the girl had tried that the first night, after she made her way back into her home, when she had slept on a pile of strangers' summer clothes in her old, cold attic. And it hadn't worked.

Brody had seen her home, seen the spaces between, where she hid. Seen her things, the belongings of her and her parents, hidden in the nook below the plywood. There was no more hiding, at least from him.

Backed yourself into a corner.

She had.

So, she yelled up to him, through the dark, as loud as her voice could manage. "Hey, Brody! My name's Elise!"

WHO SHE WAS

SHE WAS HALF-DEAD AND NOT-DEAD—SHE WAS LOSING AND REFUSING TO lose. She was not with the world as it moved on; she was its wake.

This Girl in the Walls was a girl in the rooms of a house—this house—and now a spider in a broken web, who feared footsteps, the wind, falling limbs.

The Girl in the Walls was a girl who didn't understand when she would be old enough to say: I have lost my mom and my dad, and I will never see them again. She didn't understand how she could ever grow to be that woman.

In the walls, nothing ever changes. There was dust that was her parents' moldered skin, warm before, but cool now, infinite. This girl lived in her walls because there was no other place that would still hold them.

The Girl in the Walls wanted to live, but she had to be careful, as each day was a step across a deadfall, the branches bending beneath her feet, threatening to snap. She had to be careful, or she'd lose them.

Before Brody left that afternoon, Elise told him all this, in so many words. She brought him around the house and showed him each of the places she hid.

She revealed her hiding places, and she gave herself up. So, she told him who she was, who she'd become. She said it all as much to herself as to him.

HIDDEN THINGS

WHEN SHE FINISHED, BRODY CLOSED HIS EYES. NODDED, TWO CURT bobs of the chin. For the rest of that morning, he helped search the house with her. Careful, cautiously moving objects, lifting couch cushions, peering beneath dressers and along the backs of closets— he helped her look through her home for things that had been lost. Eventually, it was Brody that found one first. A fresh set of eyes is a good help.

In one of the floor vents in the library, with the metal grate pulled up and placed to the side, the air duct was a compartment like a small chest. A bookmark, blue and leather and frayed at the edges, dusty at the bottom of the vent, but—as Elise remembered—one of her father's. Brody handed it to her, and Elise squeezed it like a living hand.

"I don't remember my parents," Brody said to her. "But I know I like when something I got was theirs."

Elise pressed it into the pocket of her jeans. Kept her hand in there with it.

THINGS BROUGHT

SUPPLIES, OR AT LEAST THAT'S HOW HE REFERRED TO THEM, NEW things each time he came, tucked away in a muddy blue tote bag he carried over his shoulder.

He brought Mardi Gras beads and a small, stuffed bear; a plastic grocery bag filled with rocks he had collected from the riverside of the levee. He brought games—Jewels in the Attic and chess, wet and dried leaves and a magnolia cone bursting with smooth red seeds. He brought an old miniature water gun made of plastic gone brittle from heat, and a half-empty container of Silly String she refused to let him spray, even out in the yard.

He brought her useful things: Listerine, napkins, and girl's deodorant. He brought things she had absolutely no use for, like sunglasses, a badminton birdie, a set of rusted keys, and a bell for a bicycle. Useless things she told him to take back at each morning's end. Some things Brody forgot to take at the end of the day. And sometimes, after keeping them beside her in her nook overnight, she changed her mind, and wanted them after all. Things like an antique stopwatch, a vial of bright-blue nail polish, and a miniature cactus she placed in a patch of light from the attic dormer, camouflaged within a large Christmas wreath.

He brought food—cans of beans and peaches, a sleeve of Ritz crackers, a pair of satsumas fresh from a tree with the skin still speckled with black mold. He brought cereal, but never any of the good ones, no matter how much she complained ("Why on earth would I want more Raisin Bran?"). He brought useless foods, too:

"What am I supposed to do with a cake mix, Brody?"

"Make a cake?"

"I can't bake a cake, Brody."

"Well, I didn't want cake anyway."

Some things he brought were nice things. Expensive things. Like a Gameboy with a cartridge of Mortal Kombat II.

"In case you get bored," he said.

"Is this yours?" Elise asked. "It's really old." She switched the game on, and the small power light on the edge of the screen glowed a bright green. Lighting flashed across the head of a silver dragon. "Wow."

"I beat it already," Brody said. "Watch out for the ninja who comes near the end. He spits poison."

"Thanks," Elise said, and had said each time, each day he had arrived at her house. That strange tingle crawling along the back of her neck and scalp, the feeling she got when something was being done only for her. Hadn't felt it in a long time.

But when the mornings ended, after they cleaned the house together, ensuring each thing was as the Masons had left it, there'd still be signs of him there. Miniature signs, mostly gone by the time the Masons returned, or for days, or more, unnoticed. Footprints across the yard. A small puddle alongside the house by the hose. Fingerprints on the doorknob. Elise and Brody could do nothing all day, could sit in front of the television from starlings to cardinal, and there'd still be signs.

It didn't help that he was curious. When Elise left him alone, he rifled through storage bins and desk drawers. This house was so much larger than his own. So many nooks, rooms, alcoves, crannies, closets to explore. It held so many different objects, ones he'd never owned, and secret ones stashed in the back of a desk drawer.

For the Girl in the Walls to survive, these kinds of things can't last. These friendships.

Those who live in the walls must adjust, must twist themselves around in their home, stretching until they're as thin as air. Not everyone can do what they can.

Others might try, but soon enough, they can't help themselves. Signs of their presence remain in a house.

Eventually, every hidden thing is found.

RETURNING HOME

SOMETHING IS NOT RIGHT.

This is not where it's supposed to be.

Sometimes the change is ignored, forgotten nearly as quick as the realization occurs. Finding a doily shifted on the small hallway table is not such a change that a mother or father wouldn't slide it unconsciously back in place and move on. But other changes are evident. For him, the first thing was that the remote for the television had moved—not on the coffee table at the base of the sofa, where his father insisted it be kept.

Marshall looked over the table for a moment. Puzzled. A victim of a small betrayal. He gave in and went to press the power button on the side of the set.

Its black buttons were tucked around the frame of the television. Marshall curled his fingers and groped. He tested them, tapping them all to find the right one. But before he found it, with his hand along the side of the television set, he'd felt the machine's warmth, warmth like a living thing, as if it had been running all day.

Marshall turned the television on. Put its volume down low. Turned the television off.

ON THE ROOF

THEY SAT ON THE ROOF IN THE LATE NIGHT AND WATCHED THE clouds. When Brody had come, it had always been during the safe weekday hours, and on Sunday, while the Masons were at church. Evenings had always been off-limits—the Masons were home. But tonight was different. Yesterday, Mr. Nick had cleaned the gutters and had forgotten to take in the ladder, leaving a perfect route for someone to climb up to the roof from the outside. Now, it was already after midnight, but no one would miss Brody at home: his aunt worked the graveyard shift at the pharmacy, and his uncle, whenever he got home, if he came home tonight, wouldn't bother checking on him.

Up there, they doused themselves with the can of bug repellant. When they caught the bitter spray in their mouths, they spat the taste off the side of the roof. A necessary suffering; summer nights belonged to insects. It had been two weeks since Mr. Nick last cut the lawn, and the grass below teemed with bugs. Moths, mosquitoes, crickets, and black Devil's Locusts—with eyes fractured into dozens of smaller ones, thousands in total, accounting for them in the dark. Elise and Brody sprayed themselves until they reeked of chemicals, but at least they no longer worried over slapping after each itch. Elise only hoped the smell wouldn't be so strong the Masons would catch a whiff of her later on.

Brody snacked from a tin of peanuts and pointed up at the stars, showing her which constellations he knew. "You see that bright star, and the big box around it? And the tail going out the back, that goes right below the moon?"

"I think so," she said. "Yeah, I see it."

"That's Godzilla."

The shingles below them continued to radiate warmth from the hot afternoon sun. Their texture was rough, a grainier sandpaper, but to sit still kept them from rubbing too harshly, and to feel no more coarse than the black rubber of a park playground. Elise was outside, but the house held firm beneath her; it reached up to her and grabbed hold. She was still here. An owl hooted from somewhere beside them, and when a passing car's headlights flashed through the front yard, Elise made out a ruffle of feathers in the fork of an oak tree.

She looked up at the sky and told Brody which ones she knew. "That big rectangle—the one that looks like its corners are stretched out? It's Orion. He was a great hunter in the old times. You can see his bow, there. And his belt with its knife. He was quiet and patient. He could hide for days and days on his belly in a field, just like the one down there, or on a treetop, or on top of a roof. He hid so he could hunt monsters. He caught so many of them that the gods pulled him up into the night sky, so he could wait in the dark and hunt forever."

"I like him," Brody said. "He sounds like me."

"I was thinking he sounded more like me."

"Really?" Brody shoved another fistful of peanuts into his mouth and shrugged. "Okay. He sounds like you, too."

Elise smiled, kicked her legs out, and leaned back on the slanted roof, resting on a forearm. "And there's the Big Dipper. Can you see it?"

"What's a dipper?" Brody said.

"It's what I'm pointing at right now. Look."

"Yeah, but what is it?"

"It's—"

"Is it a monster?"

"No. It's a kind of—"

"I bet it's a monster."

"I mean, it's not."

"Orion should keep an eye on that dipper." Brody mimed aiming a bow and arrow at the sky. "Whoosh!" he said, releasing his arrow and skewering the constellation.

Around them, the trees rustled. It was a quiet night, and an oil tanker drifted slow down the river. Inside, the Masons would be sleeping in their beds, deaf to them. If they did hear, they heard nothing more than a murmur, a sound that might come from anywhere—neighbors shouting a half mile away, the calls of ships' crewmen. Elise might as well have had her own house that night, out on the roof, one she shared. While she told Brody about Hercules and his twelve labors, the monsters he slew to prove he had become a better man, Elise thought about how much this, this night, reminded her of home.

INSIDE

EDDIE LAY AWAKE AND LISTENED TO THE HOUSE.

His ears had grown sensitive enough to hear the bird clock singing on the hour, and his father snoring faintly down the hall. Eddie's room lay open around him. All he needed was to sit up and see into every crevice. Eddie wasn't sure how long he'd keep it this way. Earlier that day, his father had opened the door to ask for help with something in the shed. His father had looked over the room, mouth tightening into a thin line, but had said nothing about what Eddie had done to it. Eddie wondered why his dad didn't ask him. He wouldn't have known what to say, but the question, maybe, might have helped.

Not long after he had gone to bed that night, Eddie woke to his parents fighting in their bedroom. Their voices sounded tired. They weren't yelling, but he knew an argument when he heard it. As summer neared, his parents built up momentum in the daylight hours, churning, no chance to stop moving. His mom's work heels left in the hallway outside the guest room, where she mumbled as she, again, worked. His father shouting through the house, demanding to know who had moved his grade book. Hurricane season coming, and his mom talked of needing to sell properties. Summer school coming, which meant more of the same work for his father. The guest room floor was taking longer than they'd expected, and they still planned to paint the walls by the end of the month. Eddie waking to their strained, drowsy anger: it made too much sense. It'd become harder now to imagine them ever at rest, asleep.

Then, Eddie had stayed awake, kept up by the patter of Marshall's fingers at the computer keyboard and the groan of its processor. Another hour passed, and Eddie wanted to free himself of his bed, to stretch and pace, and sit by the window, but he didn't want Marshall to hear him again, moving at night. When the older brother finally shut the machine down, and the dim crack of light disappeared beneath the bathroom door, Eddie dozed, falling in and out of sleep while the house adjusted itself around him.

Sounds grew blurred by encroaching sleep. What might be footsteps, or a finger tapping against a glass of water. What might be a window opening, or nothing at all. Voices. The feeling that someone crouched outside his bedroom door, to see if his breathing had slowed.

In the mythology and fantasy books Eddie used to read, simple explanations were never good for describing what really existed. A small hole in the base of a tree, the sliver of a cave opening—each might descend into an entirely different world. The solid ground could shake loose beneath a person's feet, creatures could wriggle themselves from moss, ancient empires could thrive beneath mountains. When he was younger, Eddie used to imagine that science could only account for one part of the machinations around him, and that gods perched atop the cumulonimbus clouds, and beneath his feet, down within the Earth's molten mantle, goblins stoked the flames.

He'd given up those thoughts. A teenager now; at night, it was harder to remember.

With school ending, Eddie knew he should be different, the way his classmates were different. Like at his old school on the Northshore, he sat in the back corner of class. He spent lunches at a separate table in the cafeteria, flush against the wall by the vending machines. But at the old school, he had still made conversation at recess. Mostly with shyer boys who sat beside the hackberry tree while they scooped caterpillars from its trunk with leaves. But here, he no longer shared that history with any boys his age. No more common history to bridge the gap between one person and another.

At the school he'd go to the next day, it seemed each of his classmates might have been this age their entire lives. Eddie heard their conversations before class, the weekends they recounted, the plans they made. They spoke like they were half adult already. He was nothing like them. Somehow, over the past couple years, he'd dragged his feet with growing up and had left himself so much ground to cover.

Eddie rolled over in bed and watched the ceiling fan rotate slowly above him. He tracked one blade with his eyes for a while. He toyed with the elastic waistband of his boxer shorts. Pushed his hand through, but only left it there on the thigh. He could do it, and it would help him sleep, he'd learned. Would make him drowsy for long enough that he might nod off and stay there. But even if he lay his pillow across his face, turned on his side to minimize the rise and fall of the sheets, he'd still feel watched. How could he think of anything else?

Eddie sat up and looked at the crack beneath the hallway door. Marshall was right. He had to be normal. There was nothing here with him. He had to put away childish thoughts. Put an end to fear from imagination. It began now, at night. Each morning began the night before, when he was here alone in his bedroom.

His old books, the ones that disappeared—they must have been taken by his brother or parents, a sign that they needed him to grow up. A simple explanation. He had never asked, and he wouldn't ask, but it had to be that simple. The sounds he thought he heard, the feelings he got, those imaginations that didn't, hadn't existed?

It was these thoughts that made him weird. If Eddie could stop them, he'd stop being strange. Like in books: Rumpelstiltskin was strange, Gollum was strange. Strange made them ugly. It made them hated. It kept them alone.

PART 3

SUBJECT: SAW YOUR POST

I believe you. I understand you. Maybe better than anyone.

I know no one listens. When I was young? The same for me. I told my parents and they said I made it up. I told kids at school. They acted like I had just grown another head. I even told my pastor. For a long time had to think— it was me. But you know? We had every sign then.

Missing things. Noises in the attic. Closed doors come open in the morning. Strange sudden smells. A cough from the empty room. Rugs kicked over when home alone. Eventually I stopped telling. Mom cried. She asked why I was scaring her.

But why would I make that up?

I know how hard it is knowing. Awful and frightening. Lonely. When you know they are there in a house like yours. Hope it is alright that I emailed you directly.

I wanted to let you know over the years I have learned how to take care of this. I can help if you want. Safest to talk to someone who already knows. You are smart. But no offense I know you are young too.

First know you have to be careful what you say aloud. If they are in the house they may be listening. If they know you know? You may be in danger.

Tell me about your house. How many rooms? Count the closets separate. Stairs? Attic? Basement? Do you have pets? Rooms you do not spend much time in? List to me the sounds you hear. Look for things moved or gone. Tell me every thing you notice. Specifically. Pay attention. If you listen a house cracks open to you.

Not everybody hears like we do. Not everybody grasps the idea. You got to sort out the people to trust. Those you can and cannot. Count me with the first lot.

J.T.

ON TELEVISION

A FAMILY, GRINNING AT ONE ANOTHER, BARBECUING ON A DECK. The image lasted on the screen a few seconds before the couple and their three children disappeared, replaced by a storm. The trees of the yard roiled, the rain lashed diagonally across the screen. A man's deep, disembodied voice resonated over the rain and wind: "This is the importance of deck protection."

The camera cut to a close-up of the wood of the deck, showing how the bulbous, blue raindrops were each broken, shattered, and disseminated by the Deck Protector Formula. The storm never had a chance. With the rain defeated, the yard once again turned bright and warm, and the family huddled around the grill.

A terrible commercial, and Elise had seen it too many times to count. She tried to entertain herself by looking at all the parts of the screen she thought she wasn't supposed to. For instance, this time, just as the ad ended, Elise caught a glimpse of the space behind the family. There, past their brightly colored sundresses and polos, an even brighter bowl peeked between their limbs. Fruit salad—honeydew, cantaloupe, watermelon, even cherries.

"Oh, man," Elise said. "I would love fruit."

"They got any here?" Brody asked.

"No," she said. "They have apples, but they'd notice those missing. It's been a long time since they've had grapes."

"Hm," Brody said. He sat beside her on the sofa and picked at a callus on his heel. "You know," he said. "There's watermelons in the garden."

"Already?" Elise asked. "Mrs. Laura didn't plant those that long ago. You sure? Anyway, there's no way you could get one. She's out there every afternoon. She'd know right away."

"What if she thought an animal ate them? I saw them broke open in other yards. I think racoons get them."

"It'd be too much of a mess. The juice would get everywhere. We'd get the table sticky."

"Why can't we eat it out there?"

UNMOORED

THE SAME AIR EXISTS IN EACH PLACE, THE SAME LIGHT AND SHADOW. Something to remind herself of, as Elise turned the television's volume to its max, and left it on as they left the room. She had done it as a kind of preparation. Elise would still hear the battle cries of Xena, Warrior Princess, even as she pulled open the back door and stood in its threshold. The sound of the inside grounding her. But stepping outside for the first time in the early afternoon, in summer, for anyone in South Louisiana, would always be intoxicating, and awful.

The sudden heat wrapped her body like hot smoke from an invisible fire, and on the other side of the door, the roar of the cicadas ballooned. Sweat beaded already along the back of Elise's neck, as she stepped down the brick steps of the back porch. The grass warm and wet with dew. With each footfall, she expected a thorn to lodge in her instep, or a fire ant to sink pincers between her toes. Brody led the way, but when he saw her trailing behind, he doubled back, took her by the hand, and towed her along like she was some unruly calf.

"It's bright out today, isn't it?" Elise said. "Like, really bright."

Brody squinted at the clouds. "Not really."

"It's hot, though," Elise said. And as they neared the waist-high netting of Mrs. Laura's garden, she said, "Is Ms. Wanda outside? Does she see us?"

"Who? Wait, why are you pulling? Stop!"

"I'm just—"

The house loomed behind her, somehow both massive and very

small. She worried the breeze had blown the door shut behind them. That the door had been locked. That they were trapped out now.

"I just need to check the door," Elise said.

But Brody dug his feet into the ground and pulled her hard, swinging her back. "You've been outside before," he said. "You were fine on the roof!"

"Different!" she said. And it was. The roof was its own room. "I— was touching it."

"Listen," he said, taking her by the shoulders. He let go and pulled out of the overall front pocket the rubber mallet he had taken from the garage before they had come outside. He held it out to her like it was precious. "I'll let you have first smash."

Elise looked down at the watermelons, two of them, that lay there before them, beneath the leafy beans and tomato plants. Only fist-sized. No wonder she hadn't seen them from the house. They were nowhere near ripe.

"Picture the whole world right there, the big stupid thing, in front of you," Brody said. "And then smash it!"

Elise ignored him. She knelt beside the watermelon. Felt cool here, with the black earth on her knees, under the light shade of the plants; felt sheltered. Her mom had her own garden, not as large— smaller plants, herbs—planted alongside the house. She had let Elise work alongside her, digging holes with a spade, watering with a small bucket. Elise had been younger than Brody was now, probably, and must have been useless in helping her mom. But, those few times, she enjoyed being involved, watching the plants grow when she passed by on her way to the car. The back door was still cracked, and Elise could hear the faint mumble of the television out here in the yard— she wasn't so far. She looked around the yard. Not too far.

Elise's hands quivered as she raised the watermelon on its vine. She focused on the fruit. Tapped along its ends with her fingernails. It was dense, heavy for its size.

"You're not smashing," Brody said.

"It's not ready yet," she said.

As she brought the melon to her face, everything behind it had begun to swirl, dizzying. Each thing throwing off its own heat, the colors vibrant, the grass a yellow-green, the sky blanched. Elise couldn't last long out here.

Brody turned and wandered the yard nearby. Elise crouched, digging her toes into the ground to hold tight, and watched a dragonfly's contorted flight path through the yard. She wiped a grasshopper from her leg. She'd gone light-headed. Felt the tight ache of a sunburn on her pale skin, though she couldn't have been out there more than a few minutes. She stood, shielding her eyes from the sun. Turned back. Brody, resigned, followed her into the house. She closed the door behind him. In the other room, the television droned on as if nothing at all had happened. The house hadn't changed. The dim light around her was a dip into cold water.

Mid-May. It'd be weeks before watermelon turned ripe. Later, Elise told herself, and she'd be out there again.

Give it a few weeks. Out there, with the house looking down upon her, and the sweet, pink fruit filling her mouth.

MEETING

DURING DINNER, WHILE EDDIE ATE ALONE IN THE DINING ROOM, Marshall came in carrying a half-finished plate and a glass of milk, black and chunky with protein powder. Eddie stopped eating when Marshall sat down across from him and placed his silverware on the table, but he didn't look up from his plate.

"Marshall?" Their mother's voice from the kitchen.

"We're fine," Marshall called back. He skewered a potato with his fork, brought it to his lips, chewed it slowly in one cheek. When he spoke again, his voice was muddled with food, but low. "Look, I know this bothers you—having me here, when you're trying to—" Marshall pointed at Eddie's plate with his fork, making a circular motion. "But I need to talk to you. So, put up."

Eddie kept his head low and peered up through his bangs. On the drive to school yesterday morning, Marshall had reclined his chair nearly into Eddie's lap, as though he wasn't even there. It wasn't until their father smacked Marshall's thigh with the back of a hand that he sat upright.

"I'm asking you," Marshall said. He took another bite, and to Eddie's surprise, tugged a napkin from his back pocket and covered his lips while he chewed. The whole move seemed self-conscious. Almost girlish.

"Why?" Eddie asked.

"Because I need to talk to you about something really stupid."

"Are you mad? Mad at me?"

"No," Marshall said. He lowered the napkin. "Well—a little.

You're annoying as shit, and it's a nightmare living with you—" The smirk that had begun to tug at his brother's face dissolved. "And you clearly can't take a joke. No, Eddie, I'm not mad at you."

"You sound like you're mad."

"Shut up. For the love of—I'm not mad."

"What is it you want?"

"I want to talk!" Hands thrown in the air, as if it were the most obvious thing. "I want to talk," Marshall said again, and looked into the doorway to the living room, as if expecting to see their parents already standing there, arms folded over their chests.

They weren't there, weren't listening, but Eddie wished they were.

"Do you ever go in my room?"

Eddie said nothing. Why would he ask if he wasn't mad? Marshall must be lying—he had to be angry. The older brother's forehead ruffled into a thick crease. His face pale, the muscles of his thin neck like tense cords. Marshall checked the doorway again, and when he turned to look Eddie in the face, his eyes were humorless, flat.

Eddie shook his head no.

"You don't go in my room? When I'm not there?"

"No," Eddie said. He shifted in his chair, the curve of his spine pressed into its back. Maybe once he would have crossed into his brother's room, when they were younger, but it was off-limits now, and had been the whole time they'd lived in this house. The space wasn't his, he wouldn't belong, would feel watched even if he knew Marshall was away. Even so, he realized this might end with a fist brought down on his arm, with a plate of food flipped into his lap.

"You don't eat the stuff that's meant for me in the pantry?" Marshall asked. "The granola bars, the Pop-Tarts I'd specifically asked Mom for?"

"I don't." Eddie never even wanted them—the granola bars too dry, the Pop-Tarts too sweet, they made his stomach ache—but Marshall leaned across the table, close enough to stab a fork into Eddie's green beans and eat them right from the plate. "I don't," Eddie said.

Marshall turned and checked the doorway once again. He exhaled, and Eddie felt the passing of his brother's breath on his face. Marshall slouched back in his chair, sinking low, until the difference in height between them was gone. "Eddie," he said. "I believe you."

Marshall closed his eyes and tapped his fingers along the edge of the table. Opened them and looked up at the ceiling. "What if I had something stupid to tell you? I mean, I think it's pretty stupid. I just—I don't know. Can you just tell me this? I feel pretty dumb asking you, but I'm thinking I'd much rather say it to you than probably anybody else—definitely more than Mom and Dad. Obviously. Because I sure as hell know what Dad's going to say. And because they've already totally blown it all off. And, well, I'm realizing I'm being twice as confusing as I should be when talking to someone who doesn't understand half the shit going on, so . . . I don't know."

"What do you want, Marshall?" Eddie's stomach hadn't stopped churning since Marshall had entered the room. Get it over with, he wanted to say. Please. And then go away.

"Here's my question: Eddie, do you, or have you ever felt, that besides me, and you, and Mom and Dad, that somebody else is here with us in the house?"

Marshall stared at him, unblinking. An intense feeling, like a rope tied between their eyes was being pulled taut. Eddie had no memory of the last time Marshall waited for anything he had to say. But the question Marshall asked wasn't one he wanted to answer. The second he did, the room would grow larger around him, the ceilings craning higher, the doorway farther away. The walls might as well be human skin, their sensitive hairs twitching.

"I think," Eddie said. He kneaded the napkin in his lap between his fingers. "Yeah. I have."

Marshall nodded. With a voice little more than a sigh, he said, "I think so, too."

BROTHERS

THAT NIGHT, AFTER DINNER, MARSHALL LED EDDIE TO HIS ROOM. "Check this out," Marshall said, sitting down in his desk chair. He woke the computer from sleep and motioned Eddie to go across the hall. "Grab a chair from the office."

Eddie returned with a blue, vinyl beanbag. He plopped to the floor while his brother opened the browser. Eddie sank into the bag, feeling its insides swell up and around him. He realized the last time he'd sat in it was on the Northshore, years ago, when he used to watch Marshall play Mario on the old Nintendo 64. Eddie had been too afraid to play the game himself—too afraid of falling from a ledge or finding a ghost materialized behind him—but watching his brother had been like a movie that listened to him, that accommodated his requests to stop, go back, and look at something a little longer.

Marshall gave him a puzzled look. "I thought you'd bring a real chair."

"I like this one," Eddie said.

Marshall stood and went to close his bedroom door. Then he opened his closet and went into the bathroom to check behind the shower curtain. Then he sat back down, as though nothing he had done was out of the ordinary. Eddie wondered how long they had both been checking.

"So," Marshall said. "Look at what I found."

Marshall opened a bookmarked web page, and a forum with strips of text loaded from the top of the page down. Small images of avatars loaded to the left of the screen, most with a default outline of a face with a question mark in place of its features.

"I posted a question on this site a few days back about some of the things I might, you know, have been feeling about our house. Just describing some things. Not much. But look at the responses." Marshall scrolled to the bottom of the screen, which showed a full three pages of posts. "Some of them are the same people a number of times," he said. "But, Eddie—it's kind of blown my mind. This kind of thing happens."

"It happens?"

"People believe us. Some have even said, like this one here with the bloodhound picture, they know of people it's happened to, they've got news article links. When I posted something, this guy started emailing me with actual advice. They all swear it's happened to them."

"That someone . . ."

"That someone was hiding there, in their home. Sometimes for a really long time. Coming out at night and raiding the pantry, taking things, living in old folks' homes who can't move around much. The guy sent a link to an article about this lady that had passed away, and nobody knew it for a long time because, every night, the inside lights kept coming on. The mail stacked up and the lawn grew long, and nobody had any idea."

"Why?" Eddie said. "I mean, why did you start thinking about this? What made you start?"

Marshall turned his chin and regarded him with a single eye. "There's been a lot of things."

"Like what? Did you hear? Or see?"

"How about this?" Marshall shimmied his chair back and pulled open the desk drawer. At the very back, wedged into the back corner, he pulled out an old, green pencil bag. He looked at Eddie, not at the bag, when he unzipped it. From inside, Marshall pulled a switchblade, folded, with a plastic, black hilt. A small knife, but the shape of the blade when he sprang it open—curved, jagged near the base, with a long, sloping tip—made it an entirely different tool than their mother's kitchen knives, even if they were mostly larger, or sharper.

"Mom would kill me if she knew I had these," Marshall said. "Or, had them. There were two." Marshall considered the knife in the palm of his hand, closed the blade, and handed it to Eddie, holding it with his thumb and finger in a way that said to be careful. "I bought two from a kid at school. The other knife's smaller, but it's the same kind. It's the type some real kind of enforcer would have. The blade springs out if you press the button. I've kept them both in this drawer, and yesterday night, I take the bag out—and one's gone. Mom and Dad wouldn't have taken it. Not without fully losing their shit with me. And they sure wouldn't have taken just one. And you—you said you don't come in my room."

"No," Eddie said.

"Well." Marshall took the knife from Eddie. "There's been a lot of things that go on in this house. But this is something that can't be explained away." He closed the blade, and instead of putting it into his drawer, tucked it into his front pocket.

Eddie felt sick. Someone, in his room, in his brother's room, touching and taking his things. All those times he had sensed someone— whoever it was—something had been in their house. This entire time, he and his family had been in danger. He resisted the urge to stand and search Marshall's room again himself. The air felt malignant.

Marshall scrolled through the on-screen pages while Eddie looked down at his hands. "You can see, all sorts of people talking about them," Marshall said. "Whether ours comes in and out, or if it's holed up somewhere in the house, I'm not sure. Whether it's a 'he' or 'she' either, I don't know. But I'm thinking—I'm pretty sure it's just one. It's an 'it' to me for now."

An "it." The pronoun didn't seem like an accurate word at all. An "it" was a mouse in the wall, or a cat at dusk skulking too far off to make out its eyes. An "it" was like the weather, was like a house— around you, but something separate and removed. An "it" doesn't listen to you, respond to the words you say, doesn't stand up when you tell it to leave.

"What do you think it wants?" Eddie asked. The sounds he heard, the footsteps and thumps in the wall, the missing, borrowed books, the little plastic witch and the feeling he got sometimes when he was alone in his room, the day of his birthday—what had been in the foot space of his desk in the closet? And after, from under his bed, the sounds of something leaving. But how could he tell Marshall any of this? How could he explain that it hadn't seemed dangerous before? That instead—he just hadn't known what it had seemed. He hadn't thought about it. Hadn't realized.

How stupid would he look? How could he say that the times when it seemed so real, he hadn't said anything because, yes, the thought of someone there, someone less than a full person, like a small cloud, had made him feel good. Had made him feel like when he was alone, he wasn't, that when he sat down on the carpet, the floor rose up to meet him, that when he entered a room, something shapeless welcomed him silently in.

And what if, maybe, none of this was real. Marshall might be playing a trick on him. Or it could be a test to see whether Eddie really was still a frightened little boy. Or even if Marshall really did believe, like Eddie had, maybe he had been carried away by his own imagination. An old house makes many noises, their parents had told them after their first few nights here. What if they were giving a face to a configuration of noisy crossbeams and walls? What if Marshall had simply forgotten where he had hid the other knife? And even if there was something here with them, what if the thing Marshall talked about was something completely different from what Eddie had heard, what he thought he heard?

"Some of my books disappeared," Eddie said. "Some of them, from my room. A couple weeks back. Like somebody took them."

"Really."

"I hear stuff sometimes, too."

"Like what?"

"Footsteps. I don't know if they're real."

"They're real."

"Are we going to tell Mom and Dad?"

Marshall squinted into the screen. After a time, he shook his head slowly. "They won't ever believe us," he said. "Honestly, I'm thinking the more convinced we seem, the less they'll be."

"But why won't they?" Eddie's voice cracked as he said the words, and a sudden shame swelled in him. He wanted to mention the missing knife—his fear that it would hurt them, now that it knew they knew—but he was afraid his voice would squeak and tremble—unable to be anything but a little boy's again.

"Shh." Marshall twisted in his chair to face his brother, lip curling at the corner. Faces showed so many expressions, were hard sometimes in how they showed many things at once, but Eddie knew this one well. An asymmetry. It only meant two things: embarrassment or contempt. He deserved them both.

"Where have you been?" Marshall said. "Have you not been paying any attention, wrapped up in that little world you live in? I have been telling Dad and Mom this. I've been saying something's not right, that I've heard things, that food goes missing, and Eddie, they laugh it off quicker each time. Dad calls me a child. Dad acts like I'm weird. Then they treat me . . . like I'm you."

Eddie winced.

"And what?" Marshall continued. "I should tell them about the knife? I'd have to tell them where I bought the thing—that'll look good, Eddie. 'Hey Mom, I bought weapons from some older dude at school, and now I think a stranger is sneaking around in our house.' Seriously. I'm not looking for appointments with a counselor."

Eddie considered the floor. He regretted coming here, to Marshall's room. Should have just said no at the dinner table, said no, there was nothing, he never noticed anything. Marshall, eventually, would have left, given up. And the thing in their home? Maybe it would have heard. So, nothing would change. Eddie would avoid the noises in the dark, and it would continue to leave them alone.

"You know I didn't mean that," Marshall said. "About you—about you being weird. I meant that it's actually part of the reason I'm talking to you. Only you, really. Because, well? You are weird. You're the only damn person here who isn't going to call me a freak for thinking this."

Eddie looked up.

"Also, stupid, you're my brother. Who else do I have? All my classmates suck ass."

Marshall clicked the mouse and loaded another page on the forum. For a while, the two sat like that: Marshall reading him posts, Eddie sitting behind, listening to the titles of the linked news articles. *Man Found Living in Ex-girlfriend's Shed. Remnants of Trespassers in Deceased Elder's Home.*

"You don't think," Eddie asked, "the house is haunted, or something, do you?"

"Jesus, Eddie," Marshall said. "I'm freaking out enough—don't give us a ghost, too."

Eddie smiled in spite of the fear. Marshall was joking. This was something you could joke about. Terrifying, but ridiculous, too. And Eddie wasn't alone in knowing.

His brother had confided in him. Eddie was someone worth confiding in.

"Here's what we do," Marshall said. "We fucking deal with it. We look around the house, and if we find proof, we show Dad and Mom. And if we see something, there's two of us. We make it get out."

"That's it?"

"That's it. Dad and Mom can suck it. Until they believe us, they can't help us. They'd probably just want to get in our way." Marshall smiled and leaned over toward Eddie. "Who knows? Maybe after, Dad and Mom might finally listen to us. Treat us with some respect.

We might not have to spend every free weekend doing their damn 'projects.'"

"Really?"

"Well, knowing them, probably no," Marshall said. "But, you know, we might make the news. People at school will look at you different. It'd be like in all these articles, except with a good ending. We find out how the person's getting in and out, where they're hiding when they're here, and we get 'em out, keep 'em out."

Marshall's face was right by his own. Eddie could see the swath of patchy stubble on his cheeks, a constellation of pimples above his eyebrows. He was grinning at Eddie. His neck tense with excitement.

"We can do this?" Eddie said. "Are you sure?"

"Yeah," Marshall said, squeezing his brother's bicep. "Fuck yeah, we can."

THE GUEST ROOM

ELISE LAY ON HER BACK WITHIN THE GUEST ROOM WALL AND LIS-
tened to the short strokes of Mrs. Laura's paintbrush against the baseboard. She had seen the paint bucket in the back porch the evening
before, with the little spatter of color on the tin lid. Brown. Chocolate brown. They had painted the walls beige, and the trim would
be brown. With the white windowpanes, the transformation of the
room into an enormous s'more would be complete. Elise imagined
her mom's face: her mouth falling open in pure horror.

Another thing that had been her parents'—the peach walls and
pearl trim—would be gone. She hadn't yet had the chance to look, but
Elise assumed the new coat of paint would also erase the faint impressions of her horses by the door. Elise had been five when she had made
them. While her parents installed a dishwasher downstairs, she'd taken
her school pencils to the baseboard, drawing three horses, realistic as
she could manage. She'd been punished, of course, sent to bed a full
two (!) hours early—brutal, but Elise had known what she was getting
into, though she'd only done it out of boredom. When her mom, who
hardly got upset, first saw them, she bowed her head and bit her forefinger to fight back tears. Elise still remembered the shame in seeing
her that way, waiting for her to say anything at all. How Elise wanted
simultaneously to be taken in her arms, and to be far away, out of her
sight. The house seeming so broken-down and big, her mom so tired.

But when her dad came, he dropped to the floor, crossed his legs,
and studied the drawings. Recognized the simple fix: a pencil's eraser
would clean away the graphite animals. Once clean, there'd be noth-

ing left but her pressmarks, the semi-invisible inversions of bones. Of course, like all projects in that house, it still took him over a week to finally erase them, long enough that Elise began to wonder if he actually liked seeing them there, with their elongated legs and wild eyelashes.

But now, even the pressmarks would be gone. Normally, Elise would be in a foul mood all day, grieving over the remnants of a memory painted over and cleared away. But she'd had a good morning, and the feeling clung to her like warmth from a nap in a patch of sun. Earlier that day, she'd shown Brody how to hide, to really hide, the way she did—to nothing himself to the point that even she couldn't find him. No sounds of his fidgeting, no sense of his breathing; she could almost convince herself that he wasn't hiding, that he hadn't come over, that she'd only dreamt up him coming over that morning. Brody wasn't behind the living room sofa, or in any of the closets, and she knew he had no interest in ever climbing into any of the spaces between walls. ("That's a no," he had said to her once, looking up into the access panel in the pantry.) So, he'd gotten good with what he had. Too good. She'd begun to search ridiculous places—the bell of the dryer, the freezer—afraid that he crawled in somewhere and suffocated himself. She gave up.

"All right!" she cried. "Game over! You win! Come out!"

And out he popped, smiling with self-satisfaction, from beneath the guest room's armoire. He had slid into the opening on the back bottom that'd been exposed when the Masons had pulled it away from the wall.

"Look at this!" Brody had said, coming over to her and thrusting his cupped hands into her face, as if to show her some bug he'd captured. In his hands were paint chips, fat and curled like worms, the guest room's new beige color on one side and the old, flesh-colored peach on the other. Elise had been mad, first from being beaten in their game, and then thinking that he'd scratched the strips loose from the wall with his fingernail as he waited for her to find him. But

Brody told her how he'd only scooped them from the floor into his palm. She wanted to believe him.

"They're beautiful," she'd said. And they were, in a way. "Don't eat them."

Now, that afternoon, Elise listened to Mrs. Laura hum while she painted. No melody, just the occasional, disjointed notes. Every few minutes, the woman grunted as she stood, took a few paces over, and sat back down. She hadn't wanted the boys' or even her husband's help on this step. This was careful work. The painter's tape had been removed, and now the Mason mother filled in the spaces that had been overlooked and touched up the mistakes. Elise enjoyed the time beside her. Why was it? Women somehow felt different, Elise figured, even having them nearby, not speaking. There's something in a mother that's in all mothers, maybe. There's something in a mother that's there already in girls.

It was a Wednesday night, and tomorrow evening the boys would be done with school. They couldn't possibly be doing homework, but even so, they were closed off in their rooms. (Or was Eddie outside, in that space of his between the two trees beside the shed? Elise hadn't been keeping track as well lately as she might have.) Mr. Nick finished grading in his office. The house was next to quiet, empty-feeling. Elise had always preferred a loud house in the evening, one that drowned her own sounds in its own, but tonight, this was what she wanted. Mrs. Laura stood again and yawned. She was stretching.

Earlier that day, when it was nearly time for Brody to leave, the two of them had discussed how they would do it: how he would be able to come back when the Mason boys were home for summer. They always had Sunday mornings, when the family went to church. And the Masons were sure to have vacations, weekend trips to the beach, or visits to their family up north. And there'd be other times, times when Mr. Nick would be teaching summer school and Mrs. Laura away at work, Marshall would find another part-time job somewhere, and Eddie—well, hopefully a summer camp was in his future.

In the event of impromptu Mason departures, for a family lunch out or something else, Elise would hang her unicorn T-shirt in the guest room window—a flag for Brody, if passing by on the levee, to know the coast was clear. They could make it work, and while they planned, a weight on her shoulders that had been building over the last few days—or longer—had risen from her.

In the guest room wall, the book of Norse mythology was her pillow. She'd stopped reading it for a while, taking the time to flip through the other books she had taken from Eddie's room. She had nearly finished the book, and had become apprehensive about allowing it to become another in her small stack in the nook of ones she had already read. A finished book is one that no longer feels like it can crawl around while you sleep. Once completed, it's just an object, one to keep, to be remembered, but one that no longer lives a life of its own. Dead weight she had to keep hidden. She continued to read the stories, but with hesitation. In the most recent one she'd read, Odin's sons, Thor and Loki, were sent to investigate the wicked ice giants' kingdom. To safely slip unknown throughout the giants' borders, the two manly gods disguised themselves as beautiful, dainty women. The whole story was silly, but it was loaded full of action and adventure and deceit, and as Elise read through it, she had to force herself not to turn the book's pages too quickly. At one point, when the king of the ice giants told Thor that he'd never seen a woman with such a full, flowing beard, Elise had to chomp full-down on her hand from releasing a thunderous guffaw. In her mind, Thor stroked his bushy red beard thoughtfully before tucking it back where he had had it hidden, beneath the frilly lace around his neck. Thor told the Ice King how he kept the hair so smooth—conditioned every evening. Beside him, his brother Loki nodded in agreement. To Elise, Loki looked just like Brody, wearing a black party mask and cape, and an enormous, beflowered sun hat.

Someone moved through the hall, and she heard Mr. Nick's voice in the doorway. "Hey," he said, with a softness in his voice Elise hadn't heard from him in a while. "How's it going in here?"

"Coming along," Mrs. Laura said.

"It looks good." He stood there in the doorway, quiet. He must have been watching her work. "It's been crazy, hasn't it? This year. This house."

Mrs. Laura's brush tapped against the side of her paint cup. Elise pictured her turned to her husband, her lips pursed into another tired smile.

"You know it's coming up?" he asked. "Or have you been too busy reconstructing this impossible mansion of ours to remember?"

Mrs. Laura laughed softly. "Remember what?" She shifted her legs atop the plastic on the floor. "Remember you? Remember me?" She sighed. "All I can recall are each of Home Depot's separate aisles, and the exact names of all the shades of paint cards."

Elise could sense Mr. Nick smirking. "So, no celebration this year?"

"This year?" Mrs. Laura said. "Let's get the house in order first. That'll be . . . 2055? Our seventieth anniversary?"

"I think we need a celebration. Pronto. The two of us. Like, a real, actual break."

"I mean, if that were something that was possible."

"Let's go out of town," Mr. Nick said.

Mrs. Laura was quiet. She dabbed her brush against the cup and went back to painting.

"Just one evening," he said. "Get out of the house. I don't bring any papers to grade with me. We leave the work. Leave it all here."

"Where are you thinking we'd go?"

"Burloway—the old plantation house outside Baton Rouge? I looked into it. They rent out rooms. We could stay there for a night."

"And trade one oversized, crumpling plantation-style house for another?"

"And trade a busted-up house for one that's not our problem."

Mrs. Laura snorted. "Okay," she said. "But what about the boys?"

"What about them?"

"Are they coming?"

"It's one night. They're sixteen and thirteen."

"Eddie's not," Mrs. Laura said, and hesitated. "You know what I mean. You can't just say he's thirteen and act like that's all there is to it. And Marshall's . . ."

"He's Marshall," said Mr. Nick. He exhaled sharply through his nose. "Look."

"And Eddie's moved all those things in his room . . ."

"We've talked about that—"

"Have we?"

"Well, maybe we'd get the chance to? Maybe we could talk without one of us losing our shit? Without us being exhausted? Without falling asleep before—" A firmness had formed in his voice. When he spoke again, it was with a conscious attempt to soften it. "Laura, it's one night. Honey, I think we need this."

Mr. Nick crossed the room. The floor creaked when he knelt beside her, and his voice lowered, not much more than a whisper. "I just went by Marshall's room. I heard them. They're in there together. They're talking."

"Okay?"

"I heard Eddie laugh," he said. "Both of them were. Think about that. When was the last time you heard Eddie laugh?"

"I'm glad to hear it." The bristles of Mrs. Laura's paintbrush slid along the trim once more.

Mr. Nick stood beside her. He waited in silence. "Laura?" he asked finally.

"I'm thinking," she said. She placed the paint cup on the floor. "What did it sound like? When you heard Eddie laugh?"

ONCE DONE, DECIDED

IN THE DARK, ELISE FOUND SHE COULDN'T HELP BUT GRIN, HER cheeks full and squeezed tight. The parents would be gone, for a night. Not as happy as she'd known anniversaries to be, but it still reminded her of her own parents, the times she remembered her mom standing barefoot in her dress in front of her bedroom's full-length mirror. Elise, on the bed, helping untangle her earrings. As a reward, receiving a spritz of the lavender perfume on the wrists. Elise's dad's razor buzzing in the bathroom. They'd go out—his jacket folded over his arm, her high heels clicking across the foyer—like some actor and actress in an old movie. Elise would be left home with the sitter, which, to be fair, made for its own fun, as almost as soon as the gray-haired woman came she fell asleep in a living room armchair. One year, Elise had taken advantage and eaten the remainder of the Mardi Gras Moon Pies she'd gathered from the parades the week before, four or five of the cakes in one triumphant binge. She read out on the front porch after dark, and when the sugar finally left her veins, she grew tired, and on her way to bed, buried her sitter's sleeping body with pillows.

An anniversary, even one for the Mason parents, was good. For them, and for her—fewer people home, more space. Eddie and Marshall stuffed away in their bedrooms as night rolled in, and the whole empty house around them? If she was careful, she might even have Brody over. Convince him to be quiet enough, and she might be able to play a game of checkers in the back porch. The boys' bedrooms were so far away from the stairs, they wouldn't hear.

Well, more likely, maybe not checkers, with the rumble of its pieces in the box, and clicking of the pieces on the board. Too risky. Instead, maybe they could read beside one another, down in the library. Or outside, on the front porch. Or, well, maybe since Brody wasn't such a good reader, maybe she could just tell him what was happening in her book. Quietly.

"So, next weekend?" Mrs. Laura had told her husband, before she finished touching up the trim and crumpled up the loose strips of painter's tape on the floor into a ball. "Saturday. We put it all away. We leave it here. Recharge, I guess. The boys can keep an eye on themselves, and we're back first thing in the morning?"

"It's a date."

TOGETHER, NO
STONE UNTURNED

THE BOYS' FIRST DAY OF SUMMER VACATION, AND THEIR FATHER HAD GONE in to prep for summer school. Their mom had a weekend appointment for a house showing, and she wouldn't be home until three.

Outside, it rained, and the windows glossed from the water, while droplets pattered against the roof. The boys began in the garage. They searched for incongruous things. What would the signs look like? They imagined matted blankets, a stranger's shoes and backpack, maybe even a large cardboard box tucked behind the kayaks, as if someone homeless from one of the downtown streets had brought his meager belongings here. The brothers weren't sure what they were looking for. They'd know when they found it.

They picked up the loose boards from the woodpile in the garage and squinted into the tight spaces within, checked around the backside of the pressure washer and tiller and ladders, around the bucket of old baseball mitts and balls that Marshall used, when he was Eddie's age, before tryouts got competitive and he failed to make the team. They looked behind the heaped mess of badminton netting and racquets, bought by their dad for the family, which they had tried only twice in the backyard of their old Northshore home.

They moved on. They crawled into the back of the living room closet and split their parents' hanging coats to either side; they opened kitchen cabinets, pulling out a Crock-Pot and a food dehydrator, looking behind. In the pantry, Eddie climbed on his brother's back and peered into the access panel, but saw only the swallowing dark, the hollow insides of the house. They went on hands and knees to search beneath the beds upstairs. They pulled out a stack of towels in the linen closet and sifted through the clothes hanging in the armoire.

They were prepared if they found someone. Marshall carried, in his back pocket, the other switchblade. He had tried to sharpen it further with one of his mother's kitchen whetstones, but poorly, so now the blade was scratched along its sides. Still sharp enough to sting when he pressed it into his finger, though. The point more than sharp enough to jab.

Eddie wore the backpack Marshall had given him for his birthday. An old aluminum baseball bat poked out its top. Each time they opened another closet door, or dropped to a knee to see beneath a bed, Eddie held it out, its end wobbling in front of him. The width of the bat was as big as his upper arm, larger even, and he'd never actually swung one before during PE, he'd always sat on the balance beam to the side by the pull-up bars. It felt good to hold it out between him and the dark of a closet as Marshall reached in and switched the light on. When he closed his eyes and squeezed the handle, the bat was like a sword, large and ornate, something a knight carried. But every time they searched somewhere new, threw open a door, looked behind a corner, he had to make sure he kept his eyes open. Tried not to blink.

THE ATTIC FOR LAST

THAT WAS THE PLACE, MOST LIKELY. WHEN THEY SEARCHED THE house, they passed by the door time and again, ignoring it for now, as if they'd jinx it. Though the outcome they wanted to prevent wasn't fully clear to them: whether they hoped no one was there, and their imaginations had gotten the better of them, or that someone, hiding, was.

When they stood before the attic door, there was a true, small comfort in Eddie, knowing that the house, searched, behind him was safe, and that whatever it was now waited in a direction he could point to. The drawback was that the attic might as well be hunched and waiting.

"Are you ready?" Marshall asked. He opened the door without a response.

Below the sounds of the rain on the roof, the ventilation fan hummed, and up the length of the staircase, the dim glow from the dormer window awaited them. They climbed the stairs slowly, side by side, the wood popping beneath their feet. Halfway up a sudden torrent of heat swallowed them. Warm air rises to the top, Eddie remembered. Like stepping into a warm pool, from the top down.

At the head of the stairs, the boys paused to look around them through the shadows in the spaces behind the boxes and spare furniture and equipment. Thick roofing nails jutted through the wood-like weeds. "I'll get the light," Marshall said, and he crossed over to the pull chain that brought an orange, incandescent glow. The center-heart of the room burst into color, but the place beyond the cardboard and plastic bins and dark suitcases remained gray and shapeless.

"How do we do it?" Eddie asked. They were surrounded on every side. They might as well have been in an entirely different house.

"I guess," Marshall said, "we just move the boxes?" He weaved his way between a stack of paintings and full garbage bags to the perimeter, ducking below the low ceiling's nails. "We look from the outside in." He pulled a flashlight from his back pocket and shone it into the crevice where the ceiling met the floor. He pivoted and pointed its beam as far as he could to the other side of the attic. "Here we go."

The boys moved, and the attic floor moaned as if the house itself was stirring, one massive, slumbering body turning to its side. The boys opened boxes, began pulling out winter clothes and old toys. They wanted to see whether something had coiled up beneath them. They rifled through piles of seasonal decorations. At one point, Marshall let out a yelp. Eddie shouted in return and clutched wildly at his baseball bat in the bag behind him.

"It's nothing!" Marshall said. He raised a hand and motioned his brother to calm himself. "Just a cactus. Stuck my finger. Damn thing was in a Christmas wreath." He sucked at his finger and looked around him. "The fuck is that doing in there anyway?"

They continued, opening the drawers of an ancient cabinet, getting on their hands and knees to shine a light into the space below the large metal AC unit. The wind spattered moisture against the small window, and the rain continued against the roof above. The boys searched ten minutes, twenty minutes. When finally Eddie found it, he was surprised to see how small it was. All this searching, and he could lay his palms flat against the floor and cover it completely. Eddie called his brother over to the dormer. "There," he said.

A print, from some bare foot smaller than their own, drying already, half-gone on the wood beneath them. Outside the window, the puddles on the roof rippled with each new falling drop of rain. On the floor, the toes of the print pointed inside. As if someone, hearing them in their search downstairs, had opened the dormer window to escape to the roof outside. Then, halfway out, one foot down upon the wet shingles, had paused, had decided against leaving, and had come back inside.

"Someone's still in here," Eddie said.

THEY STOOD ABOVE HER

BENEATH THEIR FEET, THE PLYWOOD FLOOR BOWED INTO HER belly. The crossbeams pinned Elise's arms to her sides. They stood on her chest. Their weight compressed her lungs. This was being buried. Elise resisted her urges to kick up at the floor with her knees. Above, they weren't speaking. Only standing there. She sensed them motioning to each other. Turning all around. Elise forced gulps of air into her tight chest, miniature gulps, her lips working like a goldfish's.

Were they trying to crush her?

Finally, the boys moved, released her. Elise shuddered. Couldn't help it. The plywood above her tapped against the frame—her whole body tensed, but they didn't stop walking. Didn't hear. The boys went on to the center of the attic and stood for a moment in the stairwell.

Elise's forehead pressed against the plywood. The bones of her chest ached as she breathed. Blood pulsed through her temples. She tried to hear what they said.

Earlier, when Elise had tried to run after she heard them searching beneath her, to crawl out on the roof, she couldn't. The heavy, cold drops of rain on her leg, the sudden shift in temperature and humidity, the windowsill slipping from her grip—the inside had still felt safer.

But now, they were whispering. Elise couldn't hear them. Their voices so quiet, she realized, they knew she was close.

Marshall and Eddie descended the staircase, their steps falling in unison. The attic door's hinges squealed, the door coming shut very slowly.

Elise did not move, for as long as she could manage.

GO AWAY

WHEN THE NEXT MORNING ARRIVED, THE RAIN HAD FINISHED, AND the sky was cloudless at sunrise. The light through the windows was a vibrant pink, fog-like in the air. For those who hardly slept, the color was unreal, the fatigue must be playing tricks on their sight—no way could a sunrise turn a house so clouded, lambent. To look out in the yard was to see the same: the oak trees, mud of the lawn, gray gravel of the driveway—all doused in the orange-rose hue. The old rhyme: red sky in the morning.

Hours passed while the birds downstairs, like gatekeepers, announced their alternating shifts. The Masons rose from bed and readied themselves for Mass. They left together, the lot of them, piling into Mr. Nick's red Saturn, the boys to the backseat, the older brother turning for one last glance at the house, a hard look, as though daring it to reveal its maw and to snap at him as he left. But how could Marshall be any more wrong? With the car pulling out the long length of the driveway, the house did not bite, but instead finally exhaled, slouching into something shapeless and beaten. How far will crossbeams sink before they crack? How quickly can composite parts—shingles, siding, ducts and vents, floorboards—collapse and separate, decay into the ground before even Odin the All-Seeing wouldn't recognize what they'd been?

To bend is to bow down, as the One-Eyed would say. And to bow too low prevents one from ever standing again.

Even so, she bent.

The boy arrived when he was told, the robins' time, shortly after the Masons had left. He rapped on the back door with the knock she had taught him: one, one-two, one. But she wasn't there, waiting for him. Minutes passed, and Brody knocked their pattern again—he'd never needed to knock twice before—and still waited. He grew impatient and bored, and then worried: had she been found out? Taken away? Worse? Alone between those walls, had she made a miscalculation; some grip she'd used for months finally worn smooth, that failed to hold her. Fallen into a narrow, hidden space? Should he try the side door again, even though she'd told him to leave it alone? He stood on his toes, but couldn't see far enough into the house through the windows. He knocked their pattern again and again.

Then Elise appeared.

She wasn't the same. An old woman now in a small girl's body. Dark rings below her eyes, shoulders drooping—a girl like a tallow tree bent from a storm, an abandoned cabin slumping in the woods. She stood in the doorway on the other side of the screen, her limp hand on the latch, keeping it shut. And she told him what happened. How they'd come for her.

Two brothers who knew to look for her, and who had nearly found her. They tore her home apart searching, then sewed it back up as if it had never happened. And after, they went back to their rooms, whispering for what must have been hours, halting with each sound heard, quieting to listen for her. Their parents came home, but the boys said nothing, from as much as she could tell. But they knew. She heard their doors swinging open throughout the night, as if expecting to surprise her, to come at her there, in the spotlight of their rooms' overhead lamps, and grip her in their hands. She was hunted now. Abruptly, now. Something had changed.

Did he know why?

"No," he said. "I don't. I really don't. But wait. Didn't the younger one know about you before?"

"He'd never come looking for me. Not until now."

"Are you okay?"

Elise lay her forehead against the screen, turning her pale skin dimpled. She held the handle shut, looked at him through the upper halves of her eyes. When she spoke, she hardly moved her lips.

"You steal the things you bring me," she said. "The fingernail polish. Food. The Gameboy. Board games. Everything you've brought here—you stole from other houses."

Brody plucked at the screen door handle with his fingertips. "I brought some things I thought you'd like."

"Did you take things from this house, too?"

"Not really," he said. "Not much."

"What did you steal?"

"I was going to bring them back!"

"What's missing? What exactly?"

Brody cocked his head to one side. Gritted his teeth. Chewed on something imaginary. A caricature of nervousness.

"I don't know. Just a couple things. A movie maybe. A couple coins, some dollars. A seashell. A flip knife. Some things."

"Get away."

"I can bring them all back right now!" He tugged on the screen door with both hands, but she wrenched the door back shut and hooked its small latch.

"But I can go back home right now," he said. "I've got them all under my bed. I wasn't stealing—I just took some things, Elise. I take things sometimes, but I can bring them back—"

"Don't say my name."

"What?"

"Don't call me by my name. Don't think you can say it!"

Brody took a step back down the porch steps, as though she'd lifted her heel and thrust it into his belly. "But I can fix it," he said. "I can bring it all back."

"You've never seen me before," she said. "You've never seen me here at all. I've never existed, and if anyone asks, you never knew me.

A hundred years from now, if you think you remember me—you're wrong. It was a dream and a lie."

"But I'm sorry."

"It's too late for that!" She was shouting now. "Brody, you've ruined it for me." The girl's lips pulled across her face. Her cheeks red, eyes wet. "It's my home, Brody. This is my home, and you're ruining it!"

"I'm sorry."

"Don't come back," she said. "Don't ever come back. Get away."

Door shut, and locked.

"Go away!" she said.

Said again inside. Go away. And again, again, until she was sure he had gone. Go away, she said, until the walls of her home echoed along with her, cried with her, too.

THE FRONT PORCH

EDDIE SAT ON THE GLIDER BENCH AND TRACED THE SHADOWS IN the yard with his eyes: across the azalea bushes whose flowers had begun to fade, speckles and the strips in the yard where the setting sun shone through the trees, and the roof's stark shape angled on the patch of pampas grass a full acre away. The river was high. Eddie could see the white top of a cruise ship, huge as a cloud, sailing down for the Gulf. The music playing through the ship's loudspeakers sounded like the buzz of a mosquito just behind his ear. Eddie closed his eyes until the ship had passed.

Earlier today, his parents told him how they'd leave in a few days for an anniversary trip, and he and Marshall would have the house alone for a night. Even so, neither of the boys had mentioned the footprint in the attic. Yesterday evening, they'd spoken in low voices to one another, tapping on the shared bathroom door whenever something ballooned in them they needed to say. Broken thoughts, in halting sentences. But had anything been said?

Marshall's words, most often. He had the most to say. Spoken as much to his younger brother as to himself. Saying:

We're right. We were actually right—but can we tell them?

We can't.

Because what proof was the print? Hardly there—already drying—couldn't even think to grab Mom's camera before it had evaporated.

—I'm not crazy, right? You remember it, too? Shaped like? There was the heel, a missing space for the arch, and the big toe—looked like a toe, didn't it? Crescent-shaped, skinny, but if you stepped, pushed off on your foot like this? A callus on the toe might form the print. Toes missing, the balls of the foot not all there, but they might have dried already.

Right?

The window wasn't leaking, the ceiling wasn't—we watched it to make sure. It was a print—a person's print. Stepped on the wet roof, then came back in.

Someone small. Smaller than us, for sure. We can do this, I think.

But how? Eddie thought.

We still can't tell them. They still won't believe us! We need proof. We need to do something. We need—to know what to do. We both have to stay calm. I can ask those people online. That one guy would know. He believes us already anyway. We need to—Eddie, we can do this. We can do this.

But how?

Eddie rocked on the glider bench. There was no going back to before. No more pretending noises were nothing, that inconsistencies—missing and moved things—didn't happen, weren't there. A door half open when he'd left it mostly closed, the rise and fall of a dust ruffle half-seen out of the corner of his eye. Once a person knew, there was no going back.

The balance was gone. Balance of not really knowing. Of walking through the upstairs hallway in the evening, passing darkened rooms to either side, and not flipping their light switches, leaving them be. Of hearing, while sitting at his desk, the groan of a floor behind him, and not turning because the weird belief—one felt more than thought—that what he didn't know couldn't hurt him. Whoever that boy had been weeks ago who heard the noises in the walls, who'd even left his damn books out for the thing, Eddie no longer understood him. His reasoning, his stupidity. Eddie had kept this hidden from his own family. He'd protected it. Why?

"Fuck you, Eddie," he whispered at himself. "Fuck you. You idiot traitor. Goddamn weirdo."

The only consolation Eddie had was that he had told it to leave. He had tried. Even if he'd kept it secret, he still knew it had to go. He still couldn't tell Marshall that. Couldn't tell anything of before, of how he used to think. Eddie didn't need his brother finding out, getting angry at him for being so useless for so long.

Eddie rocked on the bench, aggressively now, until the back of his seat bounced against the house's siding and jarred his neck with each collision. It hurt, was dizzying, but Eddie did it anyway—if only he could be shaken all over, shaken like that old Etch-a-Sketch toy, somewhere up there now in the attic, until everything that had happened a few days, few weeks, months, could be shaken clean from him. Hell, if he could, he'd shake himself clear from this whole house, clean away the present until he was back at the Northshore, back further, all the way until he was an infant. So he could try again. One more time to try to be someone else. Anyone else. Just not the person he was right here, now. Frightened, and stupid.

Footsteps sounded from inside the house. Tennis shoes dragging on the foyer's tile floor. The old antique doorknob twisting, its cast-iron clunking against cypress wood in the socket, and the whine of the large hinges. Marshall's face appeared around the door's lip.

"Hey," he said. "How you holding up?"

Eddie covered the lower half of his face with his hand. He wasn't so sure what he meant by the movement, but his brother acted as though he was. Marshall closed the door behind him and took a seat next to Eddie on the bench. "Yup," he said. They sat together as an elderly man on horseback passed on the levee, and as the patches of orange sunlight on the lawn diminished into gray. Their parents were somewhere inside, finishing their work in the guest room, maybe, or reading, working, or watching the small television in their room.

Eddie said, "You remember the termites?"

Marshall snorted. "I still find little bodies in the corners of my room. I remember."

"Sometimes I still think I've got some crawling on me."

"Oh, God," he said. "Yeah, I know the feeling."

"It's awful."

"You just gotta " Marshall scrunched his shoulders up and shook himself as if trying to shiver away a chill. "You got to get those thoughts off you."

Wind blew, and trees responded in the yard. Marshall leaned back and his knobby knees bobbed while he tapped his heels on the porch. Dark, coarse hair showed from where his pants pulled up on his thighs, above the knees, and for the first time Eddie realized his own legs would be covered soon enough. Marshall held a solid four or five inches of height on him, but Eddie could not imagine, once he grew to be that tall, he'd ever feel as big as how Marshall looked to him. The older brother was a giant. There were bigger boys, some in Eddie's own grade, but it didn't make it any less true.

"Hey," Marshall said. "I really need to show you something."

ANOTHER BELIEVER

UPSTAIRS IN THE BEDROOM, MARSHALL'S COMPUTER SHOWED AN email thread of short responses. Eddie followed Marshall's cue and stood, hunched, elbows on the computer desk, not bothering to take a seat. Their parents' voices were an undertone from down the hallway. Marshall went over and closed his bedroom door while Eddie read.

"It's that guy from the forum I showed you before," Marshall said. "The one who emailed me. He's been sending advice. We've gone back and forth a few times. And since now, well, since we know for sure that there's actually someone here . . . I told him about what we found in the attic, the print, and—" Marshall grabbed the mouse and scrolled too quickly for Eddie to understand the conversation, but the younger brother's eyes clung to certain words:

food go missing?
Stairs? Attic? Basement?
noises in the attic and hallway
footprint, it looked like
What else have you found?
We looked through the whole house and
exactly where is your
Plaquemines parish
will be coming

Eddie saw Marshall had sent their full address.

"He said it'd help if he knew where we were," Marshall said, almost as if it were an apology. Once at the bottom of the thread, he scrolled up again, still too quick. Marshall nervous, or embarrassed. He looked only at the computer. "I figured he was trying to help by looking at online blueprints or satellite pictures of us, or something. I wasn't thinking he'd actually want to come."

Abruptly, Marshall closed the browser, and the desktop appeared— beneath the icons, a shadowed, leering grin. Artwork from one of his favorite Disturbed albums. Marshall turned from the computer and took a seat on his bed, staring at a space somewhere behind Eddie. "I really didn't ask for it, but he said he'd go ahead and come down to check things out for us. I told him if we just knew what to do, we could handle it, but I guess . . . I don't know. I'm not sure. He said it wouldn't be a big deal. He's an electrician. Or he's done work like that. Pest control, too. He said he knows houses, and it'd be quick. He seems weird, but . . . He won't charge us or anything. He—with this kind of thing, he said it's just something he wants to help with. I guess, probably more so because we're young."

"Do Mom and Dad know he's coming?" Eddie asked.

"He wanted to come as soon as tomorrow," Marshall said. "He wanted to drive all evening and get here before morning. I got him to wait. He'll come on Saturday, when the parents are doing their anniversary thing."

"Mom and Dad don't know."

"I still don't really feel like they'd believe us."

"Oh," Eddie said. He looked down at the carpet, at its separate threads. Gradually, Eddie realized he was angry. He had curled his lips between his teeth and was biting them hard enough to hurt. He wanted the email conversation in front of him again. Marshall had closed it too soon. Eddie wanted to read it and to dwell on each word. He wanted each stupid word to boil while he looked at it. To evaporate. He wanted the feeling they evoked in him to boil, too. Those emails made him feel like half the ground below them was sinking. At this point, Eddie didn't care if their parents didn't believe them. He just wanted them to know. But Marshall was holding them out. He was making it worse. He was keeping them alone.

"I'm pretty sure I know what you're thinking." Marshall's voice had softened. "I wish we could tell them, too. But you know they're not going to help us. If Dad and Mom knew we were trying to— they'd only try to convince us it's in our heads. Anything we hear, or see. It'd all get drawn out. Every day would be another day where something—something might happen. To us, or them. This way is doing something about it. Quicker. And maybe safer for everybody."

Eddie had no idea what this was and wasn't.

Marshall sighed and wiped his face with the palm of his hand. Kept his eyes pinched shut while he continued to talk. "Earlier, when I was up here. I was listening, you know? I freaked out. I needed to talk to someone, someone who believed us, and I mean, he's believed even before anything . . . It's just, I'm sorry . . . it should have been with you. I should have at least checked in with you first. We should have written him back together."

Eddie stared at Marshall's shoes.

"But," Marshall said, "I don't know. Maybe, it's pretty good this guy's offered to come down. Like a contractor. What if he actually helps? You know, he said he has tools that would make it pretty simple."

"Tools?"

"Yeah. I'm not sure what. But he told me he'd come and set them up when Dad and Mom leave. That the whole thing would be quick, and they wouldn't even have to know. If he comes and finds someone here, we'll tell them once it's over. But if he doesn't, yeah, we'll look stupid, but only to him. We'll be right back where we are. Then we'll think again about what to do."

Marshall looked him in the eyes. His jaw muscles had knotted, a small bulge forming like a rock, a hard ripple beneath a current of water. He needed reassurance, Eddie realized. When had that happened before? How small Marshall seemed here, in the middle of the room, with the walls and white expanse of ceiling above them. How small did that make him, too?

Eddie wanted to bellow, bellow deep from his chest, loud as he could, and purge all that bile that brimmed in him. Wanted to shout in his brother's face, and shout at everything around them. Incomprehensible words—it didn't matter. But he didn't. Eddie sat quiet. Listened as their father went into his office and closed the door behind him.

"I mean, besides," Marshall said. He bent over, dipped slowly to look beneath the bed. When he sat up again, he looked tired. "I really didn't want us to be alone here that night anyway."

Eddie swallowed. Looked away, and nodded. He hadn't thought of that. Eddie guessed he must have figured with Marshall being there in the bedroom beside his own—hadn't considered it being alone.

"We can do this." Marshall stressed each word, as if saying them was enough.

JUNE

LOUISIANA SUMMER IN FULL EARNEST. HUMIDITY AND THE HEAT OF the air out there like the threat of a vise grip, invisible arms waiting to wrap and tighten around the chest. Louisiana summer, and impossible even to stay inside without feeling it there, too: the pockets of heat collected in closets and crawl spaces, each its own hot, dark belly of a beast. The AC vents did what they could, but their air, with its unnatural chill, felt little better, the way it changed a drop of lukewarm sweat sliding down a lower back into some frigid, twitching thing—not a fire but an ice ant. The cold air hyperthermic, making the heat of the safe, hidden places, when returned to, seem even hotter than before.

Mr. and Mrs. Mason packed their weekend suitcases. They thumped around their room, water pipes squeaking when they stopped to scrub their hands and forearms again, cleaning them of the lingering spots of paint. They took showers and cried out to each other, in a game they'd begun to play, each time they discovered another remnant of their projects still clinging to their bodies and hair. Downstairs, the refrigerator became stocked with food—frozen TV dinners, two half-gallons of milk, apples and oranges, shrink-wrapped tilapia, corn dogs, frozen vegetables—more than enough to sustain the boys for an afternoon and night.

"You sure you'll be okay here?" Mrs. Laura asked Eddie from his doorway. She squinted one eye and pointed in the direction of Marshall's bedroom. She mouthed the words, "He bothering you?"

"I'm fine, Mom," Eddie said.

It would be the same as any other time the boys spent at home. After all, Marshall still only had his learner's permit, could still only drive with an adult riding beside him. His mother's car would rest in the driveway, useless to them both, its odometer checked and noted, and casually mentioned by their father that it had been checked and noted.

Marshall still hadn't finished cleaning out the garage. But the task had become less pressing, after one of the roofing shingles above inexplicably had broken through and had begun to leak, through the sub-roof, onto the worktable. "Just wait on it," their dad said. In the meantime, Marshall was to use his computer "for work, for once," and to search for another job. Beggars can't be choosers, and Marshall was to beg. He was to have a list of prospective businesses by the time they returned. The boys were given other instructions—to water the outside plants, bring in the mail, turn off the lights at night— which Mr. Nick listed separately to each boy, declaring them loudly into each boy's doorway. When it was Marshall's turn, Mr. Nick was interrupted halfway when his son shouted that he had heard it the first time.

"Dear God," Marshall said. "Please stop, and get on with the damn trip already."

LEAVING

SATURDAY MORNING, THEIR MOTHER OUTSIDE IN HER NAVY-BLUE dress, back bent between the garden leaves, doing a last-minute sweep for anything amiss. Their father bringing the bags out to the car. Eddie watched them both through his open window. His mom had learned last night their neighbor Ms. Wanda was visiting family that weekend, so instead of her phone number taped to the fridge, the boys had the number of a family friend, living on the Northshore, who'd drive an hour and a half down the long Causeway and through the city, if need be.

While Eddie watched his parents, his bedroom wall twitched. Marshall's room thumping from his morning pushups. Eddie's mom sensed him watching through the window. She looked up and waved.

When his parents drove out, the driveway puddles splashed brown specks on their side windows. Eddie listened as their car tires beat over the seams of the road as they followed the length of the levee away.

WAITING

QUIET, FOR A TIME. NO SOUNDS BUT CICADAS OUTSIDE, AND INSIDE
the mechanical birds crying out on the hours. The whir and rumble
of Marshall's desktop computer. Eddie rose from his bed to return a
book to the shelf. No sound anywhere else but the ragged breath of
someone, returning into the blind dark. That girl, cautious and tired
and reduced, feeling rivets and scars of the walls beneath her fingertips, finding her way through.

NEARER

ON THE ROAD, EACH HOUSE PASSED IS A BLURRED FACE.

Their facades cry out—a flash of brick or color or pale siding—one after another. Windows like eyes. They're all reaching out to brush the side of his face.

Each moment passing, he tells himself, is one closer.

WHEN HE ARRIVES

SOON, AT THE TIME THEY'D AGREED, OR EVEN SOONER, THE MAN'S truck tires churned through the driveway, splashing potholes. His big, black Ford, rocking on its chassis, pulling up outside the back door where the steps met the grass.

The engine cut out, and a car door thumped shut. The boys' footsteps pattered through the house as they left their rooms and descended the staircase steps to meet him. The screen door squealed open, then a hard knock on the back door. A man's voice, deep and resounding, carrying the sluggish drawl of one of the Southern states to the north and east. He'd come a long way.

"Here we are," the man said. "Here it is."

His voice, deep like a god's. The thought shot through the girl's mind, as if she weren't the one to think it.

He led the boys back inside. "So, this is it." His voice went against the grain of the house, vibrated against its wood and tile, sounded like it could come from several rooms at once.

Not a god's voice. A god's voice was deep, but hidden. Like the rustling of leaves. Like a heartbeat. This was a voice like a king's. Not a good one.

Elise pressed her ear against the wall to better hear.

Who was he?

The thud of his boots crossing from the foyer onto the rug of the library, then through the rooms downstairs. He moved through the house like he'd been there before. With the confidence of a man who built a home, and who was comfortable taking it apart again. He spoke as if he heard her question.

"The name's Jonah," he said. "But you boys can call me Mr. Traust."

He tapped on the walls.

PART 4

MR. TRAUST

HIS SKIN WAS SENSITIVE AS A CHILD'S, PRONE TO BLOTCHING. HE wasn't much taller than the older brother, with the same short-cropped hair. But he was thick, with rounded shoulders. Not fat but solid around the waist, and bigger around the chest. One of those men who look as though, in their change to manhood, he'd inflated, his rib cage expanded. He breathed through his nose in short takes, as if testing the air. Seemed somehow to be looking at more than one place at any time.

"You're Marshall," Mr. Traust said, cocking his pointer finger at the boy. "And you are?"

"He's Eddie," Marshall said.

Eddie stood in the doorframe to the foyer—he'd backed into it when the man entered through the laundry room—and Mr. Traust raised his chin to look behind him. "Good to meet you both," he said. "It's odd, I understand, having me here. But I want to say, I can help."

He moved past Eddie into the living room, the way workers did who already knew the house, who'd done a half-dozen projects there in the past. He touched the walls with the tips of his knuckles as he passed them, drummed on them.

"Will this be quick?" Marshall asked, following after him.

"Can be," Mr. Traust said, passing on, filling each door's frame as he passed through. The smell of his sweat trailed behind. "Tell me again about the sounds you hear. Tell me about the feelings you get, and the footprint you two found in the attic. I want to hear it all from the beginning, now that I'm here. Now I know where to look."

THE FEAR IN BEING KNOWN

ELISE AVOIDED HIM. SHE AVOIDED FOOTSTEPS AND THEIR MUFFLED voices, Marshall and Eddie talking to the man, telling him about the creaking of a stair in the night, the rush of water in the downstairs bathroom, the constant shifting and popping of the floors and walls.

"Sometimes it feels like even the house is alive," Marshall said, his voice directly beside her, in the kitchen.

Traust pulled himself up on the counter and tapped on the stained-glass window above the stove. He circled back to the dining room, where the piano sang out three unmelodic notes. Then screeching, like a bird under attack, as he pulled the instrument away from the wall. He knocked along the piano's wooden back. "You'd be surprised by all the hollow spaces," Elise heard him say.

She needed to get farther away. Forcing herself to move slowly, she reached for her handholds in the dark, cautious that her fingers and toes didn't thump against the wood and plaster while she found her grip. Couldn't let the fabric of the back of her shirt drag against the wall. The sound like a dry brush over paper—if she heard it, they might. By the time she'd nearly made it up to the second floor, they were up there, too. In the office, the boys' bedrooms—doors opening and shutting, the big man grunting, furniture squealing across the wood floor, dragging against carpet, what must have been Eddie's bed pulled from the wall. Footsteps and voices echoing through the joists and bones, rapping on the walls through her own bones and skin.

Marshall's voice: "I've heard things in the hallway at night. When

I leave my bedroom door open, sometimes I swear I see shadows moving.

"Once, when I was home alone, I think I heard something like pages turning. Like someone was flipping through a book. Over here.

"There's movement up in the attic sometimes. Like a person crouching around."

Within the walls, Elise held herself suspended. Had she always been this obvious? Had they known even from the beginning? The boys trailed behind the man while he moved, Marshall closer, Eddie farther behind. A part of her wanted to speak, loud enough that only they would hear, "Just stop." As ridiculous as the thought was, still, she had it: if they'd really heard her all those times, why wouldn't they have done something earlier? Months ago? Why wouldn't they have let her know?

"My brother has heard it all, too," Marshall said. "Right, Eddie?"

Their voices above her, talking about her. Elise was no Girl in the Walls. She was a little girl stuffed up and hiding. A trespasser in the dark of someone else's house. Both the brothers had known. They must have heard her every day. And if they had heard her, they could hear her now. They could find her now.

Elise lowered herself back down to the first story. She sidestepped through the narrow walls around the library, then crawled into the void space beneath the staircase. She stayed there, crouched on all fours. Listened.

"Are you finding anything?" Marshall's voice upstairs, calling to the man, who must now have gone into the attic. For some time, he didn't respond. Elise could hear him moving around, repositioning things up there, heavy things being dropped. He had boots on, and they beat down on the floor. Elise wondered whether it would be safer beneath the house. To get there, she'd need to go back the way she'd come, between the library and dining room. But already they were moving again, heading back through the hallway toward the staircase.

"It's really like two houses," the man, Traust, said to the boys, as they came down the stairs together. "One stacked inside the other."

"Have you seen anything?" Marshall asked. "Like any evidence?"

Traust laughed from somewhere deep in his belly. "Do you believe in spirits?"

"No," Marshall said, with a trace of shock. "Do you?"

The stairs creaked directly above the girl. She looked up to the crack of light that broke where their feet fell. She placed her eye against the hole and could see him there for a brief second before he passed over the cracks and moved down. A big man, though not too tall—he didn't have to duck under the lip of the ceiling where the staircase curved, the way Mr. Nick always had to.

"Absolutely not," Traust said. "Everything we sense has its source in something natural. But, you know, I think it's something like that. A whole world happening just outside what we see. Like wall shadows going wild the second we close our eyes." Traust stepped down from the stairs into the foyer. "Nice clock."

"Is someone here now?" Marshall asked. "Do you know?"

Traust didn't answer right away. There was rummaging on the floor. He must have been searching through some kit he'd dropped when he came in. Once he found what he was looking for, he showed it to the boys. He told them, "It's not what you think it's for."

THE NOISE WILL SEARCH

EDDIE, STILL HALFWAY UP THE STAIRS BEHIND THEM, SAT DOWN carefully on the steps, perching at a safe distance. The girl, beneath, kept her eyes open wide. Did Eddie hear her? He was right there. She could reach up through the crack in the middle of the stair and graze the seat of his pants with her thumbnail. Was she too loud—should she hold her breath? The walls thumped around her as if massive knuckles were knocking against the house's side. She thought for a second it must be a hammer, he must be nailing something into the wall. But it was something else. Ellse felt it through her, its pulse throbbing through her teeth.

"That thing isn't taking any of the paint off," Marshall said, "is it?"

"Go ahead. Try it yourself."

Movement on the tile of the foyer. An exchange.

"Isn't this just a nightstick?" Marshall asked. "I thought cops used this for, you know, hitting people. Rioters. Not walls. What're you doing with it?"

"It lets us hear."

"How?"

"Like bats in a cave, or ships at sea. Echolocation. Sonar."

"No way," Marshall said. But his own knocking against the walls followed, hesitant and irregular. "Like this?"

"Give it a real man's swing," Traust said.

"I don't want to chip the paint off."

"A house as big as this?" Traust said. "I'm thinking your pop and mom won't even notice. When we're done, they won't know."

The pounding grew stronger.

"Look," the man said. "Now try here. Find what's around and beneath you. Get an understanding of a place."

The sound moved in a semicircle around the foyer.

"You've got a knack for it. Now, you hear where the studs are. Normal stud-finders won't work on old walls like this. Density's irregular. Each inch is slightly different. But now, using this, we can hear. This is an old balloon frame house. Most of it, anyway. Here, the space between connects through the rooms. If you come over here—"

The walls pounded all around Elise. She risked the movement to cover her ears.

"That space beneath the stairs is nearly hollow."

"You think the person's in our walls?" Eddie asked.

"The littler boy speaks," Traust said. "Thought you might have been a mute. But your question? No. Not all the time in the walls. Maybe not right now—but maybe now. We'll have to open it all up, everything up, and see."

"Have you found them before?" Marshall asked. "Did you have them in your house?"

There was rustling, the object being put back into the toolkit on the floor. No one in the room spoke.

"Y'all hear that?" Traust said.

Eddie shifted on the stairs. The wood creaked.

"You hear it, don't you?" Traust said. "There's a feeling you get when you know, right? All the proof in the world can say otherwise, but you know it. I knew it well enough by your age, like I told you on our emails. Both of you, look around. I think we all know there's someone listening to us, right now."

Elise bit tightly into her knuckles; the taste of dust on her tongue. She wouldn't scream—she wouldn't. But she needed the knuckles filling her mouth to know it wasn't possible.

"Think of me as a tool," Traust said. "A divining rod. Think of me, for today, as an extension of you boys. For what you want—which is an empty house. This house being your house again, alone. Does that make sense?"

The palms of Eddie's hands pressed down on the seam in the stair.

"When I was your age, I think I would have killed to have someone like me come. Who believed and who could take 'em away. Would've slept a lot better at night, I can tell you that. Would have been a lot healthier and happier for it." The man laughed, walked over, and placed his hand on the banister. "What I'm asking is that, for now, y'all follow my example. Do as I do. We work as a team. And when this is over, and have that person out here before us, we can all know. We'll have that. But until then—we do as I say. We get it?"

"Yeah," Marshall said. "We got it."

"When I say grab, we grab. Does the little brother get it?"

"He gets it," Marshall said.

"Good," Traust said. "And at the end, what we find is mine."

UNPACKING A TOOLKIT

THE MAN MOTIONED THE BOYS TO HIM, THERE WITH HIS CLOTH toolkit on the foyer floor. Marshall bent over, looked up at his brother, and jerked his head to tell Eddie to come down from the staircase. The boy did, conscious of the feel of the cool wood beneath his bare feet, of the emptiness behind him upstairs, and the sweaty stink of the man below. Whatever balance there had been in the house was all gone now. A seal broken, and what was with them—silent in the house, a presence light as cobwebs against the skin—was coming undone.

Eddie stood beside Marshall as the man gave them the tools they would be using. He put them in their hands until their hands were full and they looked at each other, and then stacked the items on the floor around them. An odd assortment of objects, like the belongings in the shopping cart of someone without a home: Ziploc bags holding things that were hard to tell what they were, and others, obvious enough, but hard to tell what they would be used for.

Handkerchiefs, rubber bands, a coil of wire.

Bells, like ones that would dangle from a cat's collar.

Small fireworks—M-80s.

Zip ties and a doctor's stethoscope. A kit of wire cutters.

Six small containers of pesticide. Cotton balls.

A headlamp and three small flashlights. A Leatherman.

A hammer and rubber mallet, a small electric drill.

Handcuffs.

"You know," Marshall said. "We just want it out of our house."

Mr. Traust stood up between them. He said, "That's right."

The big man put his hands on his hips and opened his mouth as if to speak. Then he stopped, his eyes wide and flitting as if something had startled him. He looked into the library, then turned and checked the living room. Stood there for a minute, his back to them, a downward arrow of sweat darkening the broad back of his old, gray T-shirt. He composed himself and grinned at the boys with a smile dense with teeth.

"Daylight's wasting," he said. "Let's get to work."

WOODS HAVE EYES

BEYOND THE CHEST-HIGH GRASS AND THISTLES OF THE BACK FIELD stood the tree line, with its wall of dense underbrush, the glossy poison ivy, tallow saplings, and the oak's and maple's low branches. Inside, past the range of sight, were the noises of bodies moving. The rustle and crunch of litterfall, palmetto leaves rustling. In a bizarre trick of acoustics, some sounds in the woods were muted, while others were amplified, their sources seeming larger—not that different from the workings of a house's walls.

An armadillo's small claws rifling along the ground sounded like the full paws of a black bear. A squirrel leaping from a low-hanging branch like the kick-up of a coyote's back legs. The buzz of a beehive, somehow, lost completely. These woods were dense with life. Birds, opossums, and raccoons. Snakes and boar, bobcat and bear. The trees looked inward upon themselves with hard, knotted eyes. They felt every tremor of the wind through their branches, every vibration of the ground through their roots and trunk. They looked outward along Stanton Road, to the boy leaving his home to duck beneath the low palmetto branches and orb-weaver's webs, his bare feet soon squelching in the mud of his trails. They saw out to the field, and the levee, and the large, white house. Sometimes, small things would climb their branches. They'd been keeping their own steady watch.

The truck in the backyard was now unloaded. It was the middle of the afternoon and the sun, though half-covered by a film of clouds, beat down bright and hot. But, for whatever reason, the lights in the home were lit—the boys' bedrooms, the guest room, even the attic—

dim bulbs like small, golden bodies through the windowpanes. The occasional flutter behind the glass, someone passing from room to room, and in another, a large piece of furniture moved in front of a window to seal off an eye.

But the house itself stood immobile, seemed even half-asleep—like a tree drooping after heavy rain. From across a field, it's hard to tell something's wrong. A tree afflicted with termites takes time before the fissures in its trunk show.

WHAT IT MEANS TO FIND THEM

THERE'S A STORY THE MAN GREW UP WITH THAT HE'S THOUGHT OF often. He can't remember where he first heard it, who told it to him, whether he dreamt it himself. Another story about a haunted house.

A man inherits a house. It is huge, and its rooms and hallways tumble after one another like a ball down stairs. It is remote, and he must make sure all the lights remain turned on. The house has many lights. The overhead bulbs burn one hundred watts apiece, with lamps positioned in the corners of those rooms, their shades taken off and the naked glass glowing bright and hot. The air is sickly warm with the heat, day and night. Even the closet lights are on. In cabinets and dressers, flashlights, left on, roll and clank against one another when the drawers are pulled open.

The man finds spare light bulbs stored in boxes in the corners throughout the house—thousands in total. The bulbs have hundreds of different styles and shapes, tubed and twisting, fluorescent, hexagonal, and pear-shaped. With the heat all around him, even when he is alone it doesn't feel that way.

At first, out of curiosity, he turns out a light, and a slow, flickering feeling builds in him. It feels as if something lost is now swelling, and it has a sour, rotten smell. His fingers fumble with the switch. When he turns the light back on, the feeling leaves. He wipes the sweat from his brow, suddenly grateful. He lives in the house for some time.

When the bulbs burn out, somewhere in the house, he knows it, wherever he is, because the feeling is there with that little dark building. The man is frantic to replace them. He's noticed how, in the patches of house where the light doesn't reach, there are dead things: insects, spiders, mice. When a fuse burns out in the basement, drowning the room in darkness, he realizes he's lost it. He boards its door shut.

But the bulbs are always burning out, and he is not always quick enough to catch them. When he turns a dead bulb, removing it from its socket, it feels as though the thread will never end. He must resist the urge to wrench the bulb free. In that pocket of shadow, he feels them there. He feels their fingers upon his forearm, pressing their nails into his skin. They've been there the whole time. Eventually, this story ends when the whole house is dark.

You boys ask me what it means to find them. To catch them, finally, in the beam of your light, to see them there, beside you, when you've known that they've been there just beyond the edge.

It's to remove the mask of the world. To pull off its face and see the wiring beneath.

When you grow up in a house like yours—not like this, no mansion, nothing this big—but a house like this in that it is a house, with the sounds of a house, and drafts, and locks, and spaces hidden away, a place with angles that prevent anyone from seeing everything at once. A house where no one believes you. And each day you're home, scribbling your homework, eating your meals, flipping through your television channels, straining step to step through the day's particulars—and somebody's up there breathing in the attic? Each day grows you into something a little different.

In church, they tell you of God and the Devil, and the keen difference between them, but when you're a kid at home in a house that's supposed to be empty, hearing a door somewhere close come open, what difference is there? There's you, and there's everything else. Every object and thought turns against you, and all you have is yourself and knowing.

But once you know, know like the feeling of those fingernails pressing into your forearm, you can fight. You can resign yourself to the fact that you'll die trying to find them. You can have that certainty. But when you don't yet know—you're alone, and nothing else helps you.

I have gone a hundred lifetimes without knowing, seems like. I have gone longer than you will understand without holding them here in my hands. I want to see their face. I want to see a face and take it back with me to show everybody who didn't believe. Everybody else who's lived a hundred lifetimes without knowing.

"Mr. Traust," Eddie said from down the hallway, with his voice shrinking as he spoke. "This isn't about us, is it?"

"Boys," Traust said. "Now. How's about you go check the closets again."

SHE MUST MOVE

THE CLOCK IN THE FOYER TOLLED. THEY'D BEEN SEARCHING FOR OVER AN hour. Doors and cabinets opened and slammed shut, footsteps moving in all directions. The walls were not safe. Elise heard the click along the hallway, in the bedroom, against the wood of the stairs and the bare library wall after he took books from the shelves and stacked them on the floor. She wouldn't have known what it was if she hadn't heard the boys talking about it behind him. A stethoscope. Elise could hold her breath long enough. But she couldn't stop her heart. The organ had become so loud now, throbbing in her chest, hammering in her ears, so loud she thought he'd hear it from another room, that he'd follow it, along the house's ventricles to its source.

In short spurts, as Elise found the opportunity, she shimmied through the walls to the other side of the house to the kitchen, working herself up and over doorframes, passing by the dim, warm light of the stained-glass window. Once there, she used the studs to wedge herself up to the top of the pantry to the access panel. She opened it and dangled her feet down onto the shelves, finding a place to stand between the boxes of cereal and rice. She closed the panel behind her. Elise descended the shelves and flattened herself against the ground, her cheek against the cool tile, to peek through the crack beneath the door. She rose to her haunches and touched her ear against the wood of the door to listen.

Here—her opening.

Elise turned the knob and crawled through the kitchen on her hands and knees, pausing at the doorway to the living room to ensure no one else was lurking there, silent. Then she turned the corner and slipped into the living room's coat closet.

They'd checked here already, hadn't they? She parted the hanging jackets, grabbed hold of the metal coatrack, pulled herself up, swung her foot on the shelf above, and inched herself on top. The shelf was full with a collection of small boxes, picture frames, and flashlights, and Elise lifted herself up and over them. Once behind, she reached back through and, mindful of the squeak of metal hangers on the pole, pulled them back toward the center of the rack. In the narrow space behind the boxes and frames, she curled her shoulders forward, pressing her back and legs flush against the wall. She breathed.

Elise realized now she'd nearly been discovered in this closet before, back during Eddie's birthday party. Nearly. But she hadn't been found. She didn't know whether that meant this place was good or bad luck. She wished she had someone who could tell her. Her dad, her mom. Even Brody.

Minutes later, Elise heard footsteps against the living room carpet. Was it the man? She grabbed one of the flashlights in front of her on the shelf. Metal, hefty, at least four or five pounds. Slippery in her sweaty palm. Elise figured if she saw those big hands come reaching at her, snatching at her, she might swing the flashlight down with enough force to stagger him away. She waited. Another set of footsteps entered the room from the foyer.

"What's he doing now?" Eddie asked, his slender voice.

"He's going through it all again," Marshall said. "All the towels out of the linen closet, and in my room, he's taken the sheets off my bed. Clothes out of my dressers. My CDs and textbooks are all over the floor."

"What about my room?"

"I think he's doing yours next."

The boys were quiet for a moment. Someone sat down on the reclining chair. From the foyer, the cardinal called out the midpoint of the afternoon. The sound of the birds surprised Elise. As if she'd expected the painted birds to have taken flight and fled.

"He was talking about putting trip wire up there," Marshall said. "He was actually going to nail it into the doorframes."

"To nail it?"

"I told him he had to use tape instead. Masking tape, so it wouldn't leave the goop behind."

"Are we going to be able to clean this all up before Mom and Dad get back?"

"We're going to have to."

"I don't want him here," Eddie said. "I want him gone."

"Yeah," Marshall said. "Me too." He sounded tired. "I'm thinking the sooner he finds someone, the sooner he'll be out of here. But we can't forget what this is all about. He said he thinks we're close. And . . . after all this—I mean could you even imagine after all this still not finding anything? Still having whoever in our house? Eddie, we can't live the rest of our lives scared of the fucking dark."

"I wish we told Mom and Dad."

"No," Marshall said. "Seriously?" There was frustration now in his voice. Elise could picture him there, standing in the center of the room in front of his seated brother, eyes squeezed shut, fingers rising to his brow, shaking his head. "Eddie, they wouldn't have believed us. Why is that so hard to get through? Something that's been stolen, they'd say we lost. Something like the footprint, they'd say we imagined. Something we heard, they'd say was only the house. You're not dumb, so please, quit acting like it. Do I have to say this? That either, one night, that person will finally slit our throats in our sleep, or else—I don't know—we'll both go insane."

"Like him?"

"Eddie," Marshall said. "What the hell? Don't you think someone who sneaks around, who steals our shit—a knife!—isn't more of a problem? If not, well, then you actually have gone insane, or else you're more stupid than I even thought you were. This guy comes in, and you just cringe, and complain, and hardly even look. I mean, I don't like him, either, but you're not making this go any faster. All you've done is whimper and sniffle behind me. Tiptoeing around. Barefoot. You're making the guy think we're both just little fucking kids. We don't need that."

Marshall went across the room and began tearing the cushions from the sofa and tossing them on the floor. "Get up!" he said to his brother, and Elise heard him pull the cushion from the recliner where Eddie was sitting. "Go look in the garage, or something. Just go, man, and do something."

And the younger brother left.

IN A CORNER

AFTER MARSHALL SEARCHED THE LIVING ROOM, THE CLOSET DOOR opened and light expanded into the room. He stepped in. The crown of his head was just an arm's reach below her; she saw the short, stray bristles of his hair in a crack between two small boxes. Marshall parted the hanging coats and jackets to see behind them.

The muscles of Elise's arm tensed, and she lifted the flashlight above her, as high as the ceiling would allow. If he looked up, if the balls of his eyes rose in their sockets, she couldn't even give him the chance. She pictured the globe of his skull sprouting hairline cracks from the impact. She'd push the boxes and frames between them down and hit him as many times as she could manage before his knees buckled.

If she didn't, Marshall would hold her there, under his bony knuckles, calling for Traust to come down. The big man would be there in seconds.

Marshall closed the part in the hanging coats. Elise waited for him to look up and see her. She thought to herself that this was something she could do, wasn't it?

Marshall's eyes rose. They skimmed over the picture frames and boxes. Only a flutter of the eyes, but she made out the deep brown of his irises. Elise didn't move. Couldn't.

He turned and closed the closet door behind him.

KEEP MOVING

OUTSIDE, THE TREE LINE OF THE WOODS WAS A WALL. THE DOMED sky a ceiling. The steep, grassed levee a wall. On the other side of the levee, the river was a constant, silent force. Removed from her view for months now, but alive and streaming.

Elise listened to the men in her home, tracked their movements, projecting and extrapolating them in her mind, as the clock in the foyer tolled on the quarter, and then on the half-hour. When she felt it was safe, she dripped, like a single bulb of water, down from the shelf. She left the living room closet, darting behind the piano, now dragged into the center of the dining room. She waited, the pressure of standing still in the open room welling within her, as steps crossed through the foyer, into the living room, then into the kitchen. Marshall saying something to his brother, who was still in the attached garage. Elise rose up the curving stairs, quiet. Traust in the parents' bedroom, but she passed the doorway as little more than the flicker of a ghost. The rooms around her in disarray, like the furniture had come alive into open revolt. Laundry hampers spilled. Drawers emptied on the beds. Clothes taken down from their hangers. Towels covering the hallway floor beneath her feet. They were taking apart their home to find her.

Keep moving. This was her home, too.

The river on the other side of the levee rises and falls. Swells and recedes.

Elise, the river. A current outside of sight.

POISON THE WELL

BY LATE AFTERNOON, MR. TRAUST HAD GONE OUT INTO THE YARD. EDDIE had caught a glimpse of him there, the dark shape of his head passing the first-floor windows in the bronzing sunlight. Soon, Eddie heard him below the house. At first, Eddie thought it might have been the other, the hidden one, but he heard the man's grunting, involuntary and beast-like, and the thick weight of his body bumping against the house's foundations. That wasn't their intruder—theirs was quiet, almost imperceptible, even delicate. Mr. Traust's noises made Eddie realize for the first time how small this person must be. Below, something began to hiss.

"What the hell is he doing down there?" Marshall said, from the staircase.

Eddie shook his head.

"You're going to want to step outside," said Mr. Traust's muffled voice, calling up from below.

The boys met him at the crawl space behind the azaleas. It was a shock to see his flushed, strained face in the dark rectangle in the house's siding—Eddie would have never guessed he could fit through there in the first place—and he emerged coughing, wriggling himself free, his face and shirt streaked with gray dirt. Halfway out on the grass, he covered his mouth with a handkerchief. He thrust up the other hand for Marshall to grab hold. Trails of thin smoke twisted from the hole behind him. The man's eyes had turned watery and pink.

"Fumigation," Mr. Traust said, getting to his feet. He didn't com-

pose himself long, and motioned with two fingers for the boys to follow him back around the house. While he walked, he gave an animal
attention to the windows—his body partly facing them, but his boots
falling directly in front of one another. He reached his truck and
pulled three mouth masks from the bed. He tossed two to Marshall,
who wasn't expecting it. Marshall dropped one and had to bend and
pick it up.

"So," Marshall said. "What is this? Are you poisoning our house
now?" There was resignation in his voice. "I said our parents are getting home tomorrow. We don't have time to wash every dish and
bedsheet—"

"Your house is too big," Mr. Traust said. "We don't have enough
eyes to pin it all down at once. Besides, I only set 'em off beneath the
house. The foggers' smoke goes up, but it's going exactly where I want
it. The spaces between. Only there. Just those spots our friend has to
hide. Get it?"

"You sure?"

The man locked eyes with Marshall. Pursed his lips.

Marshall handed Eddie a mask, while Mr. Traust grabbed his
toolkit from the side of the house and went back inside.

"Put it on," Marshall said. He avoided Eddie's gaze as he handed it
to him. Instead, he looked back toward the crawl space, where wisps
of smoke twined.

THE BODY CRIES OUT

IN THE FOYER, THEY STOOD AND WAITED FOR THE HISS OF THE FOG-gers beneath them to cut out.

Mr. Traust looked around at the walls. He placed his toolkit down and stepped into the living room, his head cocked to the side, one ear turned up like a dog. The boys didn't know what else to do but follow. The man stopped abruptly and frowned when he turned to find them in his way. The boys backed into the foyer, and then followed him into the library.

"How many of those things did you put down there?" Marshall asked.

"Shh," Mr. Traust said. He brought a finger to his lips. He looked around, then he pointed at the floor as if to say, "Wait here." He went on through the laundry room and disappeared around the corner into the back porch.

The boys waited in the library beside the books that had been pulled and stacked in short towers, beside the rolled-up rug and the sofa pulled perpendicular to the wall. The sun was dipping in the sky and the lamp cast soft shadows across the floor.

One minute. Two minutes, and the hissing beneath them went quiet. The ghosts of smoke rose up from the floor vent—hard to tell whether Eddie was actually seeing it. A car passed on the road, its windows down, country music warped by speed. The house around them was still.

The smoke rose through the house's insides. Eddie could imagine it just on the other side of the wall, twisting in the dark around the studs and beams. Tendrils, gray worms in black mud, around them on every side. Eddie's breath felt hot in his mask. Sweat gathered on his upper lip. Mr. Traust was now standing, silhouetted by the windows in the back porch. His big legs splayed, arms raised, elbows jutting, his hands covering his eyes. He was listening. The lights of every room gently hummed.

And then, finally, finally above them, through the ceiling, somewhere from the empty rooms overhead, they heard someone cough.

STORM'S BEGINNING

MR. TRAUST THUNDERED THROUGH THE HOUSE. PASSING THE BOYS in the library, he kicked the books on the floor out of his way, whole stacks crumbling before his shins. The boys pressed themselves against the shelves to let him by. Up the stairs, three at a time, his boots so loud it seemed like he might break through the wood. So loud, half-way up, he needed to stop. Couldn't hear the sound. The boys came after, paused at the foot of the stairs, and watched as he listened, watched his big hands white-knuckled on the banister, his chest rising and rising. Anxious, ready, but somehow his face didn't seem to belong to the rest of him. Its brows pinched, its lips stretched back, he held an expression they'd expect from a boy who was afraid. It took a moment for Eddie to realize Marshall was gripping his shoulder.

Then there it was again, the coughing—hacking now—and Mr. Traust was after it. They ran up behind him and saw the rug in the hallway catch air under his boots. Outside the parents' bedroom, he stopped and listened, moved on, the sharp tip of his nose turning up at the spaces above each doorframe. He went past the guest room and the office, began trotting down the hall to the end, the boys still behind him, to where their rooms were. The man threw open the door to Eddie's bedroom as if it were barricaded and entered. The coughing was coming from here, so loud now, it seemed, the boys barely noticed Mr. Traust drag the desk across the floor to the other wall.

They watched as he climbed, with one large step then another, up on the desk. He seemed so huge now, the top of his head grazing the ceiling. He stretched his arms wide and felt the wall with the tips of his thick fingers, laid his head against it, as someone was coughing right there, just on the other side. Then Mr. Traust stepped back, heels hanging off the edge of the desk, cocked his elbow back, and brought one meaty fist against the plaster.

Her screaming. The house itself might have been screaming.

The wall's blue paint cracked white around the small black hole. Whatever was inside now scrambled and kicked at the walls like a bird trapped in a box.

Mr. Traust gripped the knuckles of his hand. They might have been bleeding. "What the fuck are y'all kids doing?" he shouted. "Get my damn toolkit—my hammer—go!"

As Marshall turned and ran, Mr. Traust threw an elbow into the plaster.

HE TAKES HOLD

EDDIE WATCHED HIM FROM THE CENTER OF HIS ROOM. HE FELT ALmost as if he'd never been here before. The man leaping from his desk to rip the alarm clock from its socket, to bring it back up and beat the clock against the plaster. This place could not have been his. This room, not his. The man left impacts like the craters of rectangular meteors. Green and gold stress marks—wall colors from different coats of paint—shot out of each blow like jagged lightning.

Eddie listened to her—it was a her, now; all that uncertainty of what she might have been narrowing, tightening focus. Young, younger than he was, and inside the walls, fumbling and scratching, trying to pull herself away. She was crying. Mr. Traust brought the plastic clock again against the wall, its power cord whipping behind him, until it snapped into two pieces, its red and green wires exposed. A hole in the wall opened, and he focused on widening it. Something fluttered past in the shadow—did Mr. Traust see it?—and Eddie realized that the girl was someone physical, real, whose body took up space, whose skin had texture.

"Where the fuck are my tools?" Mr. Traust cried. "I need my hammer! I need my—" He turned back to Eddie, tossing the broken clock to the floor. Then he wrenched his hand inside the hole, his forearm disappearing, the plaster chipping away as he forced his upper arm farther into the dark. He groped through the inside of the wall by feel. His eyes flat, motionless in their sockets, staring emptily at a place just above Eddie's forehead. Nothing, finding nothing, then he was grinning—eyes huge, oversized, even startled—his fingers found her. His whole body quivered as he grabbed hold and yanked.

Thumping in the walls. She shrieked again, but the sound was cut short by her coughing. Mr. Traust's neck had gone blotched with red so deep it might be purple. He contorted his body while his arm pivoted in the hole, like the minute hand of a clock become insane. Feet, small ones, were slapping against the house's insides.

"Got her! By her hair!"

He had grabbed hold. Seized the filament-thin fibers of a net that had been spread all over the house, that they'd walked on every day, that no one had been able to see. Each of those moments now held in the man's hand. In this room, there'd been the exhale of a breath from behind the overstuffed armchair. Or when, in the middle of the night, just outside, someone had stepped out of Eddie's way in the hallway. In the morning, when he turned the water of the shower on and adjusted the temperature, the rustle in the attic above him, like some bird turning in its nest. Recollected sounds, her sounds. A sudden flash through Eddie's mind: just beyond Mr. Traust, through the wall, the image of a face—compact, outlined in half-light—being pulled, scraped raw against the wood beams. Being yanked by the hair, out through the small hole. The man would press the tips of his fingers into her eye sockets, taking hold like he would the holes of a bowling ball.

Eddie ran across the room and was on him. Gripped the man by the shirt and pulled, trying to get him off the desk. Mr. Traust cursed. He kicked at Eddie with the heel of his boot. "Stop it!" he said, but Eddie kept on, yanking at the pockets of his jeans, bracing his knees against the desk drawers, trying to unhinge Mr. Traust for a moment away from the wall and the girl inside.

"What the hell are you doing?" the man yelled. "She's pulling away!"

Mr. Traust thrust his boot down on the bridge of Eddie's nose, and set the boy's face searing. Eddie fell back to the floor with the world weightless around him. The smell of something familiar—flowers or dust—and his brother leaping across him. Eddie on the carpet, seeing Marshall's fist thrown into the back of the big man's knee, forcing him to buckle, bending as if he were stuck with a hot poker. He came unhooked from the wall and dropped to all fours on the desk. Marshall's hands were under Eddie's armpits, tugging him harshly across the carpet to the door.

Mr. Traust was agape at them. "What the fuck!"

"Stay away from my brother," Marshall said, firm.

Mr. Traust turned to look back up toward the wall, and they all heard her: that thumping in the wall, scratching—she'd found her grip now, was climbing out of their reach.

"Dumbasses!" the man said, stuffing his arm back in the hole, grabbing at nothing.

"You kicked my brother!" Marshall said. "The fuck is wrong with you?"

Eddie's fingers found his face and brought back blood from his nostrils. He looked at it, two drops sliding across the back of his hand. The room around him wobbled.

"I had them by the hair!" Mr. Traust said. "I had one in my hand!"

Marshall bent Eddie and looked him over. "Are you all right?"

Eddie shrugged, and Marshall pulled him to his feet.

"You and the little retard made me lose them," Mr. Traust said.

"Fuck you, man," Marshall said.

"Y'all are just in my way now."

"You kicked my brother in the face, asshole!"

Mr. Traust stepped down from the desk. His face gone dark. Thick arms rising up from his sides. His hand bleeding, and the arm cut from the wall, too—the meaty forearm trailing a red, seeping line.

"It's a little kid in there," Eddie said. He didn't know what else to say.

"Stupid little shits." Spit fell to the floor with the words.

"Get behind me, Eddie," Marshall said.

Mr. Traust took a step forward. Sweat speckled the man's shirt. Without looking back, Marshall turned halfway and reached behind him. His hand found Eddie's shoulder and pushed him in the direction of the doorway.

"That won't happen again," Mr. Traust said. "It's your house, and I've tried to respect that. But you boys are going away. I'm putting you boys away."

"Go, Eddie," Marshall said. "Go. Get out of here. Call 911."

"That isn't going to help," Mr. Traust said.

Eddie backed into the hallway, watched as his brother floundered at the pants pocket where he kept his knife. The boy's hands shaking too much; the blade clattered to the floor. Mr. Traust came up to Marshall and slapped the boy's fists away like they belonged to a doll. The man grabbed him by the wrist and wrenched his arm around his back.

Eddie fled into the office. The cordless phone was mounted on the desk. He slammed the door shut and twisted the small lock on the handle. Eddie crossed the room and grabbed the phone with both hands and typed the buttons. He held the receiver so tight to his face it hurt. He shouted so the man would hear, "I'm calling them!"

Calling would be enough to make him leave. Would have to be. The man couldn't stay if the police were coming. Eddie didn't know what he would say to the operator when the call went through. The receiver was still silent in his ear, and Eddie waited. He wouldn't know what he'd say, but he'd shout and cry if he had to. "Just come," he'd tell the operator, "and help us."

"I'm calling!"

"Hey," Mr. Traust said. He was standing right outside the door. "How do you think that'll happen?" He grunted, and there was the sound of a body struggling against another. The man was holding Marshall tight against him. "Little boy, unlock the door, and come on out. I cut that phone line some time back."

THE GIRL IN THE WALLS

ELISE PULLED HERSELF THROUGH THE CRAWL SPACE IN THE ATTIC and pushed free the plywood floor. She sucked in the warm, fresh air. Coughed again. Her eyes and nostrils scalded. Whatever the man had released into her house felt like broken glass down her throat. Elise needed to spit, but it hurt to spit. She reached down into her nook and took out one of her water bottles and doused her face, letting it run over her open eyes. Beehive buzzing in her head. Dizzy. She swirled the warm water in her mouth, letting it leak out on its own, dribbling down her chin to the floor. A puddle left there for anyone to see. Didn't matter.

The Eater of the Dead had come for her. Nidhogg, who ate the roots of the World Tree. All the names from her books. Hel. The Jabberwock. Satan. He'd come for her, and he wanted to hurt her. He'd come to take her. He'd sent a pillar of smog through her walls to choke and find her.

What was she to do?

He had poisoned her home. When he first punched the wall, the impact had come into her thigh—she'd buckled and come loose from her footholds, dangled by her hands like a spider in a broken web. He had come to take her, as he had her parents. His black smoke rising to the sky. Elise needed another place to hide.

Elise rinsed her face with the remaining water. The attic wouldn't keep her safe. If she hid here, he would tear the room apart and find her.

Breathe. The memory of her dad's voice: *Let's think.*

Without the walls, only one way down, through the attic door. But it would lead her right to Traust. Waiting for her, arms stretched out wide, an owl's wings. Could she barricade the door?

Raised voices downstairs, heavy footsteps pounding through the hallway—but they were leading away. They had to know this was where she'd gone. But they weren't yet coming up for her. She had time. Elise went to the crawl space and grabbed a wide plywood board next to the loose one she had used as a cover for her bed. Unlike the other, this one was nailed down, one skinny column of metal in each corner. She planted her feet down in the crawl space, curled her fingers around the lip of the board and pulled. Her back burned, fingers ached until the skinny nail on either side came half free. She knelt in her nook and pushed with her palms up from the other side, wrenched the rest of the board free. It flipped over and dropped loudly on the floor. Elise went to another board beside it and began again.

None of the nails were deep—she remembered the quick job her mom and dad had done on the floor. When they'd moved in, most of the attic had been unusable, a bare rib cage of crossbeams stitching out from the stairs. Her parents let Elise put some of the thin boards down herself, her dad's hands wrapped around hers on the warm nail gun.

But Elise was young, still. She'd grown strong from climbing in the walls, yet her bones were small. The joints of her fingers burned. Her thighs and calves burned. Finally, the second board came up.

Beneath her, something big was being dragged across the floor. She tossed the second board to the side, and the dark crevice leading into the house's walls was massive now, like a deep-sea trench bisecting the house. From the light of the dormer, Elise thought she saw faint smoke rising, pulled by the spinning overhead vent. Allow it a way out. This would have to be enough.

All of her things were now revealed—the coats she used as a bed, her snacks and pencils and drawings, her parents' things, her clothing and books, and all of Brody's gifts. Elise grabbed Brody's old swimming goggles and wrapped a small hand towel around her mouth, tucked its ends into the collar of her shirt. The footsteps were coming back down the hallway toward the attic door.

Elise determined her path, mapping it out below her. Then she sank down into the crevice again, her feet finding their grips. She descended, the sting of the smoke against her cheeks, back into the walls.

BOYS

A CLATTERING ABOVE THEM, LIKE SHE WAS RENDING THE HOUSE AT its seams. Mr. Traust's hands were nervous. His hot palms were wet, and the brothers felt the twitch in them as he squeezed the back of their necks, leading them to their parents' bathroom. He thrust them inside, one after the other, and shut the door. They heard him grunting, the bed being pushed, carpet catching and tearing beneath its legs, and the brass foot of the bed clanking against the frame, barricading the door. From the other side: "Stay here." And he left.

Once his footsteps faded back out to the hall, Marshall turned the knob and thrust his hip against the door. "Help me push!" he told Eddie, who came alongside him, thrusting his shoulder against the heavy oak door, again and again until his entire side throbbed. The wood only clapped against the metal doorframe. Nothing moved. Marshall exhaled. He grimaced at his brother.

"Eddie, what were you doing? What were you even trying to do?"

"I don't know."

"No," Marshall said. "No. What were you thinking? I saw you. You attacked him. You were just wild, all over the guy. I mean, the man's huge. And he's fucking psycho. And there was a woman in there, actually right fucking in there, and he had her . . . Eddie, what happened?"

"It's a kid," Eddie said. "She sounds like—it's a little girl in there."

"A girl?" Marshall said. He looked at the ceiling above them. The look on his face didn't seem like he thought that was any better.

"He was trying to hurt her."

Marshall stared at Eddie, incredulous. For a second, Eddie thought Marshall would stand up, come press his thumbs against his throat and throttle him out of exasperation. But his brother did nothing, only stood there, staring at him as if Eddie had changed into someone else, something else entirely.

Marshall cupped a hand across his face. "I've fucked this up," he said. "Bad. We're in real danger. You're already hurt."

Not far off, Mr. Traust's footsteps. He was climbing the attic staircase. He was speaking; the low rumble of his voice. They couldn't make out what he said.

"What's he going to do to her?" Eddie said.

"Eddie," Marshall said, staring at him. His head jerked in short movements. "I don't care."

The footsteps above them seemed so colossal. Too big for just one man, but they were measured and steady. Whatever the girl had been doing above them, she'd stopped. She was hiding. The bathroom's overhead vent hummed. Marshall walked across the room, with his hand at his mouth, chewing on his nails. His eyes were wide, beginning to redden at their rims.

"Once he finds her," Eddie asked him, "what's he going to do to her? And us?"

"I don't know."

The walls stirred. Mr. Traust had already given up in the attic, and had begun descending the staircase. And if they were alone, Eddie didn't feel it. He felt eyes on each side of him, heard them moving in their sockets. His nose throbbed in pain from the man's boot. Each of Eddie's thoughts felt stretched out and stomped on. Soon, Mr. Traust would find her and pull every hair from that girl's head. The feeling was overwhelming. Eddie raised his fists against the side of his temples and squeezed.

"Eddie," Marshall said. "Put your hands down. You're hurting yourself."

The muscles in Eddie's jaw tightened; pressure building in his temples and working its way down his neck and shoulders. He dug his knuckles deeper.

Marshall grabbed Eddie's wrists and jerked his fists away. He held them as he spoke. "Stop it, for Christ's sake. You're hurt enough as is."

His older brother's hands on him, the sweat of Marshall's hot palms on his wrists, the spaces between his fingers—he felt a sense of relief when Marshall finally let go. But the thoughts seemed to release. It'd been like ice water thrown over a rash of poison ivy blisters. Marshall pulled a handful of toilet paper from the roll and wadded it. He brought it to Eddie's face and held it to his nose.

"Broken?" Eddie asked.

"No." Marshall pressed a thumb to Eddie's forehead to tilt his head back.

"What do we do?"

Marshall's nostrils flared with each breath. Red prints were forming on the side of his neck from where Mr. Traust had gripped him. On his arms, too. This close, Eddie could see the tremble of his chin, the one place he hadn't forced his body to go tight to keep from shaking.

Marshall said, "We're getting out of this house."

SEARCHING, FINDING

THE MAN MOVED THROUGH EACH OF THE ROOMS, LISTENING. ELISE could hear him listening. Her body cried out at her, throat swollen and aching, her thighs throbbing, her calves and toes trembling from the weight. The smoke was still strong down here. It pulled at her, sapping her, ten thousand incorporeal, grabbing hands.

Outside, tree branches scratched against the house's siding. The sounds of him, and the boys, were coming from all over. The bandana had helped, for a short time, keeping the smoke from her mouth. But now she tasted the spray; it was almost a powder clinging to the wash-cloth's insides. Hard to understand what was happening, where she was exactly in the dark. Was she on the first floor? No, not yet. Her mind was part of a body that was giving out.

Inside, the footsteps faded. They rose again. Then stopped, abruptly, as if Traust had halted mid-stride, one foot dangling in the air. They changed direction.

Deep in her belly, the muscles of her diaphragm spasmed as if she were hiccupping. She clenched her neck, tongue tight against the top of her mouth, suppressing the urge to cough. If she didn't breathe, she wouldn't have to cough.

"I found you once." Traust's voice through the hallway. "I can find you again."

Dizzy, now. A building nausea. Elise lowered herself to a knee on the floor between the walls, and then lay, one arm beneath her. The circulation in the limb would be lost, but let it be lost. Her lungs

236 A. J. GNUSE

seemed filled with fire. Her brain swelled against every sharp corner of her skull.

Elise could stay here and sleep. If she could find sleep, she might wake after he'd given up. After the man had given up on looking for her and left. The home would all be cleaned, and the Masons tucked into their separate rooms, books or newspapers in front of them, blinding them, drowsy and unconscious to everything else.

"Sounds like those boys ran off," Traust told her. He walked up and down the hall, tapping on the walls again. "So how many of us are left here? Is it just you? How many of you are there?"

Elise saw nothing in the walls, but she sensed that her eyes had begun to swirl in their sockets. They were swimming. Somewhere else, birds were calling—were they outside? or coming from inside the clock? One small exhale, then inhale. Elise would have to give in to coughing soon. Her body was scratching away at her choice. Finally, she did—she tried to muffle the sound. Lips closed tight, cheeks bulging. Her stomach contracted. Elise thought she might vomit. The bitter taste of the lingering smoke on her tongue. She retched, dry-heaving. She was loud enough to hear.

And there, beside her, on the other side of the wall. Elise heard him clear his throat. How long had he been waiting, just there? Her pulling free from his grip, the trip up into the attic, the floorboards removed, the descent back into the walls. It was as though none of it had happened. As though she'd been here, and he'd been lying right beside her the whole time.

WINDOW

THE BATHROOM WINDOW—UNOPENED FOR YEARS, PAINTED SHUT.
Two sets of hands on the window rail, thrusting up to the dimming
afternoon sky. The wood came loose from the frame like a gunshot.
Marshall wriggled himself out first, dropping down on his hands to
the narrow ledge below, swinging both his legs out to drop behind
him. His palms slipped on the shingles, sliding forward toward the
ledge, but he caught himself on the sharp edge of the rain gutter.
Eddie behind him in the window, like in a frame of a mirror. "What
about her?" the younger brother said.

"Come on," Marshall said. He reached in and tucked his hands
beneath Eddie's armpits, and helped him out.

Together, they circled the roof to the place where the hackberry
tree grew up close. Eddie stepped down on the branch. The tree
swayed beneath him, scraped against the siding—Mr. Traust would
hear that, would hear that they'd gone out; maybe she would, too—
and he lowered himself, feet into the forks of the trunk, gripping
the branches, climbing lower, his brother behind him, his back foot
catching on the gutter on his way down, the loud snap as aluminum
bent loose from the roof. But being quiet didn't matter, leaving mat-
tered more. And the boys climbed lower, until they could safely drop
down into the lawn, the ground pushing firmly against the muscles
in their legs.

The world spanned in every direction. The house was something
they could turn from, and though its windows still glared down

on them, far into the backyard, their feet could beat the gravel and grass, with each footfall a decision to put the place wholly behind.

We're only kids, Eddie told himself.

They ran, Marshall leading, holding tight to his brother's arm.

COMING IN

LIGHTS APPEARED ABOVE HER, LIKE MINIATURE SUNS. PARTICLES of wall came loose, falling as heavy flakes of snow. Elise was buried by them. They fell on her face. She coughed. She tugged the bandana down to her neck and pushed free what was inside her. She inhaled—a brief, rasping window of relief. But the need returned to purge that sharp air.

He had a hammer now, was blasting holes in her home. Each blow vibrated through her teeth. Each strike like the gong of a clock at the hour. She bit her tongue—blood and dust-taste. With her free arm, she covered her face. She pulled herself tight. Small. Trying for something smaller than she could become.

OUTSIDE, LOOKING BACK

THE BOYS CROUCHED IN THE BACK FIELD. THE TALL, MOIST GRASS clung to their arms and legs. Gnats flitted around their faces. Sweat dappled their foreheads and temples. Ms. Wanda's car wasn't parked in her yard. The nearest house was nowhere near.

"I need to think," Marshall said, as they caught their breath.

And while they crouched, Eddie still felt the pressure of eyes on him. From the house, from the woods behind. Golden orb-weavers, massive spiders, black and yellow and large as an outstretched hand, hung drowsy between the high branches of the backyard's oaks, their wide webs appearing as they caught the setting sun. The thistles bobbed in the breeze around them. Eddie could almost fully see the man up there, through their house's office window. The rise of his arm, its arch as he brought it down against the wall. Rhythmic. Like a miner in a shaft. The boys could hear the walls breaking apart like a hand patting the side of a leg. The upstairs lights had begun to flicker with each blow.

From here, Eddie could see so much of the house through its windows.

From here, they heard the siren, rising now, growing near.

BIRDS

FROM SOMEWHERE, THE CALL OF BIRDS GREW LOUDER.

Traust stopped to listen. He could hear them too.

"Oh, shit," he said. "How so soon?"

If he had been patient before, he was no longer. Hurried now, frantic, cursing and slamming at the walls. Elise let herself cough, tongue lolling, coughing though she was out of breath, and each one felt like ripping a new strip of flesh free. Seemed like he had a half-dozen hammers, in as many hands. Elise was caked in the wall's debris. Her sight swirling. Necessary to move, escape, but her limbs were lifeless. He no longer used just the hammer, he struck with the steel toes of his boots. Because birds were coming. Rising in pitch and volume. A great migration—geese, starlings, mallards. Coming all at once, crying out in wild symphony, straining voices rising and falling as one, descending from the clouds.

They came for her. They came for him, too, and they both knew it. The man, just beside her, cursed at her. Cursed again and again. Bellowed, enraged, and his voice cracked into a scream. He didn't stop. Screamed like he'd caught fire. Like something he loved had caught fire.

The siren had turned into the driveway.

He ran from her, ran through the rooms of the house. "But you're here!" he shouted while Elise coughed and coughed.

The pounding of his boots, he came back—"And you're right here! You're right fucking here!"—and she watched as his hand reached in through the holes, groping for her in the dark. His fingers, clenching and unclenching, slapping down the sides of the wall, just above her. If he could grab hold, he'd lift her up like a rag doll. He'd wrench her against the sides of the holes he'd made until her body gave way and came out.

But the hand pulled back. He pounded against the walls. Down the hall, lumbering down the stairs, two at a time. The wail of the siren in the yard now cut out. Its heavy presence still there, but silent. The sound of men's voices.

And Elise lay there until she caught her breath. The thick air through her nostrils.

Aching. Bile at the back of her throat.

But, for a moment, the house was quiet around her. An empty house.

She found a way to pull herself up. Elise wiped the dust from her face. A fingernail brushing each wet eyelash. She lay her forehead against the cool plaster. Looked out through the holes at a still room before her.

EXILED

THEY WATCHED THE HOUSE EXPEL HIM: THE SMACK OF THE SCREEN
door as he threw himself against it and out into the yard. He stumbled in the orange afternoon light, one arm curled around his toolkit,
the other tearing the white ventilator mask from his face and casting
it into the lawn.

Alongside the house, the truck pulling closer, slow through the
wet, uneven driveway, its red lights flashing, seeming more than
huge beside their mother's frail flowers and the small wooden fence
lining the driveway. The top of the truck snapped the low-hanging
oak branches in its way.

They watched as Mr. Traust climbed into his own truck and
turned its ignition. The jerk of his entire body as he pulled the vehicle into gear. His black truck tore a semicircle through the lawn,
out onto the driveway, and met the fire engine halfway. The man's
engine revved draconic, V-8 with its muffler removed, and gravel
and mud kicked into the air. He cut the front wheels right, driving
into the front yard, chassis pitching, breaking through and over the
small fence, with a long stretch bending down around the breach.
Clumps of grass coming loose beneath the tires, the man passed the
fire engine, cut back onto the driveway, and swung hard out onto
the road.

His truck disappeared behind the pampas grass and trees, out of
their sight. Gone, for one second. Two. But gone didn't mean they
didn't feel any less seen. By him, from a rearview mirror, from the
tree line behind them, from the house and the yard ahead. And even

when the roar of his truck's engine was swallowed by the quiet around them, he might as well have still hung on there, just out of sight.

For a few minutes, they watched the firemen, who circled around the house, looking beneath the brims of their black helmets into the dim windows. They shifted on their haunches in the tall grass. "Who called?" Marshall said.

The smell of the thistle flowers. The rustling of the woods behind them. An owl warbling from the trees. Finally, Marshall placed his hand on Eddie's shoulder, a firm hand, as if to hold steady something that had begun to vibrate. They left the tall grass for their home.

QUESTIONS

"WAS IT ONE OF YOU TWO WHO REPORTED THE FIRE?"

A waking dream to be here like this. Marshall's hand never left Eddie's shoulder. The whole world alive around them—mosquitoes, fluttering moths, crickets around their feet—and each part of it was oblivious. The air still hot. The leaves of their mother's garden hung heavy from the heat. Sun dipping below the reach of the cypress trees on the other side of the levee, with silhouettes of branches and tired, hanging moss. Lean shadows cast upon the house's siding. Reflections on windowpanes.

"Do you boys live here?"

The older brother said, "We do."

"Our dispatch said a boy called in a fire at this address. Said it might have been a prank."

"We didn't call. We couldn't."

"Is there a fire?"

"No fire. No."

"Little guy's got some blood on his nose. You boys okay?"

"Yeah. He's okay."

"Who was that guy who drove out?"

"Is he gone?"

"Looks like. What was going on with him? Was he doing something with you kids? What's—"

"Sir, do y'all have a cell phone? We need to talk to our mom and dad."

A SURVEY OF DAMAGES

HIS BOOTS' DARK PRINTS THROUGH EACH AND EVERY ROOM OF THE house. Scuffing and chips in the wall from the stick he used on them. Scratches from the metal stethoscope he dragged along them.

The insides of the walls fumigated.

Carpets torn. Furniture wrenched out and spilled, clothes and towels and sheets flooding the floor, trampled. Holes blown into the walls of Eddie's bedroom. Holes in the office's walls. A broken gutter outside, dangling loose beside the hackberry tree. A cut phone line.

An attic, its plywood floor pulled open, skin removed and tossed aside; a narrow fissure exposed between the crossbeams leading down into the darkness between the house's rooms like the open mouth of a cave. Like tunnels. More than anyone, besides her, had known existed.

Her.

She, whose things were there, beside the fissure, in spaces that the plywood floor had once covered. The impression of a body on their winter coats. Books that once had been Eddie's. Trash. Tissues, snack bars, and wrappers. Odd and incongruous things: a bow tie, a single sock. Beneath the blankets, there was a curled and cracked picture. Sun-bleached, like it had been placed in the crack between the storm window and a frame, and lost there, the colors bleeding dry from the daily sun. The faces of those photographed were mostly illegible, but their outlines, and the park behind them, clear enough. A mother, a father, and their little girl.

The hole in the floor of the attic was almost eye-shaped. This was a horror.

But, to the boys, looking down, after everything, how could it be—quiet? A policeman's footsteps reverberated through the rooms beneath them. But the hole itself lay like something deeper than sleep. This should be worse, they knew. They shouldn't feel as relieved as they did. Seeing it.

OUTSIDE

THE WOODS MAINTAINED THEIR WATCH.

Someone small, in a tree, who had returned. Hoping to see some sign from her. For a moment, he had. Maybe. When the sun was still up. Some flicker through the upstairs hall while the two older boys were still crouched in the back field—or maybe just the movement of his eyelids as they blinked. Since he'd come back after the call, his bare arms and feet had been bitten raw by mosquitoes. Would have to go soon. His aunt would be home, and she'd be waiting for him.

Nearby, the shape of a hawk perched on a branch. He hadn't noticed it there, behind him. He thought of the firemen's truck earlier, how, after the call, it had beat him to the house. How it had seemed so big, even at a distance. The house so large next to it. The police car that, later, had pulled alongside it, its siren off but lights flashing. The firetruck had left but the cruiser had stayed ever since. No one had come, bringing her out, yet. He hoped that was a good sign.

The levee stretched its arms out far in both directions. One day, Brody would like to grow just as large, as tall as the largest tree in the woods. The shifting faces in the patterns of their leaves would be his own. His arms as strong and hard as the thickest branches. From far away, he could reach over and pry free the roof of a home. He'd rise over, wide as a cloud, as a constellation, and watch the people living inside, like pill bugs teeming over an overturned, half-rotten log. They'd see him, too, but it wouldn't matter to anyone. He'd see Elise, in the dark lines between the rooms, and tell her how sorry he still was. That he missed her. Ask if there were any things he could bring her.

But it had grown late. Brody dropped down into the underbrush. He would come back tomorrow, when he could. To keep watch until he saw her again. Until he knew that the girl in the walls was okay.

Across the levee, a tugboat's searchlights played over the cypress trees, and the great black river flowed past. The lights of the house—the living room, the bedrooms, even the attic—remained on for hours.

FAMILY, RECOMPOSED

MRS. MASON AND MR. MASON RETURNED THAT EVENING WHEN THE tree frogs' calls permeated the black night. An officer, parked in his cruiser with its lights on in the driveway, spoke to them for a few seconds through his window before getting out. He led them into their house, into their living room, where their two boys watched television.

"I've done a run-through of the whole place," the policeman said, hands on his hips. Part impatient, part resigned. "Whatever, or whoever, these boys had him looking for, isn't here. This house is empty." He spoke to the Mason parents, listing to them some of the damage he'd seen throughout the house. He shook his head and shrugged.

"We've got enough for trespassing and vandalism charges for the guy. More, too, maybe. Assault and battery. Is your cell phone a good number to reach you?"

"Yes," Mr. Nick said. "Yeah."

"We'll let you know if or when we find him," the officer said. "If we do, we'll reach out for the follow-up. Until then . . ." He jerked the crown of his forehead toward the boys. "You should probably sort it out with them."

Their boys looked down at the floor.

"I don't understand," Mrs. Laura said. "I don't understand any of it."

The officer thanked them. He smiled at the boys, lips turned down at the corners, as he turned and left the house.

SEARCHING FOR AN ANSWER

LAURA AND NICK PASSED THROUGH THEIR HOUSE WITH THE SAME
strained, pale faces. Surveyed the damage. Surveyed the implications
about their house, and their sons.

They were children, still. Boys who needed their protection. Arms
wrapped around them, keeping them from harm, and harm they'd
bring to themselves. How long until your baby is no longer a baby?
Never, they realized, in case some part of them had forgotten. You
might be dead, buried six feet below, but they are yours, and your
body will pulse to protect them. Relentless, steady as growth through
the deep, black soil. Their home was upended—but their boys would
be protected.

Nick couldn't look his wife in the eyes. He picked towels up from
the hallway floor and held them there, dirty and bundled in his arms,
not sure where to put them down. Laura was sobbing. She held her
boys, their bodies rigid in each of her arms, while she shuffled between the rooms. She tried not to squeeze their shoulders too hard.
She realized she might hurt them.

Eddie and Marshall showed them the hiding place in the attic, the
collection beneath the floor—the nest, they called it. The items laid
out there like an exhibit of a museum. But with everything that had
happened in the house beneath, the objects seemed so small, insub-
stantial. Most all of the things had been their own, moved.

Who could believe in this? No telling how long these things had
been there, or who had put them there. Maybe they'd been there, for
weeks, months, while they moved below through their house, eating

their meals, showering, brushing their teeth, reading and sleeping—living. But maybe these items had only been laid here a few hours ago. A fabricated proof. A justification. "I don't want to hear this," Nick said, but there was no anger in his voice.

Marshall said, "This is everything. We're telling you everything."

He showed them the rooms: where they'd been locked up, where they had heard her, and the man had gone after her. In his own room, he plugged his computer back into the wall and turned it on, and showed them websites, conversations.

If any of it were true, they would understand. They'd believe. The man who came—their boys say he'd been brought, but they'd read those emails now: he came—that man was now gone. That man was the source, the singular cause of what had happened here in their home. He somehow had convinced the boys of the irrational. A madman who had stoked two children's fears.

"Are you sure he didn't hurt you?" Nick said.

And again, they said he did not. But Nick wasn't asking about the scratches along their forearms from descending the hackberry tree. Or the bruises along Marshall's shoulders from being held by the man. The pink bridge of Eddie's nose. Or how the bottom of his eye was beginning to darken.

"This is all of it?" Laura said. "You promise there's nothing else?"

The boys swore it.

Hours drifted by without their noticing. The antique clock's birds cried downstairs. Past midnight already, and soon long past it.

"I don't know what else to say," Nick said. "I don't know what else to ask you two."

"Do you want to sleep in our bedroom tonight?" Laura said. And after hesitation—only kids—they said they did not. No, they would not.

This would be talked about again, all over again, tomorrow. Punishments, unstated, would wait. Follow-ups, check-ins, talks—a long, unwinding future of them—would wait. They were all too tired. You have to give in eventually. They walked their boys to their rooms. They watched them crawl into their beds.

That night, Mr. and Mrs. Mason paced the rooms of their house. Of course, the doors were locked. The black of each windowpane was smooth as the eyes of statues. The two separated as they walked, passed each other at times, only sometimes catching each other's gaze. Their slack cheeks, the softness at the bottom of their jawlines. They each might have been much older. They wouldn't talk for some time.

But every time they were in a room alone, they felt it. Not much different about a man and a woman from a boy and a girl. Just bodies that had been grown and expanded. But they couldn't believe their boys. Instinctually, this truth immovable in their chests.

Still, more than other nights, it was hard to turn out a light.

NO ONE EVER LEAVES

SOMETHING HAD BEGUN.

Elise felt it in the musty dead air. He was still there in the boys as they moved above her. He was in their parents now, too.

Each time her eyes closed, the man was above and beside her, searching. She knew that, although weeks could pass, her scalp would still ache when she remembered him, holding tight the ends of her hair in his hand.

No one ever fully leaves. The man had left his imprint here before he went. In each of the moonlit rooms, the furniture all cast his shadow.

He'd be here, around her, in the weather. The heat, the muggy humidity, its pressure as she lay there, nauseated, as though someone was resting on her chest. He was in the quiet, whenever the birds went silent in the yard.

Still here, wherever he was. Passing their house in his truck with his brights on in the middle of the night. He'd still be here, even if he were hundreds of miles away in his own scoured, emptied-out home. He was here and he was a thousand miles away, in the shifting patterns of weather and nature. He'd been in the dew point, and temperature, and barometric pressure that had been formulating, even as Elise turned the loose knob of the library's door to return into her home. The natural order of the world building, in the months while she hid, to come. This home was no longer hers and he sought to take it away.

The strongest storms never actually arrive. They've been here, almost silent beneath it all, rising the entire time.

PART 5

THE RIVER IS A
SLEEPING GIANT

IN A STORY, THOR, THE BRAVE CHILD OF ODIN, JOURNEYED FAR TO the north, beyond the marshes and mountains, great plains and lakes, and cold expanses of forests under a frozen, gray sun, to a house he discovered, half-buried in the snow and ice. His brother, Loki, had betrayed him, and the weight of the world had finally grown too heavy. He had been looking for a place to be alone.

The God of Thunder entered the old house and closed the door behind him, shutting out the blistering wind. He walked through the old rooms, past antique furniture that had turned pearlescent with frost. Upstairs, he found a bed, and he lay there until he felt the cold seep through the thick ribbons of his muscles, until his bones drank that cold, until each of his limbs fell numb and asleep.

During his time in that house, Thor was visited by corpses. They were his ancestors, whose flesh hung in strips from their faces. They were his old teachers and neighbors with decayed, dusty eyes. All were silent; rigor mortis had frozen their jaws shut. They cooked meals for Thor, brought soup to his bed and laid the bowls on his chest. They implored him, as best they could, to sit up and eat.

Thor would do this for them, but it was all he would do. The wind whistled outside between the great drifts of snow, and the sky was a spiral of spent charcoal. Days here lasted six months. He spent them all knowing how each passing moment brought everything closer to their end. The corpses in the house pleaded with him to please get up and go home. But he did not understand. He was already home. He was in the last place he would ever be.

This was not a story from Elise's book of Norse myths. She made this one on her own. She no longer had the book. Mr. and Mrs. Mason cleared out her nook beneath the plywood in the attic. They had turned each thing over in their hands before they dropped it into a garbage bag, which they brought to the curb. They had thrown away the books. Did they think the books were cursed?

Elise's story of Thor was one she told herself while she lay beneath the house on the cool, dark soil, waiting through the sweltering days with the footsteps of the family above her. She told the story to herself, and to Odin. He told her to stop before she even finished—couldn't stand hearing one so sad. (He then mentioned, kindly as he could, that he didn't think it good for a young girl to lose such a deal of weight.)

Elise arose to life at night, but only to check off the barest minimums. Summer wore on above her, and she waited for the changing of the season; she waited until the seasons would whirl around her, wrapping her bones like thread around a finger.

She lay, and across the levee, barges, resting along the batture, were locked onto tugboats and pushed onward away. The river was a corpse in the coffin of its levees. As the girl dozed beneath the floors of her home, the river sat upright.

SECURITY

THE MAN INSTALLING THE SECURITY SYSTEM TOLD LAURA ITS WEAK-nesses. "We say motion detectors, but in a house like this, as big as it is, we really mean window guards. If the door is opened, or a window is broken, it'll set off."

"There's nothing for all the interior rooms then?" Laura asked.

The man raised an eyebrow. "Nothing like the security system from a *Mission: Impossible* movie, no."

Laura ignored the insult. Odd that, more than anything, she just wished he were quieter when he spoke.

"This is fine," she said. Good enough to keep someone out, which is what they needed. Avoid another break-in, which is how she and Nick now referred to that day, when they referred to it openly at all. She'd become more aware of the objects in her home, what they would mean to another person, and how thin the boundaries were that retained them. Each piece of furniture, VCR, desktop computer, jewelry, china—had become a charged item. There was nothing intrinsic about the objects they owned that insisted it was they who owned them. Nothing about the boundaries of a house—the metal mechanics of a lock, the pane of a window—that did anything other than slow a trespasser down.

And theirs, their trespasser, had been invited in by their boys. Laura wanted to think of it as a robbery, but that man hadn't stolen anything. Nothing at all, from what she could tell, which made it worse. Her jewelry, outside a single necklace, all accounted for—and he wouldn't have taken only one slender, rope chain. Nick had left sixty dollars in a wooden box on their nightstand. Untouched. Made the whole thing seem more perverse. Invasive. He hadn't come for their things. He had hurt her boys, had attacked their home, and had left. To her, nothing about that seemed finished.

"It's fine," Laura said again, and left the man to his installation. An expensive system, and over whatever budget they'd been clinging to since moving into this damn, huge house. No wonder the family before them had moved out, with as much of a mansion as it was, as much of a sinkhole. Draining them, the whole family. Maybe these were punishments for moving into a place too big for a family, one that extended beyond their needs.

She left the back porch and stood for a minute in the library, one of the rooms that had been put well enough back into order. She looked over the books and pulled one of the older periodicals from a lower shelf where it didn't belong. The boys hadn't known how they'd been organized—she figured she would be finding little mistakes in them for months. Little reminders. As Laura stepped up on the shelves to place the periodical with the other old journals and books higher up, she saw, in the glass of her and her husband's diplomas, the outline of her reflection. The white windows behind her, the room a still life. A smudge of a woman, dwarfed by the gray shapes of the library.

A few days ago, one of the other teachers at Nick's school had offered to give them old ADT alarm stickers for the windows. Said he thought it might be enough to scare off any potential, returning intruder, without having to pay the monthly fees. "Burglars only go for the easiest houses in the neighborhood," Nick had told her before bed. "Why spend money we don't have to?"

Laura had asked him if he had mentioned to his friend at work that theirs had been no typical thief. "How much did you tell him, Nick?" she asked.

Nick went quiet. Sat down in bed and turned his keys in his hands. "I didn't tell him much, Laura."

They didn't speak that night until they had finished readying themselves for bed. With the lights turned out, Nick agreed to buy the whole system.

If only the repairs that needed to be done throughout the house could be finished, Laura would have it so that evening would never be mentioned again. Never acknowledged. The house repaired, her boys repaired, everything safe and accounted for, and forgotten. Laura hadn't even told her mother when she'd called earlier that afternoon. "Our summer's going well," Laura had told her. "Very hot, very busy. Lots and lots of projects. How are you?"

The security system wouldn't change much. But it was that button Laura wanted more than anything, that button she could press before bed. The one that lit the machine's screen blue, with the robotic voice she'd heard advertised in the video online that declared, loud enough to be heard through an entire first floor, "Doors and windows armed!" With the system, she wanted to give their house a voice. One that told them it was watching for others, instead of them.

Laura left the library and paused in the living room's doorframe. Both her sons sprawled on the same sofa, barefoot in shorts, watching television. Nick must have given them a break from the work upstairs.

She wondered if they should have taken TV away, too. They'd withheld allowance, banned Marshall from his computer, required of them a hundred hours of work in the house before the summer's end—and that was after they'd finished cleaning, repairing—but maybe they should have taken the TV, too. Laura hated that slack-eyed, sleepy look they made when they rewatched shows they'd already rewatched before. But seeing them there now, she realized maybe she'd been projecting that look of lethargy on their faces. That it wasn't actually there.

An alertness to them somehow, she couldn't explain it, a readiness to the way Marshall held the remote on the arm of the sofa, a tenseness to Eddie's posture, like he was paying attention to something completely different. Startling almost, once she'd noticed it, like turning around to find someone sneering at you. How long had her boys been this way? Was it something Traust—she hated that name—was it something he had done to them? Something he told her boys, a threat? Or was it something he did to them they weren't telling her? That they'd remember, and carry with them for the rest of their lives? Was this something she'd failed to notice, always had? Laura wanted to know now, to sit down on the sofa between them, to grab them against her, and take it wholly from them, whatever they knew. Let it all drain from them into her.

But she knew her boys. She knew they'd pull from her arms, turn their elbows out against her. If they told her what they were thinking, it would be of their own accord. She would have to wait. To be primed for a hesitation, a weight bogging down the middle of some daily perfunctory conversation, and to be there for them, receptive and open when finally they spoke to her. But also, she was their mother. There was shame in how she didn't know already.

"Hey," she said. "If I'm not down when the guy finishes, call up after me, okay?"

Nodding, not looking away from the television. A quick bobbing of the chins. Her boys had reached out to that man. Marshall had, and Eddie had known he had, but didn't tell her or their father. They'd been afraid here, in their own home, and they hadn't told her anything. They'd reached out to that man and not her.

Laura climbed the stairs, hearing the creak of the wood beneath her, the sound sinking down into the black beneath them. Unaccounted space, another one, hollow. Seemed like she was now always noticing them. The nest in the attic floor flashed through her mind. Had Traust left it there? Had it been her boys? These were her only options.

Laura found Nick in their bedroom, still wearing his paint-speckled pants, the container of plaster patch and a putty knife in his hands. He stood, head half-turned over his shoulder, as if caught by their television on his way to the bathroom. The glow of the set shimmered across the lens of his glasses. Another face looking away at a screen. She felt invisible in her own home, like a specter. That might be what she preferred right now.

"Laur," Nick said when she had passed by the bedroom through the hall.

"What is it?"

"Storm in the Gulf. Like we didn't have enough going on."

"Is it big?"

"The Gulf water's hot. Record high. Should be."

She stepped back into the doorway. "Coming at us?"

"Probably."

Laura nodded.

"Okay," she said. As if that was all that could be done. Acknowledge the next blow. Move on. She entered the bedroom and stood beside him to watch the forecast. He wrapped his arm around her waist, and she let him. Eventually, she lay her head on his shoulder. A tight red, rotating eye crossed over the Florida panhandle. What land should have killed, hadn't, the weatherman said. It'd get bigger.

"We've ignored our kids," she said.

"We've ignored a lot," he said. And after a moment: "Something would have happened. Eventually. Whether we left or not."

Laura didn't reply. Bad luck always in threes, the old wives' saying. Passed down for who knows how long. Laura had learned it when her father, her grandfather, and a school friend all passed when she was in high school. The same age as her boys now. Ever since then, when someone she loved died, she braced herself for the others. She counted the losses on her fingers when she was alone in the shower. Wrote their names in cursive into the droplets of water on the tile. She dreaded the threshold of four, which meant two more to come. But the death of loved ones, at least, was easy to count. How could she count what was happening to them now?

Laura imagined the house in a storm. Wind rattling the gutters.

The sky darkened outside. A leak in the roof somewhere, and the sound of dripping water. Downstairs, she heard the buzz of the workman's drill.

The weather station had cut to the ten-day forecast. Sunny and hot, until the uncertainty at the end. Lots of variables. "We'll see," Nick said.

He looked down and scraped the side of the putty knife clean against the container's lip. "You know, they will catch him," he said. "They've got his description. They know his truck. And they can track him on those forums."

Over a week. Enough time for the man to be anywhere. Laura only wished she could have seen him. Had a face and a body to give him. Not knowing made him worse in her imagination. He hardly seemed human.

"They'll find him," Nick said. "He won't ever come back here." But Nick knew no better than her, and she didn't know at all. The words her husband said meant nothing. Even so, Laura realized she wanted them. "You know," Nick said. "It actually could be good, if the storm hits. If it's small. It could be a time-out we need. Stay home from work. Hunker down as a family, light some lanterns when the power goes. Spend a couple hot days cleaning branches from the yard."

"We won't be staying if it hits," Laura said.

Nick was quiet. "Okay," he said.

After a few minutes, once the weather report turned to commercial, he talked broadly about evacuation plans. Casual conversation, as if going over ideas for a dinner they might have on an upcoming weekend. What they'd done before when they'd needed to leave. How a couple years ago, they drove up to her mother's, which wasn't bad. Nick spoke about how they could make a vacation out of it. Have time to talk on the way. Everyone. Enjoying themselves by getting away.

But already, in her mind, Laura was counting. Her fingers extending from her fist, pressing into her thigh. The man who came—Traust—the first. Two was the storm, if it hit. Three was something else, something coming or something that had been with them here all along. On the television, the weatherman gave his predictions. "They never come when we want them to."

"Okay," Laura said, though it was the last word she would use to describe what she felt. Her home had come unhinged. She was flailing, whipped around by the wind.

The house around her was its own continent. Every room outside of their own right now might as well have been its own ecosystem. Their children downstairs. The worker in the back porch installing the window sensors. The attic above them. The sudden hush after her husband pressed the button on the remote and turned the screen dark. For a brief second, they both heard a light creak from the floorboards in the hallway. Nick rubbed the side of her arm and went into the bathroom to wash off his tools.

"Okay," Laura said, and closed her eyes.

BELOW THE FLOOR

SHE FELT FEVERED, HER FOREHEAD SLICK WITH SWEAT, AND NAU-
sea that churned like her insides were changing positions. She was
hungry, but the thought of food made it all worse. She was thirsty,
but she was too tired to once again go through it all, to pull herself
up into the walls, to listen and wait as the Masons stomped through
their home, and find a moment to sneak into the first-floor bathroom
and drink from the sink.

Odin sat near her, hunched and cross-legged, his great knees jutting like boulders.

"You're dehydrated," he said.

I think you're right. She thought the words. Too risky to speak.

The god looked at her for a moment. He tugged at his long beard.

"So," he said. "What do you think that boy, your friend, is doing
now?"

You're the all-knowing. Shouldn't you know?

Odin shrugged.

The god traced the seams of the floorboards above them with the
tip of his large thumb. "Do you think," he asked her, "it was him that
called the fire department? If so, pretty clever, for a small boy. The
police came eventually, true. But firemen don't arrest a trespassing
girl if they're to find her first."

Elise didn't answer. Maybe it was Brody who called. Maybe it
wasn't. She didn't feel like bestowing any feelings of gratitude on
that thief, on the off chance he didn't deserve it. His fault she was
down here, in the dirt below her home. His fault that Eddie and

Marshall had come after her—that the man had come. His fault she was no longer safe anywhere, and that she'd lost her things, her parents' things, from her attic nook. And his fault she now heard them, the boys, calling out to her throughout the day after every noise they heard that wasn't her, telling her they know she's still there.

"But I'm not there!" she wanted to yell. "Wherever it is you think I am! I'm hardly even here!"

It was Brody's fault, and it was her fault for letting him in, for inviting him back and being weak, for forgetting who she had become.

"You're ill," Odin said.

I know.

"That boy might be able to help."

Don't care.

Someone walked directly above them through the living room and paused in front of the television. Shifted weight between his feet, making the same floorboard creak again and again. Mr. Nick.

"Still on track for us," he called out for the house to hear. He'd been doing it for a day and a half as he watched the hurricane's projected path, regular as the chiming of the bird clock above. He called out, sometimes a voice responded to his own, then he moved on. The world had changed above her, was changing.

"You need to get up," the god told her. "You need water. There's that poison down here still, I think. Lingering around. You need to get up. To move."

Part of the reason Elise wouldn't climb up was that, even when she was alone, when the Masons were asleep upstairs, she worried that the windows themselves had turned against her. That, out there beneath the calls of tree frogs, there was the revving of his engine. Whenever she bent to wash her face in the sink, she swore she could feel a hand once again wrapping around the tail of her hair. Elise worried that she was shrinking. The house growing beyond her reach. Before, she'd been strong and quiet enough to stretch out to its every corner and hold it, like the invisible force she learned in school that holds atoms together. Hold herself and her family there in it, retain them in its house's body, retain herself. Did she now? Elise raised her hands and laid her palms against the graying insulation above her.

I'm still here, Mom and Dad. I still remember you.

Elise had been having a hard time picturing what a future with her in it would look like. Wondering if she made a mistake becoming who she was now. If a girl in the walls loses her walls, she has nothing else.

"Do you wonder now, if Brody's family will evacuate?" the god asked, even though he knew Elise wouldn't answer.

Too tired, now. Arms and legs felt rotted.

Elise lay for some time, hunger pangs in her stomach aching, then going numb. She dozed off. But before she slept, she thought of a storm she had stayed through with her parents. How when the power went out, they'd had a cookout on the front porch while the rain streamed and the lawn turned dark with water. Sure, they lived by the levee, her mom had said, but the levee wouldn't break, and it wouldn't be easy for the river to top. The wind, even in its gusts, was more sound than danger, when they were inside.

And Elise's mom had been right. At the storm's end, the damage had been small: a broken porch window, overturned yard furniture, a layer of branches throughout the yard. In the last few hours before the clouds broke, Elise and her mom had scaled the levee in their raincoats. They had stood, with their arms outstretched, polyester rippling against them, and leaned into the wind, letting it support their bodies as they bent over the edge. Finally, the wind gave out, and they fell on their bellies into the dense, wet grass.

When this storm came, Elise would climb back into her home and watch through the upstairs windows. One storm is almost any other. Day turned to night, the rest of the world wiped away. One storm might be the same storm, circled back from the past. Why couldn't it? Spending years out at sea, degrading, and growing strong again. Returning. Now, more than she ever had before, Elise needed it to be.

A FATHER

EDDIE'S ROOM. THE PAINT-SPECKLED RADIO MUMBLING FROM THE hallway. Nick, standing on the desk, and the afternoon sun bright through the window outside. Cutting the holes in the plaster to shape them into neat rectangles, and replacing them with drywall. Nick knew he should have the boys here with him. He didn't need the help, but this was a process they should see. See how much, what kind of work goes into fixing damage. See, so they could do it one day themselves. A way to make something out of a disaster.

But instead, Nick wanted nothing more than to stay, working here, alone. This way it was easier to trick himself. To think he was making something better, healing more than a physical hole in the wall. Easier to think this way when he did the work by himself.

Two spots in the house where that man had tried to break through—where the walls had been wrecked. Nick couldn't help but wonder what made him try to get into the walls here in Eddie's room, and again in the office. If he'd been searching, wouldn't it have made more sense to knock holes, helter-skelter, throughout the entire house? "Pathological," Nick muttered under his breath. Shouldn't try to understand the reasoning. No point to try.

But, even so, before Nick placed the piece of drywall into the space he'd cut, and sealed off the opening, he found himself craning his head into the dark. Tried to see as far as he could, the musty smell rising into his nostrils. He pictured himself as that man, looking down into the walls. Imagined what had been going through his mind. Before Nick leaned back and out, he spoke into the space. Felt his voice, bloated, bouncing around his head. He said, "Leave my family the fuck alone."

Nick turned and made sure no one was in the doorway who heard him. He'd left his glasses in the bathroom while he worked, and Eddie's room was blurred at the edges, the details of objects indistinct. He squinted down at the drywall, drill, spackling, and lath laid out over his son's carpet.

What should he have done? No other father's boys he knew acted out in a way like this. Boys in the classes he taught could be ridiculous, even strange. But this? Nick wasn't sure what this was. His wife's voice in his mind: *Shouldn't have left them alone.* But you have to eventually. This was their home, too. Where else can you leave them?

Nick told himself words his own father had never said. But he figured these were ones the old man would tell him if he were still alive. How, with boys, you shelter them as best you can, but there's not much you can stop. Like too much liquid in too small of a glass, you can't keep it all from brimming. You deal with the outcome, once it comes.

You so sure about that? His wife's voice again in his head.

No. Nick wasn't sure what he believed.

He knew that it wasn't fair how much they had to do, to maintain, just to live in this house. Nick was getting tired. Too many days stacking up. Yesterday's fatigue weighed heavy on him, and that of the day before. In a few hours, it'd be time to get ready for bed, but there was still so much left to do. So much always left to do. The radio crackled from the hallway—another news report. He wondered if any of his family had noticed he'd begun leaving lamps on throughout the house at night.

Nick stepped down from the desk. He thought to himself, get over it. Get over yourself.

"Marshall," he called out. "Marshall, you in your room?"

His son murmured something he couldn't make out.

"Go find your brother," Nick said. "And both of y'all come here. I want to show you two how you fix a hole in the wall."

How you make something out of it.

EDDIE AND MARSHALL

AFTER DARK, WHEN THE HEADLIGHTS OF CARS SWEPT SHADOWS across the ceilings, the family, drowsy, listened to the house around them. And when they were asleep, they dreamt of listening. Three hundred miles away, the eye of a mid-summer hurricane pivoted on its axis, directed by fingertips of wind, drinking strength from the warm Gulf water. Behind the levee, the river was already feeling the pull, the minor dips of barometric pressure—before even the birds and insects register the signs, it's there in the water—the small siphon.

Footsteps in the house, a door opening and shutting again, a body fumbling in the dark. Not her—she had always been more careful. The sounds coming from the boys' shared bathroom. From his bed, Marshall watched through the dim as the door creaked open an inch to hold there. Hard to tell whether it opened farther, the sharp corner of the door muddied by the dark. Slowly, every passing second another centimeter. Or just his imagination. Marshall pulled the blankets off him and rolled over, away from the door, to face the wall.

"Just get in here," he said, as he had every night before, since the day the man had come.

Eddie crawled into bed with his brother, pulled the blanket up around their necks. Squeezed beside one another on the twin-size mattress. Eddie's eyes found patterns in the ceiling's texture. Thirteen- and sixteen-year-old brothers, sharing a bed. They tried not to think of their ages. This wouldn't have to last forever, they knew.

"We're going to be okay," Marshall said. He said it to the wall, and for a second Eddie wondered whether he intended to say it for her as well.

But it was late. And the younger brother was too tired to ask.

Was it stupid to think of her that way? Beside him, the mountainline of his brother beneath the blankets. Even if the pressure of a body near him made Eddie tense, made him too aware of the veins in his neck and arms, of the other person's skin just there, it was still good to have his brother near. In case some noise woke Eddie in the night, it was good to be able to look over, and hear him breathing, and know, without a doubt, he was okay.

"Get some sleep," Marshall said, and the world fell away to senselessness.

WHAT'S MOST IMPORTANT

PHOTO ALBUMS OF THE BOYS. PICTURES OF MARSHALL BEFORE HE HAD HIS curls cut, of Eddie in cowboy boots, half-hidden behind a pine tree, refusing to come fully into view. Mr. and Mrs. Mason when they were only Nick and Laura at college, in cap and gown in front of the university's oaks and parapets. Photos of their own parents as children, black-and-white, sleepy-eyed, with priceless resemblances in the point of a chin or squinting eyes to themselves and their boys.

Documents in the lockbox in the parents' bedroom closet, social security cards, birth certificates, tax forms, and flood and fire and life insurance policies. Other papers that are unclear whether they can be replaced or not, whether they are necessary or not.

What else is important?

Are old report cards? Old arts and crafts, macaroni glued to paper plates in the shape of the words, "I love you"? Old stuffed rabbits, bears, and penguins, tucked in attic boxes, whose soft, worn bodies still awaken some pang in an adult's chest? Is the new knife set, the expensive one given last Christmas, important? A favorite, earmarked book? An antique quilt?

Not enough space for everything. Each thing becomes a shackle. One thing in means another out.

The need for practical things: duffel bags of a week's clothes, toiletries, and a container of gas in the trunk in case stations run out along the way. How obscene it is to picture toothpaste, baby powder, and toilet paper taking space in a car when so much will need to be left inside. The cartop carrier was already full, and seats need to be empty to hold people. A long drive to Indiana, and hotels will be full throughout the South. Their bodies need space to stretch and shift. Their bodies are objects, too.

Tell Marshall that an old catcher's mitt will be okay to stay at home, and that it's ridiculous to pack a computer tower. Tell Eddie that books can be replaced, as can an old Nintendo system—he doesn't even play it anymore. Tell one another for old 45 rpm records, a potted plant gifted from a deceased friend, for the large framed series of wedding photos—there are duplicates in the albums, for sure.

Tell yourself things that make you happy are not things you need to live. A shoebox of mementos that, over time, had crawled far beneath the bed. Letters from a grandmother. The house itself, with everything wrong with it, with all its hours of work. A house is a receptacle for everything else. It is only the container. It doesn't leave.

Which car—a mother's or a father's?

Whose is worth more?

Whose is worth more to us?

Certain windows will need to be boarded. Electrical cords unplugged. Every interior door closed to create barriers within the barriers. What remains must be given every chance to survive, even though the packing, by its nature, says, "I will survive losing you."

THE WHOLE WORLD WAKING

EVENTUALLY, THE SKY'S BLUE BECAME MARRED BY THE FIRST bands of gray clouds. The trees shifted in their stances, and the birds had gone. Crickets leaped, unmolested, through the lawn like miniature bottle rockets, yet the throbbing hum of cicadas had evaporated. When exactly had they gone quiet? The calm before a storm is a falsehood, a fiction. Electricity already simmered in the air.

The Masons' home, like the other houses in the neighborhood, began to echo with the hammering of windows being boarded. The sound unified the houses even through and over trees, overgrown fields, small pastures of horses, goats, and cows. The house trailers farther down the road had already been abandoned. Their owners hadn't bothered to take in their lawn chairs and potted plants—in their vulnerable homes, inside was as good as out. Stablemen loaded their horses into their trucks and drove down the rough, unpaved paths toward the levee road, while their animals looked placidly out, manes lifting in the breeze. No tugboats on the river. Their crewmen had docked the barges to the batture and had gone home to ready their families for the storm.

Commonplace for South Louisiana, as much as something like this could be. Ritualized. This storm was big, though, different in scale and wind speed—late-night satellite imaging showed a clear and defined eye that looked like it might as well belong to the entire world. Its path grew focused. Odin's lost eyeball, returned, with a vengeance. The eye of the world coming to find her. It rolled across the Gulf, pivoting up to their river.

Those who had lived here long knew their options. Same as those who'd moved south of the lake less than a year past. Stay or leave. There are risks either way. To leave meant there was no way to stop small damages from becoming larger catastrophes. A broken window wouldn't be blocked off by spare wood or a table turned on its side, a small fire couldn't be stifled. But to stay meant other risks. Meant you might not be found. There's precedent for these things. The roof might cave in. The storm surge might buckle and carry a house's walls wholly into the fields around it. Nothing to remain but the splinters of its foundation. Those who stayed inside: either escaped or lost.

In Brody's home, down the wooded road, his uncle returned home from his work to tell them they were hunkering down. Their house was short and small, but it was brick. The property was far— a half-mile—from the levee, which he said would be topped when the storm surge came. The woods all around them would drink the floodwaters. They'd bring the dogs inside, keep the mean one locked in the kitchen, and they'd stay and wait it through. And if the water still came, they all would climb into the small of their attic. Brody's uncle had already placed an axe up there. If the water still came, he'd cut through the wood of their roof.

Brody's aunt went into town and stocked up on canned foods and bottled water, batteries for radio and flashlights. While his uncle boarded windows, Brody tried to leave, to walk around their neighborhood. But his aunt told him this was no normal day, and the last thing they needed to worry about was him coming home late, because this storm was coming to them, and she didn't want him to disappear out there before the storm came. He might not find his way back.

NO PLACE IS SAFE

"ASSUMING A PLACE IS SAFE," SAID ODIN, "IS TO BELIEVE THE WORLD doesn't change, and that the people don't change in it. To know a place is to know that it is dying. With each instant, it is slipping loose from your grip. Your hands will chafe to hold it."

My hands are callused. Elise looked them over in the gloom.

"I'm telling you that you should get out now. I'm realizing you should have left long ago. I forgot who, and what, you are. Use the storm as an excuse for you now."

Elise snorted. Or, she imagined herself snorting. She dreamed it. She no longer made any noises now. She hardly breathed. The world she saw existed on the insides of her eyelids. Its sounds were ghosts through the hair of her inner ears.

"Look," Odin said. "Once, a thousand years ago, when I was still a young man, I climbed the thick base of the World Tree and tore free one of its branches. I wanted to plant the branch in the soil for it to grow, to make my own World Tree, one that was safe and separate. For me, and under my rule alone. It didn't work."

Trees don't work that way. They don't grow that way.

"What do you know about magic trees?" he said. "It had nothing to do with how regular trees do and don't work. It had to do with me."

Odin knelt down beside her, the striations of wrinkles in his cheeks like long scars. The hollow where his eye had been was its own eye now, only reversed, turned inward. "I planted the branch in the marsh, and the bark turned to plaster, glass, and brick. Its own branches soon sprouted and spread into a canopy so thick it stood impervious to the rain and wind. Its base was firm, and it would never bend or rot. It would never turn to mud within that marsh. It would never fall."

What was the problem?

"I wasn't ready. I was young. And I realized to build a home like that, as strong as it was, is to build a monolith to death. To build myself a grave. I was nowhere near ready for that. One night I broke the branches of my home to splinters. I buried it all in the soil, in a place that's since been drowned and washed away."

Odin continued: "You know, you'll never stop missing them. No matter where you are, how old you are. But hurt gets softer. Quieter, I think. You'll be an old woman, and you'll still hold them in you, in that hurt."

Why would anyone just throw it away? Of course, you could. But why would anyone else? You'd be just fine, because you're you. I won't live forever like you.

"No," said Odin. "No. I'll die."

She could tell he'd become frustrated. The god shook his head, white beard tossing. "It's my fault you're not understanding any of this. Everyone dies, eventually." Odin sprawled on the soil beside her and laid his hands across his old face. "But that you'll die, too?" His voice caught in his throat. "That's what I can't stand."

REMAINING

THE NIGHT BEFORE THE MASONS LEFT, THEY SAT TOGETHER IN THE living room. They stayed there with the news until late, the robins calling, then the mockingbird. They'd loaded their car earlier that afternoon. Holes in the wall had been patched, but the spackle needed painting. Scratches in the floor remained unbuffed. Carpet still torn. They were leaving a house in half-repair. That evening, when they had spoken to one another, their voices were worn at the edges, muffled as if under a quilt and bedsheets. After the eleven o'clock weather update, Mr. Nick woke the boys from where they sat and sent them off to bed. He woke them again in their beds long before sunrise. They left soon after. When Elise awoke, she couldn't tell how long they'd been gone.

She pulled herself into the walls and journeyed up through the home. The air was better here. Her forearms and fingers were weak, the back of her throat still ached, but the noise of her own body working against the walls energized her.

"A spider monkey!" Brody had once called her, and she felt that way again. He'd said it one day after she'd shown him the old, hidden laundry chute. She had first shown him the bottom, the space behind the painted tree. And while he squinted up into the dark, Elise had challenged him to see if he could find where the chute opened up before she climbed to it herself. Brody's lips curled into a grin, and he sprinted upstairs, pounding around, while Elise scaled the chute, hands and feet pressed against opposite sides, shimmying herself up.

Before she made it halfway up, she heard the boy knocking against the loose board at the back of the bathroom cabinet. She saw him appear, a halo of light around his face. His smile opened into a look of shock.

"What! You're just hanging there!" Brody said. "In the air! You're amazing!" And she'd felt that way, even though he'd won.

Now, Elise drank a glass of cool water from the kitchen faucet. She poured herself a bowl of cereal (Cheerios—thank God). Good enough, even with no milk—the half-gallon the Masons usually kept had been thrown out. While Elise ate, she leaned back in her chair at the kitchen table, balancing it on two legs. She refilled the bowl and carried it into the living room. While the sun rose, she watched television with the volume nearly at its max, infomercials then cartoons. Elise wanted to feel swallowed by each show, like she could turn around and see the illustrated land or cityscape behind her. Every fifteen minutes, in sync with the tones of the clock, the emergency broadcast system trailed across the bottom of the screen, a red banner with white text declaring mandatory evacuations for the southern parishes—Plaquemines, Lafourche, St. Bernard.

When the winds came, the sound was a massive tarp dragged across the yard. The light through the windows was half-formed through the clouds. Raindrops along the windowpanes gathered into small streams. Elise cooked macaroni and cheese for lunch and then lay on the library sofa, listening to Marshall's old Walkman. In the parents' bathroom, she took a long, warm bath, and watched the overhead bulb flicker, once, twice. The power stayed for now.

Elise napped in the living room recliner, and when she awoke, she microwaved the rest of the macaroni for her dinner. By eight that evening, sunset shouldn't have been for over an hour, but it was as dark as late night. The wren called out lonely from the foyer.

"I'm still here," she answered.

RISING

PEACE AT NIGHT IS A PRIVILEGE, SHE KNEW. THERE'S NOTHING about the dark that guarantees sleep. That night, Elise would not sleep at all, not for one moment. In each flash of lightning, she saw the trees tortured. Between each roar of thunder, she listened to them scream. The oak branches whipped around themselves into extreme angles. The spindly tallow tree bent until the top of its trunk bobbed into a black sheen of water. *How could the sky hold so much rain?* In a single gust, branches broke loose from the trees with the sound of gunfire. They beat against the house like massive fists.

The power had been out since ten that evening, but her birds still sang. Elise didn't hear them beneath the wind and the rain, but she knew they must be there. The cardinal, the starlings, the wren. She couldn't be alone. Outside, she saw the dark shapes rising beyond the levee. Barges, left docked along the batture, ascended with the swelling river. Lightning flashed, and she saw water brimming the levee like a tub overflowing.

Thrashing against the top of the house, loose branches turned into airborne torpedoes, the whole sky was the inside of a tornado. What must be the dormer window shattering above. Elise paced the hallway, the sound of her footsteps swallowed by the noise outside, the windows in all the rooms clattering at her. The scented candle she'd taken from the office, she had held cupped between her hands. But it had gone out. The house shook. She worried the roof would pull free. She ran down the stairs.

"I don't know where to go!" Elise screamed. A little girl's voice.

Floodwater bled in through the crack beneath the front door.

THE RIVER IS A GOD ARISEN

OKAY TO CRY.

The floodwater increasing, and the floor of the home changing into a swamp. The wind outside: a train raging on its tracks, its horn relentless, the sound throttling even the insides of her body. But safer here than anywhere else. Safer on the first floor, in the now rising water. Didn't seem real, but it was true: the wind might yet tear the second story from the building.

Elise walked through the rooms, hoping some part of the house could save her. The insides of the walls? No, they would flood as well.

Better to stay in the open. In the library. From where she sat on the sofa she could see the shape of the bird clock in the foyer. There, squatting in the dark, rising water. There it was, still, along with her.

The water felt cold against her feet, but she kept them on the floor. Measured the rising water against her ankles and legs. This was important, she sensed.

She waited. Waited until the water reached her knees, then she'd have to move. The windows might break around her, and the door might be thrown open, but she'd deal with those as they came. But until the water lapped against her knees—when that came, she'd wade for the staircase. Go to the next best place that would give her a chance to survive. Adjust when the space around her changes. And, if need be: cry.

Why not? Yell and scream, too! Let the whole world hear!

The house shook, and books from the bottom shelves rose and floated in the coal-black water around her. The water had become a living thing. But still she stayed—only at her calves. Her toes grew numb, and the chill rose through her legs and waist, but the quilt behind her was dry. She pulled it over her shoulders. As long as the water stayed, she'd be okay. The walls were strong here—she knew this old house well enough.

"Are you taking me home?" Elise shouted into the dark. "Taking me with you?"

She kept her feet in the water. If it rose too quickly, if it lapped against her knees, she'd need to climb the stairs. She told herself the sound outside was no more different than New Year's fireworks. Okay to be afraid. The whole world was being re-formed, but her mom and her dad—as always, still there with her.

MORNING

SHE WATCHED THE SKY FROM HER PARENTS' OLD BEDROOM. THE clouds hung around like inverted hills, but their gray had begun to fracture, outlined with blue and cantaloupe orange. The wind, through the open window, felt as cool as fall across her face. The world had been wasted. Gnarled, broken branches broke the surface of the yard's brown water like the twisting bodies of sea snakes. The trees had lost height from the bottom of their trunks. Strips of the house's siding had peeled free and dangled, bobbing in and out of the flood. The gutter beneath her window was gone, missing. The only sound was the lapping of the water.

Not far off, one of the river barges had broken free of its docking chains and now perched, massive as a train, on the length of the levee. Nearly teetering over the side. Elise realized that if the river had risen higher, the barge would have flowed fully over, swept across the road through the trees and yard. Through her house, maybe, too. Last night, she'd no idea how close that possibility was.

The downstairs had completed its transformation; the outside reached inside. The swamp had climbed four of the staircase steps—waist high for her—but by morning it seemed to be slowly descending. Eventually, Elise had needed to climb to the second story when the floodwater rose, and up there, she found that the attic had been leaking, with water trickling down its stairs into the hall. Elise spent the night in Mr. and Mrs. Mason's bed, with their blankets pulled over her head. With her eyes closed, it might as well have been any bed. From any time.

Over the course of the morning, Elise opened all the second-story storm windows. No worries about mosquitoes and other insects—for now, they must have been washed away by the water and wind. Her birds in the clock had gone quiet. The storm had taken them, too. Elise felt their absence through every part of her body. She was alone in the world, and it seemed nothing else had survived. Had she survived? Was this an afterlife?

When Elise needed breakfast, she waded through the downstairs water. The pressure of the flood had pushed the front door wide open. In the living room, her legs heavy through the water, she plodded past the flotsam. She noted the objects that floated: pillows, plastic picture frames, a table lamp on its side, a vase, VHS tapes, the television remote. There were other things that hadn't floated, that existed only as the outlines of forms, things she felt with her feet beneath the surface.

In the kitchen, the cabinets and pantry doors had spilled open, and she passed among the tin pots, sodden boxes of ice cream cones and taco shells, spices, a Tupperware tube of pasta noodles, and packets of chili powders—each half-obscured by the dark water and dipping below the surface as she neared them. She sloshed into the pantry and pulled herself up on the shelves. Up there, she found only a box of uncooked rice, three-quarters empty. The rest had fallen in. Elise popped the top and poured the dry rice into her mouth, trying her best to chew. Below her, a jar of peanut butter lid-up in the water, and she twisted it open and swallowed three fingerfuls. Then she went upstairs and dried off, falling across Mr. and Mrs. Mason's bed, their bedsheets her towel. Elise lay on her back, limbs outstretched, her body open to the broken house around her, and she dozed. Slept for the first time since yesterday morning. Dreamless from exhaustion.

And when she woke, she stayed in bed for a while. Wondered what it was like for the city. How was that new house? The one she and her parents had lived in for a few months, that never felt like home. Their furniture seeming awkward and out of place in the new rooms, the cardboard boxes full of their things still unpacked, until the end. Elise wondered whether the flood had washed away that antiseptic smell that clung to the building, the house's uncomfortable, unplaceable newness. She figured some new family had already moved in there by now. Her and her parents' old things shipped off to some now-flooded dump.

Elise wondered how the storm was for others in her neighborhood. Earlier that morning, she'd looked out to make sure Ms. Wanda's house had made it fine through the storm, and that the woman wasn't still home, in danger. Her land, beyond the field, was on slightly higher ground, and the water hardly reached above the bricks on which her house sat. Elise had never asked Brody what his own house was like—whether it was two or one story, if it were raised on bricks or stilts. She wished she had. Elise hoped he and his aunt, and even the uncle he said he hated, had made it out safe.

Elise wished she had someone else to talk to now, to talk about the storm, to say—what?—that it had felt like a dream, like the inside of a whirlwind, and that everything after didn't seem as real as before. This wasn't the first time Elise had felt this way. Maybe this was aging, growing up. She clenched her teeth. A progression of hells, of fires and storms that make the world seem less and less like the one you thought you knew.

After noon, the air had once again grown hot and humid. The sun-glinted water remained across the front yard to the levee. For some reason, Elise figured that the river, hidden from her view, flowed backward now. She got out of bed and instinctively flipped the switch to turn on the overhead fan. Didn't work.

Duh. Would have been more concerning if it had. She smelled the house's dampness—like a rotting log. Any electricity here might start a fire.

Elise twisted in place and stretched her torso. She must not have moved at all in her nap. It looked as though she'd slept for a couple hours. She raised an arm and smelled an armpit.

"Yeesh."

Her whole body was basted in sweat. The bedsheets would reek of her, she realized. Would the Masons notice?

"They won't," she said.

If they did, they'd probably think it was an animal. Some raccoon that made its way inside during the storm to find shelter that spent a night in their bed. Or else, well, maybe they would think it was her. Did she care anymore if they knew? Would they care? With the house flooded, Elise considered that she might go ahead and sit up in the window to wave at them as they drove in. She figured they had bigger problems than her. At least for a while.

HOMEOWNER

BUT THE DAY WAS DRIFTING BY, AND EVENTUALLY, INSECTS AND vermin would return from wherever they had hidden during the storm. Soon enough, they'd fill every room of her house. Mosquitoes bouncing against the ceilings. Tadpoles swirling in the cones of fallen lampshades. Frogs and snakes nestled between the couch cushions. Her house was still soggy as a wet sponge.

"Standing, though," she said. "Let's keep it that way."

Elise went downstairs, back into the water, to the laundry room circuit breaker. She'd never been in a flooded house before, but she'd been in hurricanes. The lights had always come back on a day or two after the winds died down. This storm might have been different, though. And lying around in the heat, with nothing much else to do, was great inspiration to think of hypothetical reasons for ways her house might yet still be broken. Elise tried to think like an adult, and she figured she couldn't have electricity returned to walls that were still filled and saturated with water.

She'd never opened the circuit-breaker box before, but she'd been there with her father a couple times after a fuse had gone out. She'd never looked into the box, only had seen the front of the metal cover swung open and her father's grim face as he looked over its insides. She figured it must have been filled with wires and complex, colored bulbs. But instead, when Elise opened the cover, she saw small, black switches. Nothing much to it. The simple, red handle on the side seemed obvious enough to pull.

"Voilà," Elise said. She had no idea whether that would even help anything—the likelihood that the power would be restored any time this week, or month maybe, might be expecting too much. But there was satisfaction in knowing that she'd taken care. She felt that her dad would be proud. Nearby, the board he had painted with the tree had come loose with the rising water, a corner jutting free like a hand gone rigid in the act of beckoning.

After, in the kitchen pantry, Elise found a collection of submerged, plastic-wrapped water bottles, and she knocked back two of them in a row. Dropped the empty bottles to the water's surface. The trash can didn't seem to hold much of a purpose right now. The floodwater felt cool against her legs, and Elise bent over and splashed it against her face and hair. Dirty water—she could imagine her mother raising her eyebrow at this particular decision—but the cool moisture felt good running down her shoulders and back.

Elise went again through all the rooms of her house. *Every branch of the World Tree.*

So different now, first floor half-submerged, but with the same floorplan, her walls all in the same places as they'd always been. Ruined but, in a way, more like her home than it had been in a long time. The quiet of the water dripping from the insides of the cabinets. The breeze, which sent the loose siding tapping against the outside walls.

Her home. Her big, dying home.

THE WORLD ENDS

ELISE HAD BEGUN TO THINK OF THE COMING NIGHT, WHETHER SHE should close the windows, seal off the home as much as she could, or embrace the break in liminality, recognize that, for now, inside and outside had joined. Tuck herself into a garbage bag, to prevent the insect bites. Pitch a small fire on the front porch tile. Become a wild girl inside her own home. There was no telling how long until the Masons returned, but it might yet be days. Roads, when drained and opened, would be clogged with sedans and trucks, cars with their trunks bungee-corded shut. Dead-eyed traffic lights. Roofing nails littering the asphalt. Elise might as well grow comfortable in the solitude. She'd have to do something about food soon, though. About clean water.

But as she once again stepped out of the flood to climb the staircase, she heard, outside, the rushing of a current, a single wave with one continuous cresting. The sound grew louder—and Elise went to the front door to look. It took a while for the source of the sound to break past the trees that bordered the yard, to enter into her view. The first of the vehicles returning after the storm. Its engine rumbled, transmission belts soaked and squealing.

When Elise saw the truck coming, she could tell it should have waited longer, for the floodwaters to drop more. It shouldn't have been driving that road. Waves splashed gray against the truck's sides, licking the door handles. Its windows rolled completely down—the inside cabin must have been soaked. If the driver so much as pressed on his brakes, the wake of the truck would catch up and sink its bed, cabin, and engine.

It was now that Elise knew where the truck would stop. It didn't turn into her driveway. But it had intended to. Didn't make it that far. The engine choked and gave out, stalling on the road just in front of her home. But close enough. The driver unbuckled himself. Fumbled with something in his passenger seat. The wake caught up, swirled around the big, black truck, leaked through the windows, continued down the road beyond him. Traust.

He'd come back. The first to return—he must have outlasted the storm nearby, close enough to return as soon as he had. Waiting through wind and lightning and flood, to come and find her.

Elise backed into the foyer. The man jumped out of his truck with a splash. Elise turned. She had to find somewhere to hide.

Not enough time to be quiet. Even so, Elise swallowed the urge to scream.

RETURN

MONTHS BEFORE, ON THE WINTER MORNING WHEN ELISE HAD RE-
turned to her home, cold air fogged all of the windowpanes. The
lawn's dry grass crunched beneath her. Her feet aching from miles of
night-time asphalt, from the roadside debris she hadn't seen that jutted into the soles of her shoes. The cold wind permeating her coat—
more than once, she'd wished she'd taken the blanket from the foster
home bed, to have thrown over her shoulders as she walked.

Elise had entered her yard as a thief would. Furtive glances over
her shoulder. Careful of the angles of sight from the road. Calculat-
ing the row of azalea bushes, the low-hanging branches of a magnolia
tree, an outcropping of the house so that they might block her from
sight as she found her way inside. Between the curtains and half-
closed window blinds, she had seen the living room's Christmas tree
had been decorated, its lights left off. No sign of movement within.

Behind her, the world had sidled behind the pampas grass, beneath
the lip of the levee. Playing the child's game Red Light, Green Light.
Elise had circled the house, palms pressed against the windowpanes
and pushing skyward. The glass moaned as her hands slid uselessly up.
She had turned doorknobs, jerking them with her wrist and rattling
them.

BRIDGING THE GAPS

AS ELISE SEARCHED FOR A PLACE TO HIDE, THIS TIME AFTER HER house had been flooded, with Traust returned, the memory of that day nagged like déjà vu. Like she'd been brought back, as if reminded by a singular, familiar smell. Her mind now in three places.

Past, searching for where her old house could take and cradle her. Present, where she searched for a place to hide. And she was also with Traust. Picturing what he now saw, wading through her yard, and climbing the submerged front porch steps.

Traust had come to break into her home, as Elise had before him. But the doors were not closed or locked. There was no one else around to hide from. So much easier for him. They were alone together. He needed only to step in.

ENTER

SHE HEARD HIM IN THE FOYER. HE TOOK LARGE STRIDES; HE LIFTED his legs high out of the water and stabbed them back below. Into the living room, where she'd been, turning in place a few moments before. Passing the dining room, with its tumbled chairs and water-logged piano. Into the kitchen. His body sent ripples through all the water in the house. Elise heard the pans and pots that floated in the kitchen clink against the flooded cabinet doors. His legs pushed through a sea of things; she imagined him gliding—his shoulders hunched, hands swimming through the air, head bobbing side to side. He elongated in her mind, his eyes becoming lidless, lips folding back to reveal the teeth. He turned back and climbed the stairs, boots dripping with each step.

When he spoke, he bellowed to her from above. He spoke to her as if they'd been speaking the whole time. "You remember the storm's eye?" he told her. "Brief here—I think. Only truly caught the edge of it. Must have lasted fifteen minutes where I was."

Elise heard him up in the attic, his boots, the heavy thump of the plywood floor being once again removed and thrown aside. The volume of his voice increased when he spoke down into the crevice that led into the walls.

"It was that—what's it called? That respite. You remember? When there was no wind or rain. When everything went so still. You know, it's that time we have to be most careful. Heard too many stories of people going outside during the eye, seeing the sky go clear with the moon and stars, and thinking the storm over. Then they get caught in the eyewall winds. One hundred fifty, two hundred miles an hour."

He was crouching up there in the attic, just talking to her.

"I was almost tempted to get out of the truck myself. Wanted it to be over! Even if I knew better. I'd watched the whole thing—that rain and lightning—all through my windshield. And I didn't think I'd make it through the second half. We did, though."

She heard him groan as he rose to his full height.

"Can you hear me? Do you know what I'm talking about, with the eye? Maybe you didn't notice. So much flooding here, I guess you might have been distracted."

In the laundry chute, Elise held herself above the water of the first floor, suspended in the dark, her hands and feet tucked into her crevices. It was a hundred degrees or more inside the walls. Sweat beaded on her forehead and gathered on her eyelashes and lips. Traust came back down the attic stairs. He had his toolkit. She heard him rummaging through it.

"You think I don't understand why you need to hide. I could ask you a hundred thousand times to come out, and I know you won't. Because, you well know, I've asked you a hundred thousand times already. In my own home, and in others. And you've never once listened."

When Elise had nightmares as a little girl, she'd pull herself from bed and go down the hall into her parents' bedroom. If they were asleep, she wouldn't wake them. She'd crawl halfway beneath their bed, feetfirst, her upper body exposed to the room. She'd lie there, the coarse carpet prickling her cheek as her parents breathed above her. Other times, if something frightened her when her parents were away, and her sitter was asleep in the living room with the television on, Elise would sit still and wait. If what frightened her couldn't hear her, it wouldn't find her.

Traust did not tap on the walls, as he had before. He knew the house now. He came up and down the stairs. He'd go quiet, for what must have been five minutes, ten minutes. Elise would only hear when he coughed or cleared his throat.

She wanted to yell at the man. Scream at him.

Who do you think I am? Why won't you leave me alone?

WHY HE HUNTS HER

THIS IS WHAT HE BELIEVES: THERE'S A GREAT SPINE TO THIS WORLD, and it's twisting beneath his feet. Rearranging what he sees. Keeping them always out of view. But every second, he knows: he's closer. He stood in the upstairs hallway, where his voice carried best. There, he told her:

Remember that woman who swears she has you, too? That you hide yourself in a suitcase she keeps in the back of her closet? And when she hears you, or thinks she hears you, she drags it out and kicks you. Kicks until her toenails have gone bloody. Until her throat's all torn from the yelling. Or that old man who says you're using his wife's perfume? That stuff he's kept in her nightstand drawer since she's passed. But now, with her gone, he's still smelling it.

When I went, he told me—he said this!—that one day, when he knows for sure you're there, he'll lock you in. He'll board all the doors and windows shut. Set the house on fire.

When I went there, to both those homes, you weren't in either. I looked and prodded. Pulled back their insulation. Ripped off the tops of their suitcases. Took their dressers all apart. Cut open the mattresses and the backs of all the couches, whether they wanted it or not. Anyone else would have to wonder if they'd been making the whole thing up.

You know, I've got so much I need from you.

Remember when I was a kid, how I'd lie in my bed and tell you that, someday, you won't snicker at me? Remember how, eventually, my parents came back to the holes I hammered in the four walls of every room in that awful house? But I'd already left. Because you'd left, too,

All those houses we've gone to! I used to pretend, when looking for others like you. I'd fix those houses' wiring, put in their overhead fans, check their circuit breakers. But, each time, every day, when I got the chance I'd squint into the closets and under the beds.

Listen, I tell you that finding you here is for us. All of us, like me. To know we're okay. And that these thoughts we've had—they're real. We're not alone. Not a single one of us is.

You're in there. You're holding tight.

I figure I'll have to tear you piecemeal.

MR. TRAUST REMOVES THE WALLS

HE BEGAN WITH THE HAMMER, PUNCHING INTO THE DINING ROOM WALL AND pulling at the space behind with a crowbar. The noise overwhelmed her. Water splashing as the plaster came loose, the blows and the wrenching, his grunting and curses. Elise safe in the chute for now, but he was tearing open the walls of her home. He roared as he pulled. He shouted out, saying he would find her. Traust went around to the library—closer now—and she heard him shoveling books by the armful into the water. He hammered at the slots of wall between the shelves.

"I will rip apart every board and fiber of this house until I find you," Traust said.

He was in the laundry room. The walls shaking, and in the chute, particulate fell around her, across her shoulders and face. Caught at the back of her throat.

"I will pull you from them," he said.

Elise held in place. So close to her, but now working back, away, toward the stairs. Trying to pull the wood away to look into the dark beneath them.

Sweat in the cracks along her palms, the webbing between her fingers. Elise supported herself in the chute, holding tighter to the walls on either side, keeping her fingers from slipping. She pictured herself, for a second, as Atlas, holding the world still.

This place was hers.

Elise clenched her teeth. Her muscles in her hands and fingers ached. But this was her old game, she told herself. There were rules. If she didn't move, he'd never find her.

STAY AWAY

PAST THE FLOODED LAWN AND FIELD, THE WOODS WERE BROKEN: cypresses snapped at their waists, deciduous leaves stripped bare, skeleton trees and spiraled, drifting deadfalls.

A dead place, except for him, Brody, already on his way. He turned from his damaged house—windows broken and the linoleum wet and the wood cabinets ghost-white and puckering, the shed partly caved from a fallen tree—and he left for the woods. His aunt and uncle were preoccupied by the broken glass and tree limbs, by covering small holes in the roof with a tarp.

Once Brody passed the tree line, he pressed on over fallen trunks and flattened underbrush, needing to forge new paths through, difficult ones, circling back long ways before being free to move forward again. At times, it was easy to lose his way, since his markers were all gone, or changed. The squinting-eye tree split in half. The empty eagle's nest vanished. Eventually, he found the waterline, where the elevation of the undeveloped land began to dip. He waded bodily into the flood, soaking his overalls. His bare feet had to feel their way over branches and roots in the gray water. He worried about snakes and snapping turtles beneath the surface.

"Get away," Elise had told him, but Brody had been to her house every day since. Just outside. Just beyond the line of trees, trying to see her if he could. "Get away" didn't mean he couldn't try to catch a glimpse of her through the windows. "Get away" meant nothing if he found that her ceiling had come down, and she'd been buried by it. If she'd broken a wrist, the bone snapped and jutting white through the skin of her forearm. If she'd stepped on broken glass, the foot swollen, wound turned purple from the brown water.

Brody looked out across a field and yard submerged in water, a marsh. The house beaten and flooded, shingles blown away, siding slashed like from the claws of a tiger. They'd been hit worse than his house. The Masons' car was still gone from the driveway—she was alone in there. Brody climbed on a fallen trunk and sat there awhile, the clouds above floating on. He heard what sounded like someone's voice, and for a moment he thought it was his uncle, shouting for him to come back and pounding the sides of trees with a hammer. It was hard to tell which direction the sound came from. Ms. Wanda's house? But her car was gone, too.

Brody shielded his eyes from the sun and squinted at the girl's house. The windows all pulled open. Upstairs, the shape of someone moving in the dim inside. There was no one else it could be.

"Get away" meant nothing to him anymore. The world had flooded, had changed. The rules changed. He'd check on her. He'd make sure she was okay.

SAFESPACE

THE LAUNDRY CHUTE WAS HERS, A WALL WITHIN THE WALLS.

Two exits, below and above. Only two ways to escape. But that meant only two entrances, too. Harder to find. Somehow, the one above worried her more, behind the stacks of toilet paper in Mr. and Mrs. Masons' bathroom cabinet. As if the obviousness of the downstairs tree painting made it safe. Traust was searching for something hidden. The board with the tree wasn't hiding. She thought of it as the sort of protective rune a Norse god might carve.

Traust took his hammer to the upstairs hallway floorboards, but he wasn't breaking through. She heard him smashing the mirrors in the bathrooms. Trying to look behind them? Maybe the thought of his reflection moving beside him felt too much like her. Eventually, he called to Elise, saying he'd found her toothbrush at the back of the cabinet beneath the boys' sink.

"Purple," Traust said. "Bristles hardly bent."

Elise couldn't help but shake her head. Small beads of sweat dripped free from her chin into the water far below. That wasn't even her brush. Hers was downstairs. Must have been one of the boys' old ones.

Elise smelled a cigarette burning. For a moment, she worried it was the smoke he'd used before, the poison, but the water on the first floor must have been preventing him setting off any more. He was resting now. She heard him exhale as he lowered himself down to the floor above.

"I want you to know," he said, "when I was a boy, I wondered, for a while, if you were a friend. But then you never came out. And with that, you made me alone. Cut off from everyone else. I was a little boy who believed, and now I'm a man who can't stop."

She heard him grunt, and the sound of boots dropping to the floor. He was taking them off. She wasn't sure if it was because his feet had begun to blister from being wet, or if he were only trying to move quieter, to surprise her in some other part of the house. If he were trying to sneak up on her, he wouldn't. Traust didn't know which of the hallway floorboards creaked, like she did, and how to avoid them. She heard him each step of the way.

"I want to let you know," Traust said, "I don't have to hurt you. I just want to see that you're real. My whole life I've needed it. Even when I'm with other people, surrounded by them, talking at each other, all I'm listening to is the sound of another empty room. A woman in bed with me, but all I ever think of is what's underneath the box springs. Life's a long thing when you're alone. Except, I'm not. I come home and sense that rustle on the other side of the door as I turn the key. I'm never alone. I'm never left alone. Finding you is finding out there's nothing wrong with me—so, come out."

A pause.

"So, come out now," he said. "Or I'll burn the house down. Or, when that family comes home, I'll kill each one of them. Do you care?"

Stay where you are.

"When I find you, I'll bag you up and bring you home with me. I'll keep you handcuffed to the radiator. When I wake up at night, I'll look over, each time, and see you were real. I'll see you're there, long after you're rotted away to bone."

MONSTER

TRAUST WAS A MAN, FAR AWAY FROM HIS HOME. AND HERE, ELISE was in hers. He wailed at her house, at her, hoping she might hear. But as long as she hid, he could never find her. She heard it in his voice—trying to frighten her, because he himself had grown frightened. Grown tired with the day passing. Elise could outwait him. And when he gave in, wading out into the water of the front yard, she would watch him go—slouched and worn. Defeated, again.

He was the bump in the night that turned out to be nothing at all.

Her mother and her father had died, but Elise was real. The Masons had gone, but she was still here. Traust was in her home, but she was more patient. She had turned herself into the dust in the walls. As long as she hid, she was incorporeal. She was the walls, the floodwater, each shift and sound and movement in every part of the house the man was not, could not reach.

"I'll hurt you," Traust said. And she believed him, but only if he got the chance.

BREAKS APART

ELISE HEARD HIM ABOVE, IN THE HALLWAY, BUT THEN, ALSO, BELOW. He'd lost all sense of himself. He'd split. Rended. The sounds of him came from two separate places at once. Traust upstairs, and softly, in the back porch. A pattern knocked steady on the door. One. One-two. One.

Elise recognized what it was. She realized who was making it. "Oh no," she said aloud. Couldn't help it.

Traust had gone quiet. He was listening now, too. The knocking continued.

"Go," Elise whispered. "Get out of here."

Slow steps above her. Cautious, almost delicate. The light squelch of the man's wet socks on the wood. Building momentum. Down-stairs, Elise heard the back door push open against the weight of the water. She heard Brody's voice, frail, winding through the damaged rooms of the house.

"Elise?" he called to her. "Are you okay in there? Are you hiding? It's me. It's okay if you come out."

SHE IS REVEALED

"ELISE?" BRODY SAID, AND ELISE KNEW EXACTLY WHAT WOULD HAPPEN.

Traust would grab him. Wrench him around the house to make the boy show him every place he knew she might hide. If he didn't, Traust would hurt him. Brody, smaller even than she was, in his mud-stained overalls and sloppy hair—stupid! So stupid! The staircase creaked beneath the man as he made his way closer to the boy, homed in on the boy. This kid, her friend. Like a stupid, younger brother.

Give it up.

"No!" Elise screamed to him. "Brody, run! Get away! Run!"

Elise's voice so loud through her throat it felt like flesh was tearing free. Brody would have to hear her, and she hoped he'd comprehend. The downstairs now sloshed and churned. Traust moved through the water fast as he could manage, one sloshing stride after another. And she heard Brody, seeing the man, cry out in surprise. Elise imagined what he must look like through the laundry doorway, coming at Brody: a real-world devil, wordless and grinning, arms pumping. The man's knees arching, legs kicking droplets high into the air.

"Run, Brody, run!" And she heard his body collide with the screen door, the boy splashing, floundering out in the yard. Elise pictured his legs bogged, hands snatching wildly at the water in front of him, trying to pull himself faster away.

"Don't trip," she said. "Please don't fall."

Don't get caught.

But a part of her knew already Brody was safe. Even if he was slow, and his legs short. Even if he stumbled, submerged himself fully, struggled to make it back to his feet. Even if somewhere safe was far, somewhere beyond the tree line, away. Because she knew the man wouldn't follow him outside of the house. Traust wouldn't go any farther than the threshold of the back door. Wouldn't risk it—a bird already in hand. Because the man had heard her voice, and knew now where Elise hid.

Traust, across the house, bounded up the stairs. Quiet at the head, where the hallway began, but only because he'd stopped in place to remember, to calculate the placement of the voice's source.

Floorboards chirping under his feet. Into the parents' bedroom. Closing in.

Elise had to get out. Get away. Somewhere in the dark of the laundry chute beneath her, the floodwater began, but until she reached it, until her foot broke the plane of its surface, she had to descend, hands and toes gripping the nooks and beams of the walls, slick with condensation. Had to move carefully. If she fell from here, she wouldn't be capable of running.

"Hear you," Traust said. He was in the bathroom. The shriek of the shower curtain being torn to one side. The click of the cabinet as it opened. Above her, Traust would be seeing medicine bottles, Band-Aids, a blood-pressure meter and thermometers, and below the shelves, at the bottom, a rough crease in the wood along the back of the cabinet. Elise had lost count of the steps she'd taken, and couldn't find the next grip. Her toes groped lower against the smooth, wet wall. She looked between her limbs down into the dark—low enough to drop?

Above, the man pulled the back of the cabinet loose with the tips of his fingernails, and the wood ground against the sides. Elise, looking down between her legs, saw the black square of water come into view, her shadow cast across its surface. And above her, the silhouette of Traust's head in the chute's frame.

"See you," he said. His shoulders swelled into the chute, eclipsing nearly all the bathroom light.

The water was too far below her. She ignored the handholds she couldn't find and used her forearms and heels and the flat of her back to wedge her way down.

The shape of Traust hesitated. Elise could sense him thinking it through. She was too far down from him. Out of reach. He could rush back downstairs, but what if she was gone when he got there?

Elise lowered herself another half-foot, a quick lurch, and that's all it took. She was getting farther away from him. Pulling back into the dark. But he wouldn't lose her again. Traust came down after her.

HE DESCENDS

SHOULDERS PINCHED TOGETHER, ARMS OUTSTRETCHED, BRIMMING over the lip of the cabinet into the chute. His body was too huge to fall, snug up against the sides. So, snake-like, he wrenched it back and forth, all face and hands and elbows.

Elise slipped, dropped a few inches, and caught herself against the chute's sides with the length of her back and knees. But already Traust was close, reaching for her. She slipped again, her feet buckling up this time, her body in a V, backside sinking—she was going to fall into the water and be stuck with her arms and legs above her. And he was going to follow, and crush her.

Traust shouting, but she couldn't understand. The words bounced around her. His shoulder digging into her thigh, and the palm of his hand engulfing her face. Her cheeks squeezed between his thumb and forefinger, and he was trying to pull her closer.

Elise fell. The water surrounded her—abrupt, cool—and Traust's voice was muted. Elise was walled in, all sides. Her feet above the surface of the water, kicking wild. Stuck in a submerged coffin. His body came down and broke the surface of the water, the current rushing around her, and then he was pushing down on her. His bulk mashing her into the floor, his back on her chest, his hard head between her hip and her arm. Her lungs compressing. The air forced from her.

Elise needed to breathe. One wall had pulled away. The painted board with the tree come loose. She reached behind her head and gripped the lips of the hole and pulled herself, wriggling from beneath him, out. She gasped into the air and dim light.

Her feet found footing beneath her, but her legs were weak, knees bending. She tried to run, turning and stepping, but the pull of the water tugged her off-balance. She fell and was swallowed by the water again. Frantic, she stood and pulled her hair from her eyes. Saw the laundry room's wall quivering—Traust pummeled it from the other side.

He raged, water splashing through the narrow hole where the board had been. His arm groping for her beneath the water. Elise stepped back. On the wall above, the plaster was cracking from the kicking of his feet. He'd already broken through the wood of the chute. The hole she'd pulled herself out of was small, but if he could fit into the chute, he could come through, too. His neck and shoulders were pinned by his weight against the submerged floor, but Traust could surely twist his arms, pull himself up and out. The water churned across the whole room, slapping against her thighs. Elise backed away, step after step. Where else could she hide? Once he pulled himself free and up, in four or five of his steps he'd catch and fall down upon her. She heard him beneath the water, muffled yelling, like the house itself was calling to her. But he wasn't coming out.

Elise stepped back and watched. The raging down there, the torrent of water reaching her, all the water in the house seeming to pitch up and down. The crack in the wall growing, the walls thumping. But with each beat, the noise grew softer. A steady heartbeat growing slow.

By the time Elise had backed into the foyer, the water around her legs had grown smooth. She stood there for a minute while the bubbles of air on the water's surface popped, two at a time, then one after another. They burst, dissolving into the water's flat, dark plane, until no more remained. Eventually, Elise went back into the room, where the man in the walls had gone quiet.

WHEN WE GO MISSING

ONCE, WE WERE CHILDREN LYING IN BED WITH OUR EYES CLOSED. The overhead lamp still on, turning the insides of our eyelids crimson. We waited to hear them enter our rooms. For the pressure at the foot of our beds, the squeal of the bedsprings as they leaned to brush the hair from our foreheads. When our parents' footsteps led away, we felt the remainder of their kiss on our faces as the room around us darkened, and our eyelids changed to indigo, the color of sleep.

It's a feeling we'll have when finally we leave this world. We hope.

When floodwaters come, they will lap at our faces, wrap our waists, and pull. Our chests will rise with the current, as if swelling for one last breath, and will be pulled free, unmoored, bodies turned by the current like the slow hands of a clock. We'll lie on the surface of the water the way a sleeper sleeps, ushered away as the water recedes.

When the girl pulled him loose from the wall, his body rose halfway. Only the hump of his back broke the surface, like the cresting shoulders of a small whale. She guided him on, steering him with her hips and the tops of her forearms. Through the rooms, on out. Out the door through which he had come, looking to find her. Outside, the world was a receding lake, and when he was with it, he receded too: a gray shape pulling away toward the trees.

The man's body would be found, eventually, or it would always be missing. There are only two ways for things to go. The setting sun shot fire across the water's surface. She might fall here, let herself be immersed. Let the murky cold sweep all over her once again.

If she weren't so tired. Weren't so unsure she would be able to stand back up.

THE PULL OF EVERY THING

THAT EVENING, ELISE LAY ON THE STAIRS, HALFWAY UP, DRAPED across them like a cat. The humid wood firm against her cheek. Hard to know how long she lay there, once night came, but over time, the water diminished out through the door until only sediment and shallow puddles lingered across the tile floor. It felt comforting to lie on the stairs, even if they were hard and narrow. This was a part of the house Elise had never lain on before. Had never embraced. That seemed important now.

Below her, the granddaughter clock had soaked in the standing water like a patch of dry and porous soil. The glossy hue vanished, its wood now soft and vulnerable as a freshly healed wound. The painted birds still there, colorful on the clock's face, yet Elise wondered how long until they faded and cracked from the ruined wood underneath.

Eventually, Elise made it up to the parents' bed once again. She slept through the remainder of the night until late in the morning, dozing through the light and the chitter of a squirrel in one of the trees in the yard. She wavered in and out of sleep, scratching where mosquitoes had bitten her along her arms, ignoring the growing pangs in her stomach and her dry throat. Elise pulled a pillow over her face. She was in no rush to get up and search the ruined kitchen again. Already she had caught the rotten smell of what was emanating from the insides of the refrigerator, whose doors hung open from the man's search, the perishables inside free to rot in the muggy heat.

But finally, when she pulled herself upright and descended the stairs, she saw that there was no longer any need to search for food

and clean water. It had been taken care of for her. In the front doorway lay a towel, two water bottles, an energy bar, and a box of Cin-
namon Life cereal. Elise stared at the collection of items.

"Brody," she said.

She took the items back upstairs. She had her breakfast in the attic. She brushed broken glass from the sill and spent the meal looking
out the dormer into the backyard. She pictured Mrs. Laura pulling
upright the trampled tomato vines. Mr. Nick with a wheelbarrow of
loose, broken limbs. Marshall and Eddie together dragging one of the
large fallen branches. Her own mom and dad working somewhere
else in the front yard.

For the rest of that morning, Elise circled her home and surveyed
the damage, and what remained. She noted the impressions of herself throughout, the signs of her presence there—tangled bedsheets,
her jeans lain out on the roof to dry, stacks of books she'd brought
upstairs from the library which she hoped to save from the humidity and mold. Elise realized how a house seems smaller once all the
windows are open. A breeze can pass through the whole building as
if the building weren't there. Ghosts bled in from outside and drifted
through the air of the rooms, and out again into the pucker of sky
that showed between the tree's branches.

Here, Odin, the All-father, came to Elise and knelt on one knee
before her. He put his face next to hers, and he told her that, somewhere out there, her parents were buried in the ground. Lying on
their backs, side by side. That every night, constellations refracted in
their glossy-white eyes. "In the end," he said, "no one is ever missing.
They're beneath us all the time."

In the next few days, the floorboards beneath her would bend and
buckle. Paint would flake from the walls, and mold would grow black
and speckled throughout their insides. Elise could make it work, if
she wanted. A new challenge, in a way, to exist hidden in a house that
was fading as fast as this one. Elise was good enough at a life like hers
to know that she could. If that's what she decided she wanted.

The floodwater had drained almost fully from the yard, and the jeans on the roof were taken back inside. The bedsheets pulled straight the way they'd been left when the Masons packed up their car and left. The windows that had been opened the morning after the storm were closed. The library books she had saved were brought back downstairs and stacked on the drying coffee table.

That afternoon, Elise left her home. She entered into the yard, and the flattened grass between the fallen branches was wet and warm beneath her feet. Mrs. Laura's flowers along the driveway were bent and weak, but alive—Elise pinched a Snapdragon's purple mouth open and shut. The scent of magnolia at the end of its bloom. The warmth of the sun on her neck and arms.

Elise passed his flooded-out truck on the road, and she scaled the steep levee. Her calf muscles strained as she climbed to its peak. The river was big and brown and churning onward, like the glistening muscles of a horse. On the other side, just above the top of the parallel levee, she could make out the roofs of other homes, the buildings peeking up at her, apprehensive, from afar. Elise walked along its length, kicking sun-baked gravel, brushing mosquitoes from her calves with the sides of her feet. Elise walked until she found the wooded road she'd known Brody to take sometimes when he'd come to her house.

Once there, she came down the levee, letting gravity pull her, catching speed. Her strides grew in length as she crossed over the ditch and pavement onto the dirt road. She followed it, sidestepping ankle-deep potholes, jumping over fallen limbs, ducking beneath the larger trunks when she had to. Mud in the cracks between her toes. Dragonflies hummed around her. Between the clouds, the sun like an apricot. The woods on each side of her, and the canopy above, were a living hallway.

The Girl in the Walls left her home to thank her friend for the things he brought her. And after, if she ever planned on returning, she must have changed her mind. Elise didn't come back.

FOUNDATION

LATER, AFTER ABANDONED AND FLOODED VEHICLES HAD BEEN towed away, the roads reopened. The return began. Patient, long lines of cars alternated through the broken traffic lights. Car tires crunched over the fallen branches and shattered glass. From the elevated interstate, the city extending in every direction, with battered shingles and pockmarked roofs, some peeled completely open as if, during the storm, something inside had shot straight up through their ceiling into the sky.

The waterline scarred the sides of homes where the floodwaters had risen and stood, stagnant. For many, the question of whether to rebuild and stay, or go on, elsewhere. Farther from the Gulf, from the turgid, hot summers, and the humidity and insects, the threat of flood, the curbside littered with sodden, rolled-up carpets and refrigerators that'd never be purged of the smell. There were other storms to come—stronger ones. Hurricane season wouldn't end for months. And next year would breed more. One storm blends into every other, when they're recollected and described. Was that Betsy that took the old shed from us? Was that Camille who took our favorite tree?

Each storm, the same—the ones that have happened, and the ones that will.

A barge teetering on top of the levee. The broken trees, the battered house, the deep divots in the yard from where it appeared some tow truck, a day or so ago, had circled round, its tires cutting into the mud, to pull along a vehicle that had stalled out on the road in front of their home.

Inside, the water had taken all of their belongings and rearranged them. Pulled from cabinets, spilled across the floor. The walls had drunk in the moisture as if they'd been thirsty for it. They were still saturated—a thumb pressed into them was like touching a doused washcloth. The whole building would need to be gutted.

And through the destruction of their home, it was clear that the man Traust had come back. Holes knocked in their walls and floors, throughout the entirety of their house. He'd left his boots upstairs. When Nick found them there, toppled on their sides in the upstairs hallway, the father tore through the house, throwing himself into each of the rooms, searching for him. But eventually, it was clear the house was empty. He wasn't here. At least not anymore. Their father's anger welled up in all of them—why won't he leave us alone? The stacked books on the coffee table in the library: what was he even doing?

As long as he was held in the frame of their anger, the man shrank to nothing more than a reoccurring pest. Like mice. Like termites. Marshall swore that if he ever saw Mr. Traust near their home again, he'd grab the nearest thing to him and crack it over the man's head. He'd taken his father's keys from the peeling foyer table and thrust them into a set of imaginary eyes.

"If I could just get my hands on him," Nick said to Marshall, and as bodiless as the man seemed to them now, hanging loose around them like water vapor, they understood the desire, and satisfaction, of pinning something down you hate.

Laura, who'd gone silent once they'd entered their home, pinched the mouths of the boots together between two fingers of one hand. And in the other, she took the toolkit they found in the office. She went out to the back field, far back, until she was nothing more than a torso pushing through the tall weeds. She swung her arms like pendulums and threw the man's things as far as she could past the tree line into the woods.

Eddie met her in the backyard. He was too old for her to reach out and take hold of his hand. He was never comfortable with touching, besides. But she could walk beside him, past her muddied garden, around the garage and the azalea bushes. They didn't need to speak. They circled around the house, catching out of the corners of their eyes their grayed reflections on the windowpanes, Eddie murmuring while he counted the steps. She could do it all night, Laura realized. Or at least as long as he wanted to.

And as the days beat on, what was lost wore on the parents. Their piano, their antique clock, their furniture, books. The wasted projects. The wainscoting in the dining room. The replaced tile and cabinets in the kitchen. New carpet in the living room. The floor and painting in the guest room. They'd lost a year here. To stay and rebuild would lose more. Mr. and Mrs. Mason silently counted the remainders of their lives.

One day, while their boys continued the process of gathering things from the first floor and chucking them out into the front yard, the parents found themselves upstairs, together in their bedroom.

They held each other. Forehead against shoulder. Face embraced by hair.

How grateful to all be alive. All of them okay. Unhurt, and breathing.

But it was still hard to lose things.

SKELETON

MONTHS LATER, IN THE FALL, WITH THE REST OF THE SEASON'S HURRI-
canes passed, workmen finished stripping the house bare. The
gutted house compressed. Each room, or what remained of them,
blended together, with the tawny wall studs seeming less like walls
than vertical window blinds. The boys, in what had been their bedrooms, could see clear through to the guest room and office, to their
parents' bedroom, and what had been the inside of the linen closet.
They could see downstairs, too, through holes in the floor that had
been for electrical wiring and ventilation. They could see up into
the attic. The whole world here lain out before them like a map.
Nothing could hide anywhere.

Their parents worked downstairs in the garage. A cold front had
moved in through the past few days, and dry, fresh air bit through
the fabric of their sweaters. Even inside, the faint suggestion of their
breath clouded in front of their mouths. When a breeze blew, the blue
plastic tarp that covered the holes in the roof flapped at its corners,
like large wings.

Eddie wondered, still, if she was all right.

Pressure welled up inside him, and Eddie told his brother that
he once knew the girl. Before it all began, before their search, and
Mr. Traust, and the storm. Or, not knew really, but had an idea of
her. Of what she was. He thought she hid sometimes behind the old
armchair in his room. For a while, he'd wanted, he'd tried, to keep
her hidden.

Eddie told this to his brother, and as he spoke, he realized, in the hesitations between words, that he expected Marshall's face to turn hard. For his brother to look him over and sneer. "Why?" Marshall would say, confused, and once he understood, he'd ask it again, appalled. Eddie was confessing betrayal.

He finished saying what he felt he had to. He'd deal with whatever came. Marshall didn't look him in the eyes. The older brother just stood there, in place. Pulled a hand from deep inside the front pockets of his sweatshirt and rubbed the bristles of his hair along the back of his head.

"Really," Marshall said. He fell quiet.

Hard now to imagine the way the house had been, since the walls had been removed. Harder to remember how it had felt—thinking you're alone in a room when something stirs outside the door. Because there were no doors anymore. The light through the windows was clear and white on the wooden floor. The house was no more than bones, stripped and silent.

Marshall asked, "So, what was she like?"

Outside, birds chirped. The boys had never known the names for them, but knew the calls—flute-like, soft trills, whistles—familiar as the contour of an old pillow. Their parents' voices murmured below. Eddie wondered what, if anything, he could say.

"She was," Eddie said. Shook his head. There weren't words for this. "I don't know. She was . . . good at hiding."

Marshall snorted. Eddie had to smile at himself.

What else was there to say? As absurd as describing a ghost.

—No, not a ghost. A house. How could anyone summarize the patches of warmth, or lingering smells of food after a meal? What do you say about the placement of furniture, the depth of doorframes, and what it's like to move around them, on instinct, when the lights have gone out?

"For a lot of the time," Eddie said, "I liked her."

THE END

SOMETIMES, WE WONDER IF SHE'S DEAD.

Maybe. Or moved on to another home, her next home, somewhere else in the neighborhood, or across the country. A girl like her no longer can exist anywhere else, we think.

As we grow older, there's a temptation to believe that every sound heard in the near-empty of our own homes is her still revolving around us. So near, we imagine that if only we closed our eyes, and waited until we heard her, and reached out our hands—we'd feel her there, reaching out to us with her own.

It's a feeling that doesn't leave us.

Sometimes, we catch ourselves. We're still listening—for what? We'll know it, maybe, when we hear it. An attic door creaking open above. A sigh, like a miracle, under the floor.

Come out!

We say it, when we can't take it anymore. When we've had enough.

But each time, when we think she's really at her nearest, our eyes are always shut.

IN THE MORNING

A THOUGHT AS SHE WAKES. A MEMORY NAGGING HER. SOME CHILD-hood thing left undone, unacknowledged. And the feeling of embarrassment with it, as if it happened only the day before. Odd how those feelings can still bite at you. Or warm you, depending. Some hardly seem to fade at all. Lying in bed in the early morning dark, her mind tumbling, she knows she won't be going back to sleep.

She finds herself, phone in her hand, typing a name into the browser. She tries again, realizing the need to amend it. Because, of course, he's grown. A man now. An "Edward," as strange as that name sounds. She smiles, not without a little shame, in recognition that now she's the one searching.

There isn't much to be found. The near absence of anything reminds her she's tried this before.

But, eventually, as her bedroom window grows pink, with City Park trees taking shape in its frame, she finds on a page an address. He still lives in town. Across the river from the old home they shared. Not so far from her now.

She gets up and readies herself for work. Eats breakfast on the front porch in air that's still cool from a storm the night before. Across the street, a stark-white egret bends in the shallow water of the park's roadside ditch. Beyond, the empty play equipment seems almost solemn in the early morning gloom, but it will be filled that afternoon. Parents will perch on the benches. Young children, crying out, will hop across the playground after one another, will pull themselves into dangling swings and take flight. She's lived in other states, with a grandfather, and then with an aunt. She's made homes elsewhere. But now she is here in this city again, like a bird returning to an old nest with the change of a season. A planet in a stable orbit. A home always is yours, even after you've gone and made others.

That morning, before she leaves, she opens her nightstand drawer and sifts past books, a sketchpad, postcards, and other kept things. She finds what she's looking for and brings it to her desk. Tucks it in an envelope. Gets in her car and drives.

She's not on her way to work. Not yet.

When she arrives in the neighborhood, Uptown, where the river bends, she parks her car several blocks away. Old houses, painted in bright pastels, press tight against restaurants and storefronts. Oak branches form a dense canopy. Rainwater drips intermittently from gutters and branches, and softly plops along the roof of her car. She sits with the door open, unwraps a peppermint from the cupholder, and pops it in her cheek. Grabs her bag and goes. Her heels tap across sidewalk pavement that has buckled over tree roots. The extra walk will likely make her late to work, but it's fine. To break the boundaries of routine on occasion, she figures, just means you're a living being.

Safer this way, too. No car means no license plate. No identifying feature. No possibility of being found. On either side of the street, windows stare blankly out. The houses seem pensive, as if sleeping.

She walks, and sunlight glints through gaps in wooden fences. A squirrel scuttles through trees above her. The breeze blows cool against her arms.

And, like anywhere else she's been, she senses they're here.

Just out of sight, but close.

Somewhere, an old plywood board is in the garage, being re-painted. A sprinkler in the garden has just been turned on. Somewhere, a child sprawls across a speckled, plastic tarp, drawing while she waits for her parents to finish up their day's work.

All three, still up to something. Wherever it is people go.

A mom, a dad, a girl.

And, every day, she holds them with her. In her.

Like a home.

MEMENTO

OUTSIDE, DRIVERS HAVE BEGUN THEIR MORNING COMMUTE. Through the narrow streets, their engines hum, their tires splashing through the puddles in the worn asphalt. In his bedroom, he knots his tie, carefully, in the mirror. He hears the wind through the oak trees and every car that passes. He hears birds chirping and each creak and cry of his own, old house.

He's always been sensitive to sounds. Always, he'll be listening.

As he readies himself to teach, he goes to his bedroom window. Opens it to the smell of rain still lingering. Checks the sill for termites, for little golden bodies remaining from the night before. His habit, for a long time now. He stands in the frame and watches the neighborhood wake.

Down the block, a pair of wrens land on the awning of a small bike shop. Fallen twigs, still plump with their leaves, lay scattered across the roadside. In the house across from his, the outline of a neighbor's cat sits in a gray window. Not far off, a woman crosses into the road. She strides across the pavement with the gentle urgency of an errand.

He turns back to his room to pick a pair of socks from the armoire. His bedsprings squeak as he sits to pull them on. But something, like breath on the back of his neck, stops him.

He gets up and returns to the window, and he sees her there, standing at the knee-high fence of his yard. She's stopped to dig in her handbag. She pulls free an envelope and tucks it into his mailbox. Her hair bound in a loose bun. Face like anyone else's.

He thinks of the very small chance that he would be right here to see her do this.

He watches her cross the road. Then he leaves his bedroom and goes out the front door.

He steps barefoot across the paving stones and opens his mailbox. The letter is bulky, bent, unmarked. He looks up to see her beneath the bike shop's awning. She's paused, for a moment, to catch a drop of water in her open palm.

He breaks the seal of the letter with his finger. Empties its contents into his hand.

An old Lego figure. A little plastic witch.

The wind is blowing, and wet leaves cling tight to the pavement.

And she goes, quick as she's always been. Stepping down from the curb, around a rippled manhole cover, checking for coming cars out the side of her eye. A woman now, he realizes.

A car passes between them. Shadow and light stipple across her beneath the branches. She turns the corner. The hem of her dress is the last trailing thing he sees. She's gone.

And so, there he is.

Lucky to have seen her.

ACKNOWLEDGMENTS

Writing a book is a communal act. I owe a great deal of gratitude.

Thank you to my parents, who have kept me more secure than any house ever could. Thanks to my brother for the mischief, and to my sister, for the best conscience. Thanks to my Georgia family, and to Grammy, for her home away from home and her bird feeders. Thank you, Aunt Dot and Uncle Virg, for getting me here.

Thank you, Susan Armstrong, for being brilliant in the million things you do for me. To Amelia Atlas, I'm grateful for all your knowledge and care.

To my editors, the Helens—Garnons-Williams and Atsma—your creativity and insight have left me in awe. Thanks for your generosity and precision, and for telling me, "Actually, you don't need to cut that." Thank you to the wonderful teams at 4th Estate and Ecco.

Thank you to Nina de Gramont, who was with this project since it was no more than a sketch on a whiteboard. I'm grateful for your encouragement, wisdom, and support. And my deepest gratitude to so many others at UNC Wilmington. Rebecca Lee and Philip Gerard. David Gessner and Clyde Edgerton. To my novel-writing cohort for your stories and brilliance. To the Sports Crew for keeping us all in high spirits, even when each of you were injured, by me (sorry). And to those talented, young writers at Roland Grise Middle—I'm just trying to keep up.

Thank you to Brad Richard, for a decade and a half (and going) of mentorship. To Donald Secreast, for your care with this novel and your shared delight in sentences. To friends in New Orleans, and

Georgia, and Saint Louis, and North Carolina, who've treated me like a sibling. Thanks to Jake Nesbit, for also listening.

And, of course, to those sounds from another room. To however the attic latch came open. To whatever was there, if anything, those times I couldn't help but think—

And to Donnie: my evacuee partner, who I come home to. You kind, patient, total bombshell—writing's always easier with you.

Thanks everyone.